THE BERLIN WIFE'S CHOICE

BOOKS BY MARION KUMMEROW

German Wives

The Berlin Wife

Margarete's Journey

A Light in the Window

From the Dark We Rise

The Girl in the Shadows

Daughter of the Dawn

Not Without My Sister

The Orphan's Mother

THE BERLIN WIFE'S CHOICE

MARION KUMMEROW

bookouture

Published by Bookouture in 2023

An imprint of Storyfire Ltd.
Carmelite House
50 Victoria Embankment
London EC4Y 0DZ

www.bookouture.com

ISBN: 978-1-83790-283-5
eBook ISBN: 978-1-83790-281-1

1

BERLIN, NOVEMBER 1938

When he slept the nightmares came. Every night the same dream haunted him, except it wasn't a dream at all. Julius Falkenstein returned to the Sachsenhausen camp, where the SS had dragged him after his arrest on that fateful day.

A day the Nazis euphemistically named the Night of Broken Glass, when so much more than glass had been broken. Synagogues, offices and shops had burnt. People had been arrested, harassed, mistreated, tortured and killed.

It should be called the Night of Broken People, because those who survived had returned broken, like him. During the day, Julius could pretend everything was normal. But at night, in his nightmares, he knew it wasn't.

His entire world had been turned upside down. He, the powerful and well-connected bank owner who used to frequent the highest circles of the German elite, had been reduced to a second-class citizen, or rather non-citizen, on sufferance. He'd never believed this could happen. He had repudiated the very notion of the Nazis treating him the same way they treated other Jews. But then, he'd never imagined they could treat any human being the way they did.

Reluctantly he had to admit—just to himself—that it was only thanks to his Aryan wife Edith that he still enjoyed some privileges. Without her insistence, he would probably be rotting away in the Sachsenhausen camp.

Each night the nightmares pull him back to that time, to endless rows of barbed wire and the cruel stares of watchmen.

The SS had invaded the Falkenstein bank, an institution that had been in the hands of Julius' family for more than a hundred years, setting ablaze his office and hauling him out, past his shocked secretary, past dozens of his employees running through the burning building and—which irked him the most—past his own armed security guards in the cashier's room. Without lifting a single finger, the guards watched the SS men drag their employer away.

In front of the building, Julius was shoved unceremoniously into the back of a truck. There, he huddled among a mass of other men, shivering in his expensive suit. Nobody dared to speak a word—everyone was too shocked about what was happening.

His unvoluntary companions seemed to be working men. Despite not recognizing their faces, it was easy to guess their professions. The leather maker was wearing his heavy apron, around the tailor's neck hung a measuring tape. One man must be an accountant judging by his oversleeves, the same ones Julius' employees used at work.

There was a single trait every man in the truck had in common. It was nothing Julius could decipher at first sight, but he knew it to be true. Every single one of them was a Jew.

"What's this all about?" someone asked.

A young-sounding voice from the opposite corner of the truck responded. "Apparently this is the Nazis' retaliation for the murder of Ernst Eduard vom Rath by a man called Herschel Grynszpan in Paris, who was a Polish Jew."

"You're kidding me?"

"Those bastards arrest all of us because of the acts of some lunatic in France?"

Julius listened with only half an ear to the ensuing discussion, since it wasn't relevant why he'd been arrested. The more important task at hand was to find a way to get out of it. Despite the gradual decline of his situation, he was still an important man with acquaintances in powerful positions. If somehow he could enlist them to pull the right strings, he might just be released.

The truck rumbled around the streets, stopping every few minutes for new men to be shoved inside, until there was no space left by any stretch of the imagination for yet another occupant. The air thickened with exhaled air, heavily laced with anxiety, causing Julius to gag repeatedly from the stench of fear, sweat and oozing blood. It took him a while to realize that some of the blood was his own, as he looked down at his hand during one of the stops and saw a gaping wound, probably incurred when the SS man had dragged him down the hallway.

Huddled together in a trembling mass, a collective sigh of relief billowed in the air, when the truck stopped once more and no new victims were shoved inside. Instead, several soldiers appeared yelling, "Out! Fast!"

Julius somehow managed to extricate himself from his huddled position, rough-and-ready, stumbling out of the truck. The guards didn't give him the time to stretch his limbs. Mercilessly they pushed him forward alongside the rest of the crowd. For a fleeting moment he thought he recognized his former chief accountant Heinrich Goldmann, propelled from one of the dozen trucks standing in the vicinity of the one Julius had traveled in.

His feet quickly moving him forward in an attempt to escape the spattering down of batons, he stumbled into the man in front of him, diverting his gaze. When he looked to his side again, Heinrich Goldmann was gone—and Julius couldn't be sure if it had actually been him or if the familiar face had been a result of his imagination.

"Keep moving!" a soldier screamed, following-up his order by ramming the butt of his rifle into the side of a prisoner's head. The man stumbled and fell, just to be beaten even harder to regain his footing, which he miraculously managed, and then kept moving along until their group reached a row of barracks.

"Inside! Fast!" yelled the guards, doling out blows, kicks and lashes.

The barracks seemed full even before Julius took a step inside, which didn't impede the guards from yelling, pushing and beating to order more people into it. His breath caught in his chest as the stench intensified and he barged against a wall of bodies.

Reflexively, he raised his arms in front of his face, although with little result. An onslaught of masses desperate to get away from the whipping guards pushed into the hut, shoving him deeper inside, until he felt as if he'd been swallowed whole by a whale, caught in a dark, stinking place without oxygen to breathe, pressed into other men's bodies on all sides.

Again, the bile rose in his throat. He forcefully swallowed it down, since the notion of adding vomit on his clothes to the horrible situation held little appeal. All around him he heard retching and just minutes later, the stench changed from merely disgusting to outright unbearable. Julius held his arm clad in fine cloth in front of his nose to alleviate the worst of the stink.

Pushed harder into the darkness, suddenly the wall of bodies pressed against him from all sides closed in on him, threatening to grind him into a powder. In that instant he began screaming at the top of his lungs. After a while, the bodies squashing him faded, giving him room to breathe. Then everything was drowned out by loud steps. The door slammed shut. His scream escalated into a glass-shattering howl, making his throat ache.

Suddenly a hand pressed down on his shoulder and a soft voice said, "Julius. Wake up! You're dreaming! You're home. You're safe."

Bewildered, he opened his eyes. The bone-chilling scream stopped, just the pain in his throat remained. His entire body sweating profusely, it took him some time to realize that his wife Edith was sitting on the edge of the bed, murmuring soothing words and brushing a moist strand of hair from his forehead.

"You've had a nightmare again." Edith held a glass of water for him.

"I'm sorry." He sat up, taking the glass from her hand and looking around the room to make sure she wasn't in his imagination. Yes, he was at home, in his bedroom. The exquisite furniture, including the mahogany wardrobe and the antique mirror with a golden frame next to it, the beautiful Art Nouveau lamp on the nightstand, everything was there. He remembered well how Edith had re-decorated the mansion on the prestigious Schwanenwerder Island in Berlin years ago and he gave her a small smile, trying to convey that he was fine.

Then, Julius emptied the glass and sank against his sweat-soaked pillow, keeping his eyes trained on Edith's face for fear the room around him might vanish and the darkness would swallow him again. It was both a relief and a shame that his wife of twenty years had come to his bedside and comforted him as if he were a frightened child.

Edith knew well that he did not like to dwell on emotions, so she pleasantly asked him, "Would you like me to call the maid to make you a cup of hot cocoa?"

Still scared stiff by the horrible nightmare, he felt infantilized by the well-meant question, and couldn't prevent a burst of ire breaking loose. "No! I want you to get out of my bedroom. I don't want anything from you, do you understand? For the last time, leave me alone."

"I'm sorry, I thought..."

Her crestfallen face filled him with remorse. It wasn't Edith's fault that he couldn't cope with the experiences he'd had at the camp. Without her he'd probably still be in there—if he were even alive.

The reversal of their roles was perhaps even harder to bear than the heinous experiences at the camp. He was her husband, who was supposed to protect her, not the other way round.

And yet, it was only thanks to Edith's intervention that he'd escaped the hell on earth. Obviously the family lawyer Dr.

Petersen had been tasked with organizing the formalities—and paying a hefty penalty for Julius' crime of being a Jew—but it was no secret that his speedy release from the Sachsenhausen camp had been orchestrated by Edith's brother, Joseph Hesse, a high-ranking SS officer, to whom she'd gone begging on her knees for her husband's safety.

"Please forgive me. It's just…" There were no words to describe what he went through. From boyhood on he'd been drilled to be self-sufficient, reflective, unemotional. His mother certainly had never consoled or pitied him. On the contrary, her standard adage for every emotional or physical pain had been, 'A boy doesn't cry' or 'What doesn't kill you only makes you stronger.'

"…perhaps I could, in fact, use a hot cocoa."

Edith's face lit up with relief. "I'll tell the maid right away."

Julius watched her as she left his bedroom, his thoughts returning to the two days he spent in the Sachsenhausen camp. Despite not having been beaten up like some of his more unfortunate fellow captives, the experience had left him scarred forever. The Nazis had marked him, claimed his spirit, captured his mind, for he would never forget the horrors of those days, they would be forever burned into his soul. And yet, he'd only caught a glimpse of what the Nazis were capable of.

All these years he'd been convinced it would all blow over, that Hitler would be reined in, if not by politicians, then at least by the military, but he now realized with sudden clarity that this would never happen. Despite not being a religious man, he sent a prayer to heaven for help—his beloved country needed it dearly.

As for himself, deep down he knew what he should do. His sister Adriana and her husband Florian had left the country two years ago to settle down in England, and Edith had begged him time upon time to follow their lead.

Contemplating emigration, the unease in his stomach turned into a fizzing fury, burning through every cell in his body. No, he would not back down. The Nazis would not defeat him, ever.

Julius Falkenstein was one of the richest men in Germany, owner of the Falkenstein bank, member of all the important business associations, moving in the highest circles, acquainted with Germany's elite, and he refused to cower in front of some crazy parvenu who called himself Führer and savior of the nation.

A little warning voice tried to be heard. "Don't let your emotions cloud your mind."

The sound advice only caused his fury to burn brighter. "I don't do emotions. I'm calm."

"It seems not," his subconscious argued. "Look at you, panting and sweating like a man in a deadly fever. You'd better have a good sleep and rethink your decision."

Julius shrugged his shoulders to silence the voice. The truth was, he was afraid to sleep, because then the nightmare would return.

2

Joseph opened the door to the office at the Sachsenhausen concentration camp, ready to get started with the huge amount of work waiting for him.

Over the past two days, almost six thousand Jews in and around Berlin had been arrested and sent to several camps. He'd waited to show up until his brother-in-law Julius had been released, because he didn't want anyone to discern the role he'd played in it.

Recently promoted to Hauptsturmführer he couldn't afford the slightest shadow of doubt about his loyalty to the Führer. His sister Edith had maneuvered him into an untenable situation when she'd come begging him to help her husband. He surely didn't have any love lost for the Jews, and wouldn't have let that fat cat banker go free otherwise, but how could he deny his little sister her wish?

Despite her cutting all ties with her family years earlier, he still loved her dearly. It was such a tragedy that she clung to the belief that a wife must stand with her husband against all obstacles. He scoffed. What a foolish concept, when one was married to a subhuman.

Joseph himself had not hesitated a single minute to divorce his long-time wife and mother of his two sons, when he'd found out that her great-great-great-grandmother had been a Jew. Admittedly, not enough to qualify her as a Jew, but sufficient to make her an unsuitable wife for an SS officer.

Had he begged and whined to the Führer to grant an exception for him? Of course he hadn't. He was better than that and always put duty to his Fatherland over personal pleasure. Whatever sacrifice the Führer asked of him, he gladly offered it.

Edith, though, his good-hearted younger sister, didn't have the inner strength to take a hard decision. It was forgivable, because she was a woman—Hitler had valid reasons for keeping them out of politics and inside the house.

For his own behavior, though, there was no excuse. He had indulged Edith, had pulled a few strings and greased some palms to get her husband free. His breathing became faster as fury burnt through him, hating himself for being so weak. The Führer despised weakness, he would despise Joseph if he ever knew.

"Hauptsturmführer Hesse," an underling greeted him, a bit too lackadaisical.

Joseph snapped his heels, shouting, "Heil Hitler!" to remind the young man about the proper way to greet a superior.

Promptly the other man followed suit and Joseph had to admit that the Sturmmann gave the revered *Hitlergruss* perfectly in form and execution.

"Can you give me a summary of the situation, Sturmmann Renk?"

"Yes, Herr Hauptsturmführer." Renk proceeded to efficiently summarize. "Altogether we arrested six thousand subjects. So far, one-hundred fifty-six have been released upon payment of a fine. We are awaiting orders for the rest."

"Well done." Joseph had instructions to release the prisoners—with a stern warning—who had the means to pay the required penalty. Those who were too poor, or had nobody to vouch for them, would be sent in due time to the Dachau camp, which sorely needed labor for the planned expansion. "Have the prisoners been separated by their ability to pay the fine for their crimes?"

"Yes, Herr Hauptsturmführer, the ones without means have been taken to barracks thirty-eight and thirty-nine."

"Have them line up, I want to make an inspection to find out who can be used for hard labor."

While Sturmmann Renk went to fetch the prisoners, Joseph settled behind the huge desk and ordered coffee from the secretary. It wasn't his usual task to sort through prisoners; the actions following the Night of Broken Glass had caused such an immense influx of prisoners that the camp administration had pleaded for help from other units. Joseph was always willing to serve wherever he was needed and volunteered without hesitation. This task might be unpleasant, but it needed to be done, so Joseph would do it.

About fifteen minutes later, Renk returned. "Hauptsturmführer Hesse, the prisoners are lined up for inspection."

"Thank you." Joseph strode outside onto the huge parade ground, where roughly two hundred men, looking rather disheveled, stood waiting. Instinctively he opened his mouth to scold them for their poor posture, then he swallowed down the words and shrugged. His advice would be wasted on the gathered scum. If these men had a spark of honor in their bones, they would have left Germany years ago.

As he inspected the prisoners, he stopped every few steps to signal the secretary shadowing him, which ones were to be sent for labor in Dachau and who remained. He wasn't privy to what the camp administration had in store for the scum unsuitable for work, but he had an inkling it wouldn't please those lazy scoundrels.

When he recognized a familiar face, he startled. Blinking twice, he scrutinized the skinny, fine-limbed man with the darkish hair and the chiseled features women liked so much. It took a few seconds before he put a name to the face. Heinrich Goldmann—they'd attended the same school. If he wasn't mistaken, Heinrich had been two years below him. He remembered him well, although he'd never suspected that Heinrich was a Jew. Back then Heinrich had been the envy of every single boy, because he'd dated the most beautiful girl in school. An exquisite black-haired girl with a porcelain complexion and the most stunning hazel eyes. Helga… something. He couldn't remember her last name, but his loins pulsated at the vivid memory of the many lustful dreams he had about her during his adolescence.

"Name?" he snapped to hide his surprise.

"Heinrich Goldmann," the other man responded, verifying Joseph's suspicion.

"Escort him to the office," Joseph ordered the Sturmmann by his side, without further explanation. As he continued to the next row of prisoners, his mind was spinning. Why had he singled out Heinrich? What should he do with him now? Heinrich was a Jew, after all. A crime for which there was no excuse nor remedy.

Joseph shook his head, wishing he hadn't said a word. But it was too late. He had to return to the office and deal with his former schoolmate. About thirty minutes later he entered an interrogation room, where an anguished-looking Heinrich was waiting for him. The moment Joseph strode inside, his former schoolmate jumped up, standing to attention. At least, he seemed to know what was good for him.

Still not quite sure what he was going to do, Joseph asked, "Did you marry Helga after all?"

Heinrich's eyes betrayed his fear as he stuttered, "H- how do you know?"

"The SS knows everything," Joseph answered, a powerful rush of euphoria coursing through his veins, creating the illusion he was floating. This always happened when he possessed absolute authority over someone. The tingling sensation heightened his senses. Relishing the taste of power, he sensed himself growing several centimeters in size.

Taking a deep breath, he smelled deathly fear, which gave him an additional kick of adrenaline. The handsome, talented Heinrich Goldmann was completely at Joseph's mercy and he could do with him anything his heart desired.

Whether he killed or humiliated the other man, made him kneel, beg or lick his boots clean, let him suffer excruciating pain, or delivered him from suffering—anything was possible and it was exclusively Joseph's choice. Heinrich's anguished face stepped the situation up a notch. It was a sight to behold. The lawless Jew and the almighty SS officer. Superior. Omnipotent. God-like.

After basking a full minute in the other man's discomfort, Joseph spoke again. "She's not a Jew though, is she?"

"No, she's an Aryan. She has nothing to do with this." The fool seemed fiercely decided not to drag his wife into this.

"She has everything to do with this. But tell me, why did the most beautiful girl in the entire school choose a Jew of all people? She could have had any man." Joseph expected Heinrich to protest, but the other man simply shrugged with a broken expression.

"I don't know. I've asked myself that same question a thousand times. I guess, when you love someone, really love them, you don't ask why."

Heinrich's self-reflecting answer took all the fun away. It transferred power back to the inferior man, by reminding Joseph that he'd never loved a woman so deeply. His loyalty belonged to the Führer above anyone else.

He cocked his head, scrutinizing the man he'd envied for the love of a girl so many years ago. The trembling mass in front of him had nothing to be envious about. "You're right. She has no logical reason to prefer you over anyone else."

Heinrich lowered his gaze, not even attempting to object.

With some satisfaction, Joseph pulled a cigarette out of his pocket and lit it up. Taking a pensive puff, he felt a strange sentiment toward Heinrich—one he shouldn't have. An SS officer did not sympathize with a Jew. "Let me give you some advice: if you truly love her, get a divorce. She'll only suffer because of you."

Heinrich seemed to crumple upon himself and it was a

wonder that he managed to stay upright. "You're right. I've been feeling guilty ever since..." He made an all-encompassing gesture, summing up the Jewish situation since Hitler had come to power.

"Look. I shouldn't do this, I really shouldn't." Joseph fought to find the proper words, or, more accurately, he struggled to find out what had possessed him to feel empathy with a Jew and why he wasted time with this conversation. "You know that you aren't strong enough to be sent for construction work?"

Looking even more miserable, Heinrich nodded.

"Do you know what happens to prisoners like you?"

Heinrich shook his head, the unvoiced sob hanging between them, since they both knew it wouldn't be pretty.

"I don't either. I mean, not in detail. You see, I'm only helping out here, because we had to arrest so many Jews after the vile assassination of Ernst von Rath..." Joseph stopped talking since he'd forgotten where he was going with this. He had no issues beating up or killing someone on Hitler's orders to defend the Fatherland, the way he'd done back in 1934 during the Röhm-Putsch when his unit had slaughtered the rogue SA-troops in their sleep, but... the man in front of him was nothing but a blubbering mess, and certainly no threat for the German nation. Inwardly shrugging the thoughts away, he asked, "What's your profession?"

"I'm an accountant." A steep frown appeared on Heinrich's forehead, expressing his confusion.

The profession suited him. Joseph could well imagine the fine-limbed man wearing oversleeves and punching numbers into a calculator. Fonder of action himself, he shuddered at the image of endless rows of numbers to be summed up. Unfortunately mathematics wouldn't help Heinrich in the slightest where he was going.

"Isn't there a way you can scrounge up the money to pay your bail?"

The crease on Heinrich's forehead steepened. "Times have been hard, and we haven't been able to save up anything."

"Don't tell me. I got laid off during the Great Depression and couldn't find another stable job, until Hitler took over. From then on, the German economy has finally been soaring." Joseph launched into a hymn of praise to the almighty Führer who'd brought so much good to his nation.

Heinrich at least had the good grace to refrain from objections, which so many other Jews would have done. His apparent pliability struck a chord in Joseph's heart. Before he thought it through, he said, "You know what? For old times' sake, I'm going to let you go free."

"Really? I mean... How can I ever thank you for this?" Heinrich's voice was choked with tears that threatened to spill.

"No thanks needed. Just don't get yourself into trouble again. And give my regards to Helga." If he were honest, Joseph did this mostly for her. He still had a soft spot for the beautiful girl who'd been the heartthrob of his adolescence.

3

Helga was like a ship without a rudder, drifting aimlessly. Without her husband she felt lost. Since that fateful Night of Broken Glass almost a week ago when he'd gone missing, she had walked all over town, asking his whereabouts. Nothing. Nobody seemed to know anything. It was as if her beloved Heinrich had vanished from the face of the earth.

Not even her well-connected sister Felicitas and her husband Ernst Ritter, the mayor of Oranienburg, had been able to find out where Heinrich was or whether—Helga's hand shot to her throat at the thought—he was still alive.

Felicitas, whom Helga loved dearly, had accompanied her to the authorities, flaunting her *Bombom,* the golden Nazi Party badge, an award given by Hitler to the first one hundred thousand people who'd joined the party and remained in good standing. Even that hadn't helped.

The only information Felicitas had been able to find out was that Heinrich had been arrested and taken to the Sachsenhausen camp. A fate which he shared with roughly six thousand other Jews, purportedly for betraying the Reich.

Helga stared at the paper peeling off the wall where moisture trickled through the ceiling in their shabby apartment. Slowly, desperation was displaced by rage at their former landlady, who'd kicked her out of their lovely home for the unforgivable crime of being married to a Jew. The subsequent humiliations she had endured while hunting for a new place to live in stoked the fire inside her, and soon a red mist clouded her vision until the rage broke the dam of her normally cool exterior. She raised a fist, cursing, "I hope you rot in hell for all eternity, dear Adolf!"

The man who called himself Führer and feigned to love and cherish the nation he ruled over, except for Jews, Gypsies, dissidents, critics, homosexuals, and other so-called asocials.

Hitler even disliked Helga, although she was a pure-blooded Aryan six generations back. A fact her sister had found out, because to become mayor her husband Ernst needed the *Große Ariernachweis*, proving his and his wife's ancestry tracing back to 1750.

Helga had become an outcast, not because of her ancestry, political opinion or a genetic disease, but because she loved the wrong man. Moreover, she had resisted the well-intentioned advice to divorce her husband and cleanse herself and her two half-Jewish children, David and Amelie, from the damaging Jewish influence.

The door opened and her son David came in. At nineteen years old he was a grown man, towering almost a head over her. He had dark hair, broad shoulders acquired by hard work in a mechanical workshop, and usually a mischievous grin on his lips. Today, there was no trace of a smile on his face.

She tried to decipher answers from his expression, wanting to know what he'd found out, yet not wanting to hear if he carried bad news.

"I'm sorry," David said.

Instantaneously the air rushed out of her lungs with a swooshing sound similar to a punctured balloon. She crumpled over, dark spots dancing in front of her eyes.

David rushed over in three big strides, caught her just in time in his strong arms and gently moved her to the sofa.

"Is he…?"

His face scrunched. "Mutti, I didn't want to scare you. Father is still alive. They continue to hold him in the Sachsenhausen camp."

"Did you find out anything else?" Her heart sunk. Friends had returned from there after paying a hefty bail, a ransom really, because there was no doubt the Nazis would never return a single cent. All the survivors she'd met featured the same hollow look, speaking of horrible experiences.

David shook his head. "Just that he's still there."

"Thanks, David." At least her Heinrich was still alive. She patted the empty spot on the sofa beside her. "I'm grateful for your help."

"He's my father," he said, settling down. Just then the door opened a second time and Amelie came inside. The fifteen-year-old had her chestnut-colored hair braided into pretzel-style braids over her ears, and was wearing a *Bund Deutscher Mädel* uniform.

"What on earth are you wearing?" Helga couldn't keep the disapproval at her daughter's appearance out of her voice. Even if Amelie had wanted to, as a half-Jew she wasn't allowed to join Hitler's youth organization for girls.

"My friend Lena loaned it to me. It's the perfect disguise. You can't imagine the SS boys toppling over each other to make eyes at me."

Helga could well imagine and didn't like it one bit.

Amelie continued without acknowledging her mother's disapproving stare. "Thing is, there's nothing they can do for Father." She flopped down between David and her mother. "There's more."

"Good or bad news?" David asked.

"Not sure. Probably bad."

Helga barely managed to breathe against the sudden pressure on her lungs.

Amelie continued unfazed. "By the end of the week a bunch of prisoners will be transferred to the Dachau camp as construction workers for its expansion."

"Father is not fit for construction work!" David objected. Since he had outgrown his father both in height and strength years ago, the family always joked that David must have been switched in the hospital. His face resembled his father's, but the stature was purportedly inherited from some distant uncle.

Helga's heart stopped beating. She was only fifteen when she'd first set eyes on the handsome boy two years older than her. What had started out as high-school sweethearts had resulted in them getting married immediately after she graduated. "Dachau is at the other end of the country! How will I ever see him again?"

"Can't Aunt Feli do something?" Amelie asked, since Helga's sister had come through for them so many times.

"I'm afraid not." Helga wrung her hands in despair. "She's already pulled so many strings. There's not much else she can do, since Ernst forbade her to publicly go and bail out a Jew, even a relative."

"Typical Uncle Ernst," David chimed in. "Always afraid of public opinion. He can shove his position of mayor up his ass!"

"David! Remember your manners!" Even if she was of the same opinion, she wouldn't allow David to use such words.

"You expect me to be well-behaved when these Nazi thugs arrest my father for no reason at all? To hell with manners."

Helga was too exhausted to give her son a piece of her mind. Secretly she admired him for his guts, although she constantly worried about his safety, since this kind of behavior out on the street would have him joining his father in Sachsenhausen in no time at all.

"I'd better prepare dinner, it's been a long and exhausting day." She got up and shuffled into the kitchen, already dreading the next day when she would have to get up extra early to pass by the police station and see whether she could work a miracle to free her husband. After work she planned to take the train to Oranienburg and visit her sister. Sachsenhausen was only a stone's throw away and perhaps with Feli's help, she might at least be allowed to visit Heinrich.

"I'll get washed up." David was usually oil-greased after a long day at the mechanics shop. While he entered the bathroom, Amelie joined her mother in the kitchen.

"Mutti?"

"Yes?" Amelie's tone of voice caused violent shivers to run down Helga's spine.

"I could… I mean… there was this young SS officer who hinted that he could get me into the camp, if…"

"If what?" Helga asked her daughter, expecting a sinister suggestion.

Amelie shrugged. "If I go out with him."

"You will not!"

"If it helps Father, don't you think I should?"

"Under no circumstances will you go out with one of them. The moment he learns that you're half-Jewish, God only knows what he'll do to you."

"He'll never find out."

Helga shook her head. "No. And that is my last word. You're much too young anyway."

"I'm almost sixteen. Other girls get married at my age."

Helga glared at her daughter. "You're not actually thinking about marrying an SS man?"

"Of course not." Amelie raised her hands in a defensive gesture. "I'd string him along until he lets me visit Papa. And then I'd drop him."

"No." Helga shook her head, feeling incredibly guilty for dragging her daughter into this mess. "I appreciate your offer, but I want you to stay out of this."

"I'm already in it, Mutti." Amelie sighed. "I can't leave you dealing alone with this."

Helga knew that arguing would be useless, so she pretended to reconsider. "I know, sweetheart. Please wait at least until tomorrow night. I'm going to visit Feli once more. She might get me inside the camp."

"Alright." Amelie seemed relieved that she didn't have to date the SS man.

About an hour later the three of them sat down to have dinner. The empty seat at the table acutely reminded Helga how much she missed Heinrich. He was the love of her life, her anchor, her soulmate, her everything. How would she cope without him?

They had hardly finished eating when the doorbell rang.

"I'll get it." Amelie jumped up and was out of the room before anyone could stop her. David gave Helga a disconcerted look. "What's up with her?"

Helga shrugged, praying the visitor wasn't the SS man Amelie had been flirting with. The next moment Amelie returned with the broadest smile. Helga gasped as behind her she saw the man she loved so much.

"Heinrich!" She jumped up and was about to throw herself around his neck when she noticed the dried blood on his face. Gently placing a kiss on his lips she asked, "My darling! What did they do to you?"

"Don't worry, that'll heal." The look in his eyes belied his comforting words. "I'm so glad to be back."

She couldn't hold onto her composure for a single second longer and launched herself into his arms, sobbing. "Dear God, I'm so glad you're back. I was so afraid I'd never see you again."

He stroked her back with his hands as if she were the one who'd endured a week in a concentration camp, until she finally stopped crying. Letting go of him, she observed how Heinrich first hugged Amelie and then David. "I'm so glad to be home and even happier to see nothing has happened to both of you."

David nodded. "I was lucky. After hearing rumors from customers, my boss warned me not to leave the workshop. He even returned late at night to bring me food and a blanket, practically ordering me to stay and not let myself be seen outside."

Herr Baumann was an old communist who'd converted to Nazism in name only. Thanks to him, David's nickname at work was Kessel and none of his co-workers knew his last name was Goldmann, so nobody suspected him of being half-Jewish. She'd have to personally thank that man for keeping her son safe.

"Are you hungry?" she asked her husband.

"Like a wolf!"

She didn't dare to ask whether they'd given him food in prison. Quickly, she vanished into the kitchen to reheat the remains of the dinner, while Heinrich stepped into the bathroom to clean himself up and change into fresh clothes. When he joined her in the kitchen, he looked almost like himself again.

"I was so worried," she whispered.

"I know, my love."

"We tried everything. I visited Felicitas at least three times, but even she was powerless to do anything for you." She thought it best not to mention that Ernst had forbidden his wife to bail him out.

"I'm home now, and that's all that matters."

Something in his voice raised a suspicion. "How come they just let you out?"

"They didn't. In fact they wanted to send me to Dachau, but then serendipity struck. Do you remember Joseph Hesse?"

Helga scrunched up her nose, thinking hard. "No, I don't."

"He's the brother of your classmate, Edith Falkenstein."

"Oh yes. She has two brothers. So what about him?"

Heinrich grinned. "It seems he remembers you very well. Looks to me as if he was very sweet on you back in school."

"Really? And what does this have to do with your release?" Helga leaned against her husband, soaking up the warmth of his body. An overwhelming sense of love, comfort and safety flooded her entire being.

"Turns out he has made a career for himself in the SS, has the rank of Hauptsturmführer. It was my luck that he had been posted to the Sachsenhausen camp to help out and that he remembered me from school. Although I think what tipped the scales in my favor was his fancy for you. I think he became nostalgic and let me go."

"Oh dear! That's the second time the Hesse family has come to our rescue, after Edith asked her husband to employ you."

Heinrich's face fell. "I believe I saw Herr Falkenstein at the camp as I arrived there, but I can't be sure."

Helga bit on her lip. "You can't imagine the mayhem on the streets the day you were arrested. Most synagogues were burning, windows smashed, stores vandalized, people beaten up. The police and even the fire workers stood by watching without lifting a finger. It was awful." She blinked a few times to dispel the images crowding in on her.

"I was so worried, about all three of you. Amelie returned home first. With her Aryan looks and working in a purely Aryan borough she had no difficulties getting home, although she told me that she made sure nobody followed her into our street, since the neighbors know." The food on the stove bubbled up. Helga turned her attention to the pot and stirred the goulash, before ladling in onto a plate. "Let's talk over dinner."

Heinrich followed her to the table, where David and Amelie were sitting with curious expressions on their faces. Helga sensed that Heinrich wasn't ready to talk about his experiences, so she cut short any possible questions by saying, "Your father has been released due to the intervention of an old acquaintance, and that's all you need to know for the moment."

Heinrich cast her a grateful gaze, before he asked, "How about you, David?"

"I'm fine. But it's not been easy these days."

Silently, Heinrich ladled his soup, until he suddenly said, "We should consider emigration."

"We tried that, remember?" David scowled. "None of the foreign countries would issue visas to us without proving to them that we own heaps of money."

"We can try again, perhaps after the recent events, they are more open to refugees?" Helga suggested.

"You're dreaming, Mutti. If anything, they'll laugh into their sleeves." David gave a brooding look.

"Then, what should we do?" Amelie's voice was small.

"I for one am not going to live in fear of the Nazis. I'm going to fight them." David grimaced as if he planned to rush out the door this very instant to beat up a Nazi.

"You will do no such thing!" Heinrich scolded his son. "There's no way you can take it up with the government, so best you stay put and keep a low profile."

"That has done us so much good during the last years." David wouldn't let up.

"Please, no fighting. Your father just returned home and must be exhausted." Helga looked between her two men. "If we don't stick together as a family, we'll never survive."

"We might not either way," David muttered.

4

Out of habit, Edith checked her presentation in the mirror, although, since the horrible November pogroms, nothing seemed to matter anymore. She couldn't shake the feeling of dread, wherever she went. Putting on her hat and her gloves, she told the driver, "I'm ready to leave."

"Where to, *gnädige Frau?*"

"The Tiergarten." Edith had an appointment with Helga in a beautiful little café in the park. She wasn't due to meet her friend for another hour, yet she wanted to arrive early, hoping that a stroll through the vast park would ease her mind.

When the driver dropped her off at the café, Edith instructed him to return for her in three hours. Then she walked across the street, past the café and into the park, relishing the pristine white snow, inhaling the crisp winter air. After walking a few minutes, she already sensed the tension in her shoulders dissipating. She took off her leather gloves and deposited them in her purse, from where she pulled out a cigarette and lit it, before putting the gloves back on.

Julius would be scandalized if he saw her, since he considered smoking unladylike. Edith huffed. Nothing in her life was the way it used to be. Gone were traditions, appearances and the need to represent. It had started out slowly after Hitler's coming to power in 1933 and gradually gone downhill from there. Julius had lost his citizenship to the Reich, she'd had to let go her trusted maid, because Jews weren't allowed to employ Aryan girls under a certain age and... Her husband's recent arrest had only been the latest blow. She feared what would come next—because she was sure the Nazis wouldn't stop.

It was only a matter of time before they'd announce their next strike. Edith had long ceased to wonder what the government would contrive next, since no sane person could guess at the atrocities the Nazis spewed out against Jews and other despised minorities. Inhaling the smoke deeply, her chest prickled with rising anger. Julius lived in a state of delirious denial. Despite all the signs to the contrary, he pretended that things would right themselves and nobody was going to hurt him.

Since he was an intelligent man, she found it difficult to fathom his gigantic misjudgment of the political situation. Taking another furious draw from her cigarette, she looked at the snow-covered trees a short distance away, musing over his peculiar behavior. Then it occurred to her that it wasn't peculiar at all. In fact, he'd shown this very trait from the first day she'd met him at a dance so many years ago in the summer of 1913.

Almost a year later on one of their dates, she'd asked him about the possibility of war. He'd assured her in the most eloquent words that a political solution for the tension would be found and she had nothing to worry about. She'd believed him—until the war broke out less than a week later and he left for the military.

Edith now realized that he'd lied to her back then and probably was doing the same today. He'd always considered her in need of his protection and had tried his best to keep unpleasant things away from her. Tears pricked at her eyes. How could Julius still believe she needed shielding from the outside world?

Her fingers trembling—not from the cold—she increased her pace. Hadn't she proven time and again that she wasn't the innocent young girl anymore, with whom he'd fallen in love twenty-five years ago? Did he really believe he could isolate her on the sheltered Schwanenwerder Island, a place in Berlin where only the highest echelons owned their mansions, and she wouldn't notice that the country around her was being run into the ground?

Had he forgotten that a multitude of their friends, including his sister Adriana and her family, had emigrated? Had he forgotten the incident when their dear friend Alexander Lobe had stumbled into their home, mangled and bloodied after being arrested by the SA, or SS, or whatever branch of government had decided to rough up the intellectual for criticizing the government.

Her steps became even faster, her booted feet stomping the snow as if she wanted to pulverize every last Nazi under her feet. It was only thanks to her brother Joseph that Julius was quickly freed after being arrested during the November pogroms, and yet he chose to carry on with the delusion that he was still a powerful member of Germany's elite.

Dragging on her cigarette, she found it to be almost finished. She looked up and didn't recognize this part of the Tiergarten park. As she turned around to look back, she noticed that she'd walked quite the distance in her angry stupor. With a quick glance at her watch she hastened to the café, since she didn't want to keep Helga waiting.

Her friend was stepping into the park, just as the café finally came in sight. Edith waved at her. At a closer distance, she could see that Helga was unusually nervous.

"What is wrong?"

"God, I hate Hitler so much!" Helga exclaimed, a bit too loud. As if on command, both women glanced over their shoulders to find out whether they had been overheard. Fortunately there was nobody in sight.

"Would you care for a walk rather than having coffee?" Edith suggested, despite her being exhausted after her furious march.

Helga's face lit up with gratitude. "That's a wonderful idea, if you don't mind."

"Not at all," Edith lied, secretly eyeing the cozy café and imagining her cold hands wrapped around a hot cup of coffee, savoring a bite of one of the delicious pastries. Her mouth watered as she tasted the fruity sweetness of the café's superb apricot torte.

"I hate that man so much. If I ever meet him in person, I won't be able to guarantee anything!"

Edith giggled at the notion. "I know that feeling. Should we walk around the lake, since it's too cold to sit down?"

"Thanks for meeting up with me," Helga said as they walked down the same path Edith had taken before on her own. After several minutes of silence, Helga suddenly stopped, looked over her shoulder and said, "Heinrich has finally been released from the Sachsenhausen camp."

A nauseating wave of guilt washed over Edith because she'd been too preoccupied with her own problems to find out whether her friend was fine. "Is he alright?"

"Yes. Shaken, but nothing that won't heal."

"I'm so sorry, I should have inquired about him much earlier, but I was so caught up with Julius…"

Helga fixed her with a curious gaze. "Heinrich mentioned that he believed he'd seen your husband at the camp. Is it true?"

The anguish about Julius' wellbeing she'd experienced hit her so hard, it pressed the air from her lungs. Coughing, it took her a while to recover her voice. "Yes. He was dragged from his office and taken there. We had to pay a hefty fine to get him out."

"That's what Heinrich mentioned. Those who were able to pay the outrageous sum were let go…"

Even though Helga hadn't accused her, Edith felt a sharp sting of inadequateness. She should have telephoned her friend and inquired after her family. It wouldn't have been a problem for Edith to pay Heinrich's fine. Shame for being the worst friend on earth crept up her spine, making her cheeks and ears burn. "I'm awfully sorry. I've been so busy with my own problems, that I forgot to ask about your family!"

"Don't." Helga gave a sad little shake of her head. "I could have asked for your help, but it never occurred to me either. Instead, I resorted to my sister, who's in the Nazi party, but even she couldn't do a thing."

"I promise to be a better friend from now on." Edith cocked her head, musing whether she should speak out loud what she knew deep in her gut. "We'll need to stick together if we want to come out of this unscathed."

Helga nodded pensively. "I'm afraid so."

Since her friend didn't offer another explanation, Edith asked, "How did Heinrich get released?"

"It's quite funny, actually. Your brother intervened."

"My brother?" Edith raised an eyebrow. Knut didn't have the clout, so that left only her older brother. "Joseph?"

"Yes. Apparently he remembered Heinrich from school and took pity on him." Helga hesitated for a moment, before she continued. "He told him to emigrate."

After the reluctance Joseph had shown to help his own brother-in-law, Edith was surprised, even annoyed, that he'd helped Heinrich so willingly. Swallowing down the emotions, she scolded herself for being resentful instead of cherishing the fact that Heinrich had been released. "I keep begging Julius to consider leaving the country, at least temporarily, but he just won't."

Helga looked astonished. "Why on earth wouldn't he?"

"Because he's deluded himself into believing the Nazis can't touch him, and because of his business. He says he has a responsibility for his employees and can't abandon them on a whim." Even as she said the words, a lump formed in her throat. Not so long ago, Julius had let go of all his Jewish employees, including Heinrich. She knew Julius had felt bad about it, but, as always, he'd insisted on sticking to the law. The Nazis demanded and Julius fulfilled—did he honestly believe this would save him in the end? Edith had her doubts.

"Couldn't someone else keep running the bank in the meantime?" They had arrived at the small lake. "Shall we go around or would you rather go back?"

"Around is fine, there's a nice café on the other shore. We could go there if you want?"

"That sounds nice, I'm getting cold feet." As if to emphasize her words, Helga shivered.

"So, have you considered emigration?"

"Personally, I can't imagine leaving Berlin, but, yes, Heinrich has been queuing in front of several embassies, albeit without results. We have neither the skills, nor the money or connections to get a preferred visa, our only chance is the lottery."

"I'm sorry." Edith wondered whether she should offer her help, but before she could think about it, Helga continued. "I mean, how much worse can it get?"

"I'm sure it will get better soon." Edith didn't have the heart to tell her friend the opposite might indeed be true.

"Come on, let's get a hot coffee," Helga suggested.

"Sounds good to me." Edith rubbed her cold fingers through the leather gloves. After a while she added. "We're both Aryans, that has to account for something, hasn't it?"

"I hope so, although some days I'm afraid it won't be enough."

"It will. It must."

"Let's hope you're right. We'll never give in to that horrible, horrible man!" Helga put a hand on Edith's arm. "I'm glad to have you. It does feel incredibly good to talk to someone in a similar position. But now, no more subversive talk, or they'll arrest us both."

"Then our husbands would be in deep trouble." The burden of responsibility weighed heavily down on Edith's shoulders. Up to now she hadn't quite come to accept it, but apparently she was the only thing between Julius and despotism. Or her Aryan genealogy to be precise.

5

Julius was sitting in his home office, which he preferred these days instead of going into the burned-out office at the bank, reading *Das Jüdische Nachrichtenblatt,* the official Jewish newspaper. He almost spilled his coffee as he read the article announcing Jews couldn't own or drive cars.

"What the hell?" he said out loud, trying to focus on the notice, according to which all Jews had to turn in their driving licenses, as well as car ownership documents to the local authority by the end of the year. Apparently, this was due to the November pogroms—allegedly instigated by rogue Jews wanting to hurt the German nation.

These days nothing seemed to make sense anymore. Hitler, and along with him most of the party bigwigs, acted in a way absolutely unheard of for any decent politician. They behaved more like a bunch of badly brought up children than grown men.

Pondering the implication of the latest rule, memories of Julius' time in Sachsenhausen bubbled up, making him sweat profusely. He took the pristine white kerchief from his breast pocket and wiped his forehead, while trying to ban the images from his mind. There was nothing gained from reliving that horrible time again and again—especially not during his waking hours when he had the power to push the memories away.

The worst had happened, and he'd come out on the other side. What else could the Nazis do to him? He squared his shoulders, walking over to the cabinet with a vast array of different brands of exquisite spirits and pouring himself a cognac. Lately he'd started drinking way more and way earlier in an effort to calm his nerves.

A knock on the door caught him by surprise. Halting mid-step, his eyes roamed the office, until they fell on the window. A wild thought of escape crossed his mind before he forced himself to relax. After his release from the camp, he'd been rather jumpy —one more reason why he preferred to stay in the safety of his Schwanenwerder mansion.

"Come in," he called, raising an eyebrow when the Edith stepped into the room, looking magnificent in a full-length midnight-blue gown, wearing the spectacular diamond necklace that had once belonged to his mother.

"Have you forgotten that we have tickets for the opera?" She looked pointedly at his business attire.

"I'm sorry." For a second, he was tempted to cancel the engagement, since he didn't want to answer questions about his time in prison. Julius Falkenstein, owner of one of Germany's biggest banks, hauled off to a camp. It was the ultimate ignominy.

Then he thought better of it. Most people wouldn't know, and those who did would take his non-appearance as an opportunity to gossip viciously about it. No, whether he liked it or not, he had to show up and pretend nothing had happened. "I'll be with you in a minute. Will you alert the driver to wait for us with the car?"

"Of course, Julius."

Even as he observed Edith leaving his office, the rage boiled in his veins. How was he supposed to get to the opera if the Nazis forbade him owning a car? To work at his city office? To attend his many social obligations?

He looked at the clock. It was approaching seven thirty. He'd have to hurry or they would be late for the opera. Would he actually be expected to walk the fifteen kilometers to the opera house by next year? Perhaps the commoners might be used to getting around without a car, but he certainly wasn't. Julius shook his head, since the notion was ridiculous. As always, the Nazis hadn't thought this law through. It was utterly impractical.

He was still standing in the same place, staring at the wall, when Edith returned. "The driver is waiting for us."

"How shall we get around without a car?" he asked more to himself.

Edith squinted her eyes at him. "Why should we?"

"Because Herr Hitler says so."

"Is this some new rule, I don't know about?" Edith seemed rather calm at the news, but then she'd grown up in a middle-class family and had only starting being driven around after their wedding.

"Yes, it is!" he yelled at her, immediately regretting his outburst. Taking a deep breath he added in a more conciliatory tone, "Apparently all Jews need to surrender the papers for their vehicles to the authorities by the end of the year. It seems we are a danger to the public if we're allowed to drive."

"Perhaps you should—"

Again, the hideous feeling of inadequacy stabbed his inside and he interrupted her. "Don't patronize me! I know what you're going to say. And no, I will not consider emigration! Ever! This is my country. I lived here long before this Austrian parvenu ever set foot in it." With the echo of his shrill voice in his ear, Julius downed the cognac still standing on the coffee table and set the glass down with a loud thud, forgetting years of education in etiquette. His mother would turn in her grave if she knew how inappropriately her son was behaving. But lately Julius couldn't keep his usual calm. At the slightest opportunity negative emotions overwhelmed his sangfroid and he exploded like fireworks at New Year's Eve.

Edith pursed her lips, giving him the indulging gaze she might give to a toddler throwing a tantrum. "That's not what I meant, Julius. Perhaps if you asked one of your acquaintances in politics for an exception. They must realize that you need to avail yourself of a car."

He was too furious to acknowledge that her idea was indeed very good. Being a member of several influential clubs, he had strong connections to the business elite and, to a lesser extent, to the political elite. In his mind, he went through his contacts, deciding which one might best serve the purpose.

Fat Hermann Göring was the obvious first choice. Julius knew him from before Hitler became chancellor, when Göring had been a boastful nobody, an opinion Julius obviously had never voiced except with his most loyal friends. Göring might even be at tonight's performance of Werner Egk's *Peer Gynt* at the Berlin State Opera. Even if not, he'd meet other important men there, to whom he might hint about his problem.

"I'll be ready in ten minutes," he said to Edith, before he hurried to his bedroom to change into his tuxedo.

Unfortunately, Göring did not attend the opera, but Julius met one of his aides, who arranged for a meeting.

A few days later Julius went to meet with the Minister of Aviation in his office in the recently built monumental complex in the Wilhelmstrasse. He'd never been inside Berlin's biggest office building featuring two thousand rooms and was deeply impressed by the stark and linear signature style of one of the most famous architects of the Reich, Ernst Sagebiel.

An aide accompanied him through long corridors into an opulent office, adorned with precious paintings. The obligatory Hitler portrait hung on the wall behind the mahogany desk, flanked by swastika flags. Herrmann Göring sat behind his desk, not bothering to get up to greet the visitor, as politeness would demand. He merely waved his hand, motioning for his guest to sit down.

The Reichsmarschall wore a fancy light-gray uniform with white piping and a double row of golden buttons, adorned with golden shoulder straps. An iron cross hung around his neck, and the Luftwaffe eagle flaunted his breast. Finally, he spoke: "Julius Falkenstein, is it?"

Julius bristled at the casual denigration. That fat man pretending not to know who he was when they had met many times before at the private business club they both frequented. Since he had come to ask for a favor, he decided to play the game. He slightly bowed his head, addressing Göring with his full title. "Yes, Herr Field Marshal General."

"Well, then, Julius Falkenstein, what can I do for you?" Göring leaned back, stapling his hands on his impressive stomach.

Julius didn't miss the second blow, by not addressing him with the appropriate Herr, or mister, in front of his name. Perhaps this hadn't been such a splendid idea. In any case, it was too late to bow out. He'd come to ask for a favor and it seemed he had to go down on his knees to grovel. "Herr Field Marshall General, I have just been made aware of a new rule requiring all people of Jewish descent"—oh, how much he hated to vocalize that under the Nazis' notorious Nuremberg race laws, he, a converted Protestant, had been classified as Jewish with one stroke of a pen—"have to resign their driving licenses and vehicle documents by the end of the year."

Göring swayed his head from left to right as if pondering the situation. "I'm well aware of that law. It's an unfortunate step the government has to take after the November pogroms. It is simply too dangerous for the German public to have Jewish subjects owning or driving a car in this dire situation."

Julius was about to explode. This so-called dire situation had been brought upon the nation by the Nazis themselves. They had arrested tens of thousands of Jewish men, vandalized their businesses, their homes, their offices and even their synagogues. To add insult to injury, they'd then made them pay one billion Reichsmarks to the state as recompense for the damages sustained. Now blaming the very victims of those pogroms for their existence was a cruel irony, to put it mildly.

"Well, you must be aware that I'm the owner of the Falkenstein bank and rely on my vehicle for work. Work that is vital for the economic health of the German nation."

Swaying his head again, Göring pouted. "I know, I know. The law causes inconveniences for some, but public safety has to be our first priority."

"You don't think I'm a threat to the public, do you?" Julius could barely keep his voice even.

"Certainly not, but the law is the law and we have to follow it. Where would we be if we made exceptions for everyone and his dog?"

"I'm certainly not anyone. If you care to remember, I'm one of the most well-respected men in Germany."

Göring stared at him coldly. "You used to be. And I feel for you. Believe me, I do. I would have preferred it if the tumults had caused the deaths of two hundred lowlifes instead of destroying invaluable properties."

Julius' eyes widened. The Field Marshall seemed to grieve destroyed office buildings over the loss of lives resulting from the atrocious attacks, which he casually called *tumults.* Thinking on his feet, he saw an opportunity to use that cold-hearted opinion for his own means. "I agree that the property damage was huge and very unfortunate. We need a thriving economy to rebuild what was destroyed. I can assure you that the Falkenstein bank will play its part in the reconstruction by providing money for this humongous task. Therefore I plead with you to grant me further use of my vehicle and driver, to best serve my nation."

A benevolent smile appeared on Göring's face. "Your commitment is laudable. Men like you are needed to form the backbone of our nation." His face fell. "But all of that doesn't matter, because you're a Jew."

"I'm not—" Julius protested.

Göring waved his objection away. "I know all about your

conversion, and in your specific case it might have been done for proper reasons instead of a ruse to delude the government. But, and here you'll have to agree with me, my hands are bound. If I make an exception for you on the grounds of being a baptized Protestant, then tomorrow a myriad of supplicants, most of them a threat to the Reich's very existence, will flood my office claiming the same for themselves."

Julius shook his head. "The Falkenstein bank—"

Again, Göring silenced him with a wave of his hand. "Look, I haven't forgotten how much you and your family have done for Germany in the past. That is the reason why you're still in a much better position than most of your kin. But"—he cast Julius a sorrowful gaze—"I can't hold out my hand to protect you forever."

Julius bowed his head. He didn't believe a single word coming out of the fat pig's mouth. Not about being sorry and certainly not about having lifted a single finger to ease Julius' descent from a powerful businessman to a nobody. An ostracized nobody.

6

David crawled out from under a jacked-up locomotive motor block. These days the workshop worked almost exclusively for the Reichsbahn, the German railway company. He earned good money, but it was grueling work. Piling the block onto a wheeled trolley he grabbed his toolbox and headed for the door.

"Hey, Kessel," Baumann called out. "I need you to pick up a few special tools in Potsdam."

David groaned. Usually he didn't mind working extra hours because it meant extra pay, which his family sorely needed since his father had been let go from his well-paying job as an accountant at the Falkenstein bank last year.

Today though, he needed to be home early. His sister was going to bring home her friend Thea Blume, a girl so beautiful and charming, and who David had been sweet on since he'd first seen her upon entering the Lemberg school. Not that Thea had ever graced him with as much as a smile. She knew very well that every single boy at the school adored her and distributed her favors sparingly.

Meanwhile, five years had passed and David prided himself on having grown from a lanky boy into a rather handsome man. There was no shortage of girls eyeing him with appreciative glances, although he'd never found one of them intriguing enough to date her. Except for Thea, of course. She had lived in his dreams for years. Tonight he fully intended to make an unforgettable impression on her.

"Can't it wait until tomorrow?" David asked his boss.

Baumann raised an eyebrow, since it was the first time David had shied away from extra work. "Something important?"

"It's just... We have a visitor tonight." David tried to act nonchalantly, despite feeling his ears burning bright.

"A girl?" David's ears seemed to catch fire, and seconds later, Baumann's mouth twisted into a bemused grin. "Thought so."

"Well, yes. I mean... it's not like... oh shit." David gathered his breath. "Tonight might be my best chance with her."

Baumann laughed good-naturedly. "Well, Kessel, then I'd say, make the best of it. As long as you get the tools here in the morning."

"You can count on me... and thanks so much." David admired the man who was not only his boss, but had also become a father figure for him. Someone who looked out for him professionally, but most especially personally by keeping David's identity as a half-Jew a secret from everyone else at the workshop. Not that the mostly rough-around-the-edges communist-leaning workers would have minded, but the fewer people who knew, the safer he was.

"Don't mention it. Just don't forget to bring the tools in the morning."

"I won't." David grabbed his jacket and rushed out the door. It was dark outside as he hurried home to scrub the grease and dirt from his person before Thea arrived. She should see him in the best possible shape—and he hoped she would be impressed.

Just as he stood in the bathroom shaving, he heard a knock on the door, sending a happy bolt through his veins, followed by a prickle of shame. After his family had been kicked out from their nice apartment, they'd had to move into this shabby place that didn't even feature doorbells.

The landlady had gleefully citied some new law depriving Jews of any rental protection rights and had added, "We don't want dirty Jews in our house." Even years later, her abject behavior made his blood boil. He squinted at his image in the mirror, thinking that moment had been the tipping point. From then on it had been a gradual, and sometimes not so gradual, decline for their family.

Thea was Jewish herself, a full Jew at that, so she must have had similar experiences. He wondered where her family lived and how she coped. He finished shaving, washed his hands and splashed aftershave on his cheeks, wondering whether he should slick back his hair as was the fashion, or rather ruffle it in the bad boy look some girls seemed to fall for.

Unfortunately he was at a loss as to what type of man Thea preferred. Since she could have anyone, he opted to stand out from the crowd. Ruffled hair it was. The image of Thea running her hand through it made his insides giddy and he quickly shoved those inappropriate thoughts away.

His sister Amelie, in equal parts a horrible nuisance and a great partner-in-crime, knew he was sweet on Thea and had agreed to letting him tag along under the condition that he invite the two girls to the motion pictures.

"Hello, Amelie. Ready to go out?" Thea's jingling voice filled the apartment.

"We have to wait for my brother David, since Mutti won't allow me to the motion pictures on my own."

"I hate the way my mother treats me like a small child," Thea said, her voice sounding so much more grown-up than he remembered.

David left the bathroom to meet the two girls in the living room that doubled up as his parents' bedroom. He'd grown used to the cramped living conditions. In comparison to all the other hardships imposed on Jews, their living quarters didn't seem so bad anymore.

"Hello, Thea." His pulse quickened at the sight of the gorgeous girl; the blonde curls framing her cute face with the big blue eyes.

"Hello, David." She cast him the most wonderful smile. "Thanks for accompanying us."

"It's my pleasure." He meant it. Thea was by far the prettiest girl he'd ever seen and he would have gone anywhere just to be by her side.

As they walked to the picture theater he made sure to walk at Thea's side, while Amelie stayed on her other side. If his sister had any misgivings about him monopolizing her friend's attention, she didn't show it. Yet, he had an inkling he'd hear about it later, which was fine with him, as long as he got to enjoy Thea's company.

"Tell me about your work," Thea encouraged him.

David jumped right into his favorite topic and described in minute detail how he overhauled all kinds of mechanical things, mostly motors. Surprisingly, Thea listened intently, her blue eyes hanging on his lips. Her gaze full of admiration filled his heart with warmth and he seemed to grow several centimeters in height.

"It's admirable of you to work so hard," Thea said, fluttering her eyelashes at him.

"Oh why, yes." David fought for poise, even as her compliment flushed out any coherent thought in his brain. He usually wasn't shy, so why didn't he have a witty response?

"Yes." She nodded to emphasize her words, her blonde curls bopping up and down. "You have so many amazing anecdotes to share."

Amelie side-glanced at him, rolling her eyes with theatrical exaggeration. Unwilling to let her ruin the moment, he cast her a stern look, warning her that she'd suffer for it if she said a wrong word. Amelie shrugged and grinned, obviously unfazed.

"Yes, yes." He ignored his sister and turned his full attention to the peachy girl walking by his side. Somehow gathering his wits, he finally managed to speak a coherent sentence. "You're right. I love my work, there's always so much happening. It's so much better than school."

"It suits you." Thea let her gaze wander across his shoulders and arms. Intuitively he stood straighter, pushing out his broad chest for her to admire. David had never been vain, but in this very instant he was incredibly grateful for the hard work of lugging heavy machinery around the workshop that had caused him to gain several kilos in pure muscle over the past months.

"I find school boring too. Thank God, this is my last year." She cast him another irresistible gaze from beneath long, black eyelashes. Slightly opening her lips, she then continued. "And the boys at school are just that: boys. I much prefer a man by my side."

"Aww." Her words stirred his loins in the most inappropriate ways.

"I wish my mother would allow me to drop classes and do something useful." She gave a dramatic sigh. "But, no! She insists I finish school and prepare for becoming a secretary. How boring! Who wants to become a secretary?"

David knew that his sister was aspiring to become one, since she had the knack for numbers like their father, so he hedged. "It's a valuable job, just not for everyone."

"See? That's what I keep telling my mother, David." She glanced at Amelie. "I'd certainly be good at being a secretary, but it's not what I want to do with my life. I want to become an actress."

"You'd look stunning on the silver screen," was all David could think to say.

"Right?" Thea's eyes lit up with delight. "So why should I be forced to learn shorthand, typing and all that incredibly boring stuff?"

Just then, they arrived at the motion picture theater. David purchased tickets for the three of them and ushered them to their seats.

"Anyone want a soft drink?" he offered.

"Yes, please," the two girls answered and he trotted off to buy three Fantas and a big box of chocolate cookies to share.

"Here you go." He distributed the drinks just in time as the lights dimmed and the film began. Thea was sitting in the middle, with him to her left and Amelie to her right. After a short newsreel, the comedy film *Five Million Look for an Heir* was shown, starring the leading actor Heinz Rühmann and the equally famous Leny Marenbach.

The hilarious comedy of mistaken identities kept David fascinated, until he sensed a hand on his thigh. Utterly unprepared, he barely managed to keep a sigh from escaping his throat. Frozen into place, he didn't dare move a single muscle while Thea's hand was doing a slow, lazy crawl up his leg.

The boldness of her actions caught him by surprise, but at the same time, he liked it very much. Perhaps a bit too much, because his blood rushed downward, causing a growing bulge in his pants. Grateful for the darkness in the theater, he swallowed down the groans of pleasure, doing his best to concentrate on the movie, in order not to lose all self-control and embarrass himself.

Thea's insistent hand moved further up, until she was about to reach his huge erection. He knew he would completely lose it if she actually touched him there, so he quickly put his hand over hers, guiding her downward again.

His breathing became a bit less labored. Over so many years he'd hoped this magnificent girl would notice him, and now he was almost too afraid to believe it actually happened. In any case, he had to keep his cool, especially because his sister was sitting less than a meter away. If she ever found out about his predicament, no power in the world would be able to stop her from teasing him for the rest of his life.

He glanced over at her, noticing that she was riveted to the screen, drooling at the male star Heinz Rühmann, similar to the way he was drooling over the very real girl sitting next to him.

Thea caught his gaze and leaned into him, her body warm and

soft. She pressed her lips against his ear as she murmured, "No reason to be worried. Your sister's attention is elsewhere."

Throughout the rest of the film, David sat with rapt attention to Thea's hand, burning hot on his thigh. The action on the screen no longer held any interest, and every once in a while he glimpsed at Thea, unbelieving of his utter luck. Every time she noticed, she turned her head and stunned him with the loving desire in her incredibly beautiful eyes.

"Oh, that was such an endearing film. Did you see how Heinz Rühmann kissed that woman?" Amelie swooned over her favorite actor.

David thought it best to agree. "Yes, it was great."

"So romantic," Thea said, her eyes sparkling with mischief, giving David the idea that she wasn't exactly talking about the film. "I'm so glad you stepped in to keep us company, David. My mother wouldn't have allowed me to come otherwise."

"My pleasure." David meant it. This evening must have been the most pleasurable occasion in his life. As they stepped outside, it was dark, a fine sleet falling down on them.

"Yuck, I hate this stuff," Thea complained.

"Who doesn't?" Amelie said. "If it were snow it would be nice, but this? It's cold and gets your feet wet."

"Let's get out of this mess." Thea started running toward the tram station.

When they disembarked the tram about a block from their apartment building, David said, "I should better take you home, Thea. Let's drop my sister first."

Amelie rolled her eyes at him, and imitated the voice of their mother: "Don't be late, David, you have to get up early in the morning."

He had half a mind to punch her on the arm for being cheeky, but he wanted to be on his best behavior for Thea. Instead he simply hissed, "You're gonna pay for it if you tell Mutti."

Amelie put up her hands in surrender. "My lips are sealed."

Then she turned toward Thea, hugging her friend. "It was a nice film. Let's do it again sometime soon."

Thea bestowed a gracious smile on her. "Yes. I enjoyed myself very much."

Again, David felt his ears burning bright, getting the impression she wasn't talking exclusively about the film. As soon as Amelie had closed the building door behind her, David took Thea's hand. "Where do you live?"

She gave him her address, about ten minutes' walk away. Despite the sleet he asked, "Would you like to walk?"

"With you? Always." The expression on her face was pure delight.

David barely believed what a lucky guy he was. The inaccessible beauty every single boy at the Lemberg school had pined for —secretly and not so secretly—was here, walking next to him, holding his hand. His skin tingled at the memory of her hand on his thigh and he was grateful for the icy temperatures cooling down his burning skin.

Much too soon they arrived in front of an ugly apartment building, similar to the one his family lived in. He wished he could accompany her upstairs and see her apartment, though her father would most certainly not approve of a male visitor this late at night. While he was trying to decide what to do, Thea suddenly said, "I hate this place!"

"But why?"

"Are you blind? Just look at the building! We used to live in such a nice place, until our landlord kicked us out."

David nodded. The same thing had happened to his own family. They had been lucky to find another place, even though it was much smaller and uglier than the one they had lost. "How long have you been living here?"

"Four weeks and I've hated every minute of it. It's so humiliating."

"You'll get used to it," he said in an effort to soothe her. In the beginning he'd hated their new apartment with a passion, but over time he'd come to accept that such was life. There were more important things to rail against.

She glared daggers at him. "I'll never get used to this… hell-hole. You have no idea how awful it is."

"I'm sorry, my comment was meant to console you." Listlessly he put an arm around her shoulder, and she immediately leaned into him, turning her face toward his.

"Thank you. But… it's so awful. I mean, I'm not even a real Jew. So why do they treat me like one?"

"You're not?" David had been under the impression that like all students at the Lemberg school, with the exception of a few Mischlinge like himself and his sister, she was a Jew.

"No." Shaking her head fiercely, her curls bobbed around her in the cutest possible way. "Do I look like a Jew to you?"

"Not at all." David gathered his courage and traced a thumb down her finely chiseled face. The blonde hair, the bright blue eyes, the rounded cheeks and the full, red lips, nothing about her resembled in the slightest the ugly caricatures of the vile Jew in *Der Stürmer*, the Nazi party's newspaper. "You look like an angel."

Her face lit up at his compliment. "My mother always says that I was born with the face of an angel."

"And you have a heart to match," David murmured. His voice grew even softer, as he leaned in closer, smelling her fresh minty scent.

"So why do the Nazis treat me like I'm the devil? I have nothing in common with those orthodox Jews coming from the East. I'm as German as any other girl and looking a lot better than most of them." She coquettishly threw her hair behind her shoulder, leaving David in awe of her stunning beauty.

"I don't know. I mean, I've been asking myself this same question for years. Why does Hitler, why do the Nazis hate us so much?" He looked deep into her eyes, trying to find the answer in there.

"It's so unjust!" She stomped her foot, hiding the pain beneath a pout.

David's heart went out to her. All these years he'd only seen the glamorous girl, the woman of his dreams and he'd never once stopped to look deeper into her soul. Just now he realized she was as vulnerable as anyone else and suffered from the same ostracization as the rest.

"Tell me about it," he groaned. "I don't feel I truly belong anywhere. The Aryans despise me for being a Jew and the Jews eye me suspiciously for being half-Aryan."

"Really? You're a mixed breed?" she asked, pressing herself against him, so he could sense her shivering in the cold.

"Yes, my mother is Aryan. Ironically, my aunt is one of Hitler's earliest supporters."

"Oh dear..."

"You're freezing. Shouldn't we go inside?"

She nodded and they walked the few steps to the entrance of her apartment building. Thea took out her keys, but before opening the door, she went up on her tiptoes. "I really liked being with you tonight," she whispered into his ear.

"Me too." David felt as if he were hovering several inches above the ground. Then she kissed him. Her full lips pressed on his, while she slung her arms around his neck. It was a kiss like he'd never experienced before and he wished it would never end. But unfortunately, that was not to be. After minutes—or hours, who could say?—he finally broke the kiss, extricated her hands from around his neck and said, "You should go inside."

"I should." Her flushed face radiated heat.

"May I see you again?" he asked, hoping she'd say yes.

"I'd love nothing more."

"What about this coming weekend?"

"That would be wonderful."

On the walk home, David was floating on clouds. The most beautiful girl on earth had agreed to date him. He truly was one lucky guy.

7

DECEMBER 20, 1938

Edith and Julius were sitting in the back of their car, as the driver took them to the house of Julius' sister Silvana.

Silvana Lemberg was the owner and head mistress of the Lemberg school for Jewish students, together with her husband Markus, who had been a celebrated author and professor of literature. First he'd been let go from his position as professor for literature due to the Nazis' purge of Jews from public offices, then they'd forbidden his books be sold in Germany.

Shortly after, he'd resigned himself to teaching seventh graders German language instead of writing award-winning novels, in the newly founded Lemberg school for Jewish children, where they not only taught them the usual subjects, but also Jewish culture and traditions, as well as Hebrew. Silvana was especially proud of the language classes and professional subjects such as sewing, mechanics and typewriting that prepared her students for emigration.

"We may not be able to visit my sister quite so often in the future," Julius suddenly said.

"But whyever not?"

"You must have forgotten that ten days from now we won't be able to avail ourselves of the Mercedes."

Edith stared at her husband. "Just because we don't own a car anymore doesn't mean we can't visit your sister."

"And how do you suggest we get there? Surely not walking all the way." He looked at her sternly over his spectacles, which he needed to use more frequently as he got older.

She shook her head with a smile. "Certainly not. It would take us at least two hours one way. We can take the tram or a bus. I'll find out which ones go there, although we'll probably have to switch route once or twice..." She trailed off at the horrified expression on his face.

"You don't honestly expect me to step into one of those metal boxes, brimming with sweating, stinking, disagreeable people?"

"Of course not. I expect you to sit on the rooftop in the fresh air and enjoy the view." He gave her a look as if she were utterly insane, and she laughed at him. "Come on, it's not that bad. I used to take public transport all the time."

"I never did." His voice was clipped.

Edith had a sharp remark on her tongue, which she swallowed down. Their social decline was so much harder on him than it was on her. He'd been born with the proverbial silver spoon in his mouth, whereas she grew up in a middle-class family. She shouldn't blame him for being so upset, since it was a stark change for him. Instead, she decided to change the subject. "Do you think Silvana will like the candles I bought for her?"

Apparently her choice for a topic hadn't been the best one, because Julius' eyes squinted into an angry glare. "That woman is utterly foolish! First the school, shouting her alliances from the rooftop and now celebrating Hanukkah. She really should try to keep a low profile."

"Do you actually believe it would do her any good? I mean, how much has it helped us to try and stay on the Nazis' good side?" Edith surprised herself with the bold remark, since she usually didn't question her husband's decisions or opinions.

During her time of betrothal, her mother-in-law had trained her to always stay silent and smile in the company of men; to graciously bow her head and obey her husband. It was the kind of behavior expected from a society lady, which Edith had become after marrying into the Falkenstein family.

But as bad as the Nazis were, they'd taught her one thing: to stand up for herself. If they didn't allow her to be a glamorous society lady anymore, she could as well shed the servile behavior and voice her own opinions—whether tradition allowed it or not.

"As long as we stay within the law, nothing will happen to us." Julius stubbornly held onto that opinion, which Edith found rather disturbing. How could an otherwise astute, intelligent man still believe in law and order where the Nazi government was concerned?

Thankfully they arrived in front of Silvana's modest, yet beautiful, home right next to the Lemberg school. The garden at this time of year laid bare, with just a few perennials giving it color. Here and there, Edith noticed hedges of rowanberry, boasting their bright red fruit. It was a delightful sight: red against green leaves and warmed her heart, making her think of Christmas.

This year, the last days of Hanukkah coincided with the Christmas celebration, which Julius considered a godsend because he'd pretended to everyone that his sister was holding a Christmas party.

Edith secretly rolled her eyes. If she were in Silvana's shoes, would she consider pretending to celebrate some other religion's holiday a serendipity? Or would she rather feel humiliated?

Perhaps the Jewish people had suffered so much already that they found respite in even such awful things as disguise? She shrugged. She'd never know and it certainly wouldn't do any good to ask her sister-in-law. Tonight she wanted to leave the political situation outside the high walls topped with barbed wire surrounding the school premises. Tonight she wished to spend happy hours with family.

Silvana and Markus' two adult sons unfortunately couldn't be with them. They had left Germany several years ago to study at Oxford University in England, and due to the November pogroms, they had canceled their trip to Berlin. Instead they were spending the holidays with Julius' other sister, Adriana, who'd emigrated to London with her husband Florian.

Edith thought it an irony that the practicing Jews Silvana and Markus had refused to leave Germany, citing their obligation to keep the many students of the Lemberg school safe, while non-practicing Adriana and her Christian husband Florian had left the country. She shook her head. If only Julius would see reason and follow their example, but apparently not even spending two days at the Sachsenhausen camp had been able to shake his confidence in the lawfulness of Hitler's regime.

If only she could make him see that his strategy to bury his head in the sand and follow every single rule to the letter wouldn't keep him safe for long.

"Welcome!" Silvana flew down the stairs, clad in the most beautiful full-length black gown with semi-transparent long sleeves made of Brussels lace. It was simple, yet stunning. As jewelry she wore a golden necklace with a pearl and the matching pearl studs. "I'm so glad you could come!"

"You look absolutely magnificent!" Edith complimented her, even as her ebullient sister-in-law fell around her neck, air-kissing both of her cheeks.

"I had it re-fitted especially for tonight," Silvana said.

A twinge of guilt hit Edith. Ever since Markus had been fired, they'd had to make do without the accustomed luxury. No doubt, the Lembergs still lived far beyond the standard of most everyone in Berlin, although compared to their former lives, it seemed much like poverty.

Edith felt self-conscious in her midnight-blue ball gown with thousands of rhinestones sewn into it which had taken hundreds of hours work by Edith's seamstress and several apprentices. She'd questioned Julius about the need to spend a fortune on a new dress when she already owned not one, but two wardrobes full of them, and his answer had been: "It is your duty to look glorious."

At her murmur of protest he'd given her a stern gaze and said, "We also have a duty to keep people in employment. This dress of yours will guarantee the seamstress and her apprentices can celebrate Hannukah, too."

Seeing it from his perspective eased some of the guilt, although Edith would rather not ostentatiously splash their money when most of their Jewish employees, household staff, or service providers had fallen into poverty.

"Happy"—Julius looked over his shoulder, despite knowing they were alone—"Hannukah, my dearest sister."

Before Silvana could fling herself around his neck, he took a step backwards, holding up a hand to ward her off. "Please don't smear my suit with your lipstick."

"Oh, stop it!" Silvana, who was without doubt the most emotional of the siblings, held her arms open for a hug. "Mother is not around to disapprove."

Edith meanwhile stepped into Markus' embrace, wondering not for the first time how Silvana had become so openly warmhearted when the rest of the family abhorred showing any kind of affection in public as well as in private. Julius' mother had gone so far as to explicitly state in her will that no one was to shed tears for her during the funeral.

"How lovely to see you, it's been much too long," Edith told Markus.

"Oh yes, there's always so much to do… we're drowning in work." Markus squeezed her hand, as he ushered them inside.

Again, a pang of guilt tore into her side. Everyone seemed to work hard, except for her. Edith Falkenstein's life had not changed much under the Nazis' reign. She still presided over household and staff, without any real work to do. In fact, her existence had become so much more boring, since they'd stopped hosting lavish parties at their mansion.

This was partly due to many of their friends emigrating, and partly because the Nazi elite looked down on them and wouldn't attend anyway. Julius might be too deluded to admit it, Edith, though saw the truth: The Falkensteins were not welcome in the city's elite anymore.

With her days devoid of organizing their social lives formerly filled with invitations to luncheons, dinner parties, theater premieres and other important events, she felt acutely how useless her life was and another dull pain she'd believed to have overcome years ago crept up, slowly spreading throughout her body like the ivy across the walls of their centuries-old mansion, and equally poisonous. If only... she'd been given the child she desired so much, her life would be filled with purpose instead of idle hours trying to be filled.

"You have decorated your house so beautifully," Edith exclaimed as Markus lead her into the dining room, where the table was set with a precious golden menorah. It stood tall and proud in the middle of the table, defying the hate showered upon its very presence by the Nazis. Since it was the fourth day of Hannukah, four white candles were lit, the other four candleholders were empty. In the middle throned a golden Star of David and above it the ninth candleholder. "Such a beautiful menorah."

The corners of Markus' mouth fell. "We received it as a gift from a dear friend who left the country and couldn't take it with him."

A chill ran down Edith's spine and she quickly pushed images of their beaten-up friend Alex away. He had left the country too... Normally, precious keepsakes were given to Aryan friends, called *Aufbewahrier*, a word made up of safe-keeping and Aryan. But understandably nobody wanted to have such an incriminating piece in their house, lest they be accused of being a friend of the Jews.

"Isn't it rather imprudent to flaunt this here?" Julius asked. After moving into his parental home, after his parents' death, he'd instructed Edith to remove all remnants of his Jewish ancestry in the house.

"We are not flaunting it." Silvana put her hands akimbo. "But I'm not going to hide it either. I'm not afraid of the Nazis!"

"You should be," Edith said, earning surprised stares from the others.

"Not as long as you stick to the laws and regulations," Julius said.

"Well, there's no regulation forbidding me to have a menorah in my home." Silvana put out her lower lip as if ready to fight her brother on that.

Markus, knowing his wife's hot temper very well, intervened. "The government knows we're Jews. After all, we own a Jewish school, approved by the education ministry."

"I always warned you about such a dangerous undertaking." Julius slightly bowed his head. He'd been adamant that his sister should not make her allegiances known in such a public way. Silvana, though, had not taken his advice. On the contrary, she'd outsmarted him and coerced him into loaning her the required money.

Edith smiled at the memory. Silvana probably was the only person in the world who had the gumption to stand up to Julius Falkenstein and she admired her immensely for it.

"Let's not talk about politics," Markus again intervened. "We're here to celebrate."

Since the Lembergs didn't employ a maid anymore, Silvana served the food herself. She loaded the table with the most deliciously looking and smelling traditional foods, including latkes, potato pancakes, fritters called *bimuelos* and the indispensable *sufganiyot* for dessert, deep-fried jelly donuts.

After a sumptuous meal, the men retreated into Markus' office to drink brandy and smoke the Cuban cigars Julius had brought, while Edith followed Silvana into the kitchen. When she saw the mess of dirty dishes, she said, "I should have brought my maid."

"It would have been nice for a change," Silvana groaned, looking around at the piles waiting to be washed. "It's been a steep fall for us."

"I'm so sorry."

"Honestly, I'm afraid this is only getting worse. Adriana called yesterday and she keeps begging us to leave Germany to live with her."

"Why don't you take her up on the offer?"

A rebellious pout appeared on Silvana's face. "Never. I'll stay here and defy the Nazis every step of the way. If they want to get rid of me, they'll have to kill me first."

They just might, Edith thought, remembering the bits and pieces she'd pried from Julius and Helga about the conditions at the Sachsenhausen camp. "I admire you for your strength. I wish I could do something useful as well."

Silvana gave Edith a look that was hard to decipher. "You could convince Julius to live with Adriana in England."

"Believe me I have tried." Edith sighed. "He just won't listen to reason. Despite all the evidence to the contrary he still believes the Nazis won't touch him."

"It's hard to fathom why he holds on to that opinion."

"After his arrest he became more obstinate, if anything. He seems to think that the Nazis already threw at him the worst they are capable of and since he came out of it unscathed, it's further proof that nothing will happen to him." Edith had never fully disclosed her, and especially Joseph's, hand in freeing Julius so quickly.

"But you don't believe that?" Silvana handed her the washed pan for drying, taking a moment to look into her eyes.

"I don't know what to believe anymore. Julius used to keep me away from politics and pampered me to the point that I had no idea about the awful things going on, but..." She hesitated for a moment, wondering whether she ought to confide in her sister-in-law. "I've reconnected with an old classmate who married a Jew as well. They are lower middle-class. The things she tells me are quite different from my own experiences. Her children had to leave the public school, they were ousted from their apartment, her husband lost his job... all because he's Jewish."

She preferred not to mention that Helga's husband had worked for the Falkenstein bank and Julius himself had let his

Jewish employees go. It wasn't something he was proud of and he'd sweetened the blow with a generous severance package to calm his conscience and telling himself this measure had to be done to protect the other employees from harm. Looking out for the many, even if it meant sacrificing a few.

Perhaps from a global point of view, this made sense. Although Edith had argued that the many didn't need protection. They were Aryans and could easily find jobs elsewhere, whereas finding new employment for the fired Jews was next to impossible.

Silvana gave a snort. "I know these stories all too well. We shelter the students as much as we can, but the moment they step outside these walls, they are fair game." Suddenly she looked much older than her fifty years.

"It must be so hard on you."

"It is," Silvana answered sheepishly. "Every time another student quits school because the family received a visa to God knows where, I'm saying goodbye with a laughing and a crying eye. Naturally, I'm more concerned about those who stay. We can only pray this will pass over soon."

"That's what Julius keeps saying. The Germans will come to their senses and get rid of Hitler and his cronies." Personally Edith didn't share his opinion, because she'd seen how her entire family, spearheaded by Joseph, had internalized the hateful propaganda. They had loved Julius for many years, not least because of his wealth and his generosity in supporting them during the Great Depression, but within weeks after the Nuremberg laws, they had disassociated themselves from the "harmful and vile Jew".

Silvana must have guessed what she was thinking, because she asked, "Are you going to see your family over Christmas?"

"I'm afraid not. They've made it clear that while I'm always welcome to visit, they won't tolerate my husband in their midst."

"We all have to take sides. It's such a shame what has become of our nation." Silvana handed her the last plate to dry and wiped the kitchen counter, before she said, "Don't break up with your family altogether. You might need them if this becomes any worse."

"Perhaps you're right." Knut was the only family member Edith was on speaking terms with, so she decided to write a letter to her sister Carsta, and send Christmas presents to her nieces and nephews, whom she hadn't seen in such a long time.

8

The New Year had brought icy cold and a flurry of snow. Helga looked out the kitchen window while washing the dishes, her gaze not seeing the dirty backyard and the dilapidated gray wall of the neighboring building. She was caught in musings about a better past when the shrill ring of the telephone cut through the silence.

Wondering who might be calling, she dried her hands on a towel and hurried into the tiny hallway, where the telephone stood next to the door.

"Helga Goldmann," she answered, hoping it wouldn't be bad news. These days she constantly feared something would happen to Heinrich or David when they were out in the streets.

"It's me," her sister Felicitas sobbed into the phone.

Helga instantly froze, barely able to breathe. Somehow she managed to whisper into the phone. "What has happened?"

"It's Ernst…" More sobs interrupted Feli's explanation.

Despite fearing horrible news, a wave of relief washed over her. Nothing had happened to her men. Almost instantly, she scolded herself for being so cruel. She might not care for Ernst all that much, but she definitely cared for her sister, who obviously was in agony.

"He's dead," Feli finally managed to spit out. "He was... it was an accident. It's so awful."

Helga couldn't get a coherent sentence from her sister, so she made a spur of the moment decision. "I'm coming to your place. Don't go anywhere. You hear me?"

"Yes... hurry..." Feli must have replaced the receiver, because after a short pause, the dial tone came over the line.

It was a strange feeling. Feli was her older sister and ever since she'd married Ernst Ritter, a powerful and wealthy man, she'd looked out for Helga and her family. She had provided them with groceries during the depression, buying David and Amelie new clothes for Christmas and their birthdays. On Ernst's recommendation Heinrich had been employed as an accountant in Neuruppin, which had brought the family back from the brink of starvation. Many times Feli had used her Nazi connections to score favors for her sister's half-Jewish family.

And now, apparently, Helga was to assume the role as the sister in charge. She scribbled a note for her family and left it on the table, before she slipped into her boots, the thick lambskin coat—a hand-me-down from Feli—put on a woolen hat and wrapped a thick scarf around her neck. As she stepped out of the building, she saw the bus approaching and raced to the nearby stop, where she arrived just in time to slip onto the bus at the last moment, before the door closed again.

Panting hard, she settled into a seat, calculating in her head the best route to take and deciding on going to Bahnhof Zoo, where she would switch to the suburban train to Oranienburg. At the huge train station she was lucky again, because the train stood waiting on the platform. She quickly bought a ticket and boarded it.

It was already dark when Helga alighted from the train and walked along a snow-filled street toward her sister's big mansion. Just now she realized that she might not be able to return to Berlin and ought to have prepared by packing a nightdress and a toothbrush at least. As she rang the bell at the manor, the maid opened the door in no time at all, giving her a very worried look. "Oh, Frau Goldmann, it's such a relief to have you here. Your sister is out of her mind with grief."

"I came as fast as I could. Do you know what has happened?"

The maid had difficulties keeping her tears at bay. "We don't know much. The police arrived around noon, informing Frau Ritter about the accident. Apparently his car spun out of control and crashed into a tree, killing him instantly." She sniffed. "They also said that the driver was severely hurt but would survive. It was just bad luck that Herr Ritter sat on the passenger side instead of the back bench."

"Oh my God!" Helga's hand involuntarily flew to her throat. Ernst had loved sitting in front, because it gave him a better view. Who would have thought that this habit would cause his death one day? "I'll go to see my sister right away."

"After she was on the telephone with you, the doctor visited and gave her a sedative. She's resting now."

"Should I wait?"

"Oh no. She'll be glad to see you." The maid motioned for Helga to follow her to Felicitas' bedroom. Like many rich couples she and Ernst used separate bedrooms, and Helga had always wondered whether the reason was because many of these couples lived in marriages of convenience and didn't enjoy cuddling at night, or whether they were afraid to be seen by their servants in bed together. Whatever the reason was, she couldn't even entertain the idea of her and Heinrich having separate bedrooms—not that their cramped apartment would allow for it.

The maid knocked on the door and after a weak "Come in", Helga stepped inside, where she found her sister lying in the big bed, her face barely distinguishable from the white linen.

"How are you holding up?" Helga embraced her sister, while the maid poured water into a glass and put it onto the nightstand next to a white tablet, presumably a sedative.

Feli's eyes filled with tears and she closed them quickly, making a wave with her hand. Helga turned her head, realizing the maid was still standing next to her, apparently eager for some juicy gossip about her late master's demise.

"Would you leave us alone, please?"

"If you wish, Frau Goldmann." The maid reluctantly retreated. Just before slipping through the door, she added, "If you need me, just ring the bell on the nightstand."

"I will. Thank you so much." Helga waited until the door closed, before she turned back to Felicitas. "I'm so sorry about Ernst."

Feli slowly opened her eyes, tears flooding down her cheeks as her entire body shook. "It's so horrible."

"Shush." Helga took her older sister into her arms, rubbed her back and made soothing murmurs like she had done with her children when they were young. After a long time, Feli seemed to calm down and pulled away from Helga's embrace.

Leaning back into the pillow, there was so much agony in her eyes that Helga's heart squeezed. Felicitas had married the much older man because it had been the wise thing to do. A well-to-do husband who'd care for her and offer her a lifestyle her parents hadn't been able to. While she and Ernst had never been passionately in love the way Helga and Heinrich still were, they had had a good marriage—as far as one could see from the outside.

Over the past two years Ernst had become sickly, suffering from frequent bad coughs—according to his doctor caused by excessive smoking—and other ailments. With his sixty-four years he'd been an old man, yet much too young to die.

"It's all my fault!" Feli sobbed anew into her sister's shoulder.

"How could you ever think such a thing?" Helga felt Feli's body shake as she buried her face in her neck.

"I should have pressured him to stay at home. He was not well. His coughing was getting worse and he was so weak."

"It was an accident. Nobody could have foreseen it would happen," Helga tried to console her.

"It wouldn't have happened if he'd stayed home," Feli cried.

"Shush, my darling. Shush. It's not your fault. There's nothing you could have done."

Feli's eyes suddenly cleared up and she said, "You know, we often fought with each other, but I'm missing him already."

"I'm so sorry." Helga could only imagine the horrible pain she'd feel if Heinrich was ripped from her side. Fearing something would happen to him day after day was pure agony, but how would she cope if it actually did?

After a while Helga asked, "Are you hungry?"

"A bit."

"I'll tell your maid to make chicken soup. That'll help." Their mother's cure for every physical or mental ailment had always been a hearty chicken broth. The memory seemed to ease Feli's pain for a little while, because she smiled. "That would be nice."

After Helga had ordered a bowl of chicken soup to be brought up, she turned to her sister again. "Do you want me to stay with you for a few days?"

"If it's not too much of an inconvenience."

"Of course not. You've helped us so many times over the years, it's the least I can do."

"Thank you." Feli's voice was thin and brittle.

"May I call Heinrich, so he'll know where I am?"

"Naturally. You can use the telephone in the sitting room."

Helga talked to Heinrich and arranged for Amelie to visit the next day, bringing a suitcase with clothes to last until the weekend when Heinrich and David would join them, since neither of them unfortunately could ask for a day off at work, being Jewish and all that.

She stayed with her sister for an entire week, helping her to cope and organizing the many inevitable tasks that came with a deceased relative. The funeral was arranged for Sunday afternoon. Ernst's family was there, along with many dignitaries of Oranienburg, the employees of the city administration, and, naturally, Helga's own family.

It was a somber affair, listening to the priest's eulogy in the mortuary chapel and then following the coffin to the open grave. There, the party leader of Oranienburg, who was an intimate friend of the family, gave a speech about Ernst and his achievements for the city. Hundreds of people attended the burial, queuing up to give their condolences to Felicitas.

Helga stayed at her side throughout the entire process. Beginning at her feet, the freezing cold spread across her entire body, making her teeth chatter. Feli though, seemed numb to any feeling, except for grief. She dutifully thanked the many visitors, her voice firm, and her posture straight. Only Helga noticed the great effort it took her to hold on.

About half of the people had passed her, murmuring expressions of sympathy, when it was the turn of a man dressed in SS uniform. After talking to Feli, he nodded his head at Helga, before his gaze fell on Heinrich standing a few steps away. He glared at him and hissed, "If that isn't Heinrich Goldmann! What's the Jew doing here?"

Felicitas followed his gaze in a slow fashion, her mouth forming an "O" as if she'd seen Heinrich for the first time. Looking back at the SS man, she wrinkled her forehead. "But why not? He's my brother-in-law."

The man's face fell. Plummeted to be precise. "You're related to such a subhuman?"

Felicitas was too mired in her grief to give the sharp retort she normally would have; her only reaction was a nod. Inwardly cringing, Helga hoped Heinrich hadn't heard the insult. She sought eye contact with him, but already the next mourner was upon them, and Feli squeezed her hand, conveying despair.

She rubbed her thumb across Feli's hand, murmuring, "You'll get through this." Occupied consoling her sister, she didn't notice the scene unfolding until it was too late to intervene.

A loud booming voice said, "You shouldn't have come here, Jew! Isn't it bad enough that the poor woman lost her husband? No, you had to show up and besmirch his good name."

"I'm sorry," Heinrich whispered, as always trying to keep out of trouble.

"Sorry! You're sorry?" the SS man shouted, before pausing to gaze around. "Did you hear this? The Jew says he's sorry. I say, we make him sorry he ever showed up, trampling the memory of an honorable member of our nation, polluting the very air we breathe, disturbing the peace of the deceased and shaming the widow's grief."

Some people murmured sounds of approval, but in contrast to the SS man, they all knew not to instigate a scandal next to the open grave. The perpetrator though, wasn't about to shut up, not even when the hurriedly arrived priest whispered reconciliatory words.

Chills ran down Helga's spine, freezing her into the ground. By her side, Felicitas struggled to keep her calm, while a few steps away, Heinrich made a face as if he wanted to flee into a mousehole. But those two weren't her biggest worry. Not even the SS man frightened her as much as the rebellious grimace on David's face, an expression she knew all too well from quarrels with her son.

If nobody intervened quickly, he was likely to launch himself at the SS man to restore his father's dignity. As much as she hated the way the SS man had humiliated Heinrich, she couldn't allow David to start a fight, or he'd soon be buried in the grave next to his uncle Ernst. But try as she might, fear—and Feli's unforgiving grip—kept her frozen in place. Unable to move, she cast a plea for help at her daughter.

Always quick to comprehend, Amelie stepped forward and began to sing in her clear voice a beautiful, yet sad, ballad. The audience, including the SS man, fell silent, listening to her. Helga whispered into Feli's ear and as soon as the song ended, Feli said, "Thank you so much, my dear Amelie. Ernst always loved that song and I'm sure he was with us to listen." Then she clapped her hands and added, "Please, I invite you all to join me for a drink in the memory of my dear husband."

She gave the address of the restaurant and people moved away from the cemetery to meet later over cake and coffee as was customary. Heinrich approached Helga, a steep frown creased into his forehead. "I guess it would be better if I did not attend. I don't want to be the cause of another scene. I'll head home."

"You are family! Of course you will come!" Feli protested.

Helga shook her head. "You know how much we love you, and the last thing you need right now is such awful excitement."

"It's Ernst's funeral and I say who will attend, not some overzealous SS man."

"You're right, but still. Don't you think Ernst would hate his memorial to become a platform for politics?"

Feli sighed. Ernst had always been concerned about what others thought of them. "Perhaps you're right, still… I don't want to exclude Heinrich."

You belong to the party that's been excluding him for the past six years. Helga didn't voice her thoughts, because she knew from experience that Feli wouldn't take any notice of it anyway.

"I'll go with him," David interjected. "I have to return to work anyway."

"Really?" Feli seemed unsure.

"It's no big deal," Heinrich added, even though his humiliation was visible in his expression.

A sudden rage caught Helga, rushing up and down her spine, urging her to scream out loud at the injustices continually committed against her family and cursing Hitler and his cronies. Feeling a small hand on her arm, she bit down the harsh words wanting to spill from her mouth. This was neither the time nor the occasion to make a scene. It was Ernst's funeral and the SS man had caused enough excitement for one day.

"If you insist." Helga kissed her husband and hugged her son. "Amelie and I will stay another night with Feli and return home tomorrow."

"I love you, my sweetheart." Heinrich pressed her tightly to him. "Don't get too worked up over that fool."

She nodded, even though both of them knew the SS man was no ordinary fool, indeed he had only spoken out loud the prevailing opinion.

"Don't make too much of it," Feli said, hugging Heinrich. "He doesn't mean it that way. He must have been grieving to be carried away like that."

Helga merely rolled her eyes, since she couldn't understand why her sister still defended the Nazis. Walking to the nearby restaurant, Amelie and Helga took Feli by the arm. Feli was wearing her golden party badge, jokingly called *Bombon,* as she usually did during official occasions.

Amelie spoke out loud what Helga only thought. "Aunt Feli, I don't understand how you can still support Hitler when he's causing so much misery."

"You're too young to understand, things never are either black or white. Hitler does many things I don't agree with, but the majority of his accomplishments is good. He's an exemplary leader, who has been making Germany great again, just like he promised."

"But what about us?" Amelie asked. "Don't you feel the way he treats people like us is exceptionally cruel and unjust?"

"Our Führer means no harm. If he knew how some overzealous bureaucrats blow things out of proportion, he'd immediately put a stop to it."

"Then, why doesn't anyone tell him?" Amelie asked with the innocence of a sixteen-year-old.

Helga was much too worldly-wise to assume Hitler might have benevolent intentions concerning the Jews, but she'd given up arguing with her sister about that topic. Felicitas would never admit that her beloved Führer was in fact the biggest prick on earth.

9

The year 1939 had brought many firsts for Julius, none of them pleasant. Since he'd been forced to sell his Mercedes and let go of the driver—because what use was a driver without a vehicle to drive?—he'd resorted to using taxis. A rather tedious affair, having to wave one down to drive him wherever he needed to go, yet it was preferable to using public transport.

One day Edith had given him a lesson in taking the bus and tram to his city office, an experience he never wished to repeat. Even weeks later his insides twisted at the thought of being pressed like a sardine into a metal box with dozens, if not hundreds, of people, none of them willing to give up his seat for an older person like Julius.

Adding to the constant delays and outages, the waiting time in the bitter cold when changing from bus to tram or vice versa, made riding public transport a nightmare and Julius swore to himself that he'd never set foot on a bus again. Cumbersome as it might be to depend on taxis, it was still a million times better.

Due to the complicated commute, he spent most weeknights in their city apartment, from where he could walk to the Falkenstein bank in less than ten minutes. Edith had offered to move there with him, using the Schwanenwerder mansion only on weekends, but he'd refused. She shouldn't be forced to leave the comfort of their home, just because the Nazis had decided that Jews weren't allow to own cars anymore.

Julius adjusted his tie, looking at himself in the mirror. The now permanent deep frown on his forehead made him look old. The past year had taken so much from him—the loss of the Mercedes had been just the last blow.

Memories of his time in Sachsenhausen attacked him out of the blue, turning his breath into frantic gasps. A sheen of sweat formed on his forehead. A rather disturbing development, which happened increasingly often.

In the beginning, he'd believed he could simply shrug the happenings at the camp away, but instead of fading, the nightmares became ever more vivid. It hurt him to admit that the unpleasant, albeit harmless, experience of riding the public transport had completely shattered his inner peace. As silly as it sounded, this little inconvenience had finally caused him to realize the Nazis had taken off their kid gloves.

All the pinpricks over the years, which he'd tried to argue away, had resulted in a deep weeping wound in his soul, attacking him not only in his nightmares, but recently also during his waking hours.

He closed his eyes, just to tear them open again in horror when vivid images of fellow prisoners being whiplashed assailed him. Sweating profusely, he locked his gaze onto an antique vase standing on the sideboard to keep him tethered to reality.

The separation from Edith during the week grated on his nerves, leaving him floating directionless in a sea of hardship. He always looked forward to being reunited with her during the weekend—just to lose the fight against his temper after a few short hours and venting his anger on her.

Usually his outburst lasted a few minutes, before his self-control regained the upper hand again and he profusely apologized for it… until it happened again… and again. It was as if after five days of tackling one injustice after another, the simmering rage inside him used the moment of their reunion to explode.

The entire situation left him puzzled. Trained from boyhood to never show emotions in public, he kept the facade all through the week, pretending not to notice the many needle pricks thrown at him. But the moment he returned to the safety of his Schwanenwerder mansion, his self-control succumbed to the vicious attack of his bottled-up emotions and however hard he tried, there was no way of keeping the rage inside.

Julius slipped into his coat, put on a fedora and left the apartment, huge by normal standards, but tiny compared to the Schwanenwerder mansion. After a short walk he arrived at the bank and greeted the security man with a terse smile, remembering all too well how that same man had watched the SS dragging Julius out of the building and hauling him onto a truck without lifting as much as a finger.

He would give the guard the benefit of the doubt, wanting to believe his employee had failed to intervene out of fear for his own and his family's lives, not because he agreed with the government's actions. As soon as he reached his upstairs office, his loyal secretary greeted him with a pained expression and a harsh whisper, "Herr Falkenstein, I'm so sorry, I couldn't prevent it."

An unprecedented fatigue washed over him, along with an awful sense of dread as he tried to imagine the newest horror lashed out by the Nazi government. "It's all right, Frau Krause. I'm sure it'll be alright."

She looked at him with the expression of a panicked rabbit, as she elaborated. "There are two men from the Gestapo waiting for you."

His blood seemed to congeal to ice in his veins. After his time in Sachsenhausen he'd turned into a shivering mess of fear at the mere sight of a man in uniform. Digging deep into his education, he somehow managed to keep his aplomb. "Thank you, Frau

Krause." Straightening his shoulders, he stepped into his office. "What can I—"

The words stuck in his throat at the sight of a man sitting behind Julius' desk with his feet up on the polished wooden surface. The man was wearing shining leather boots, a black uniform jacket, his coat carelessly thrown over one of the two chairs in front of the desk, while the younger man sat ramrod straight in the second chair.

"Ah, good morning." The leader, who must be in his mid-forties, greeted him with a sarcastic smile. "Late to work? Don't you know that being work-shy is a despicable crime?"

Julius seethed from the casual insult, since there weren't many harder-working businessmen in Berlin than him. To add insult to injury, the Gestapo officer was holding a cigar in his hand—one of Julius' cigars as corroborated by the open cabinet compartment.

The officer followed Julius' gaze and nodded. "I hope you don't mind that I availed myself of a cigar to shorten the waiting time?" Not expecting an answer to the rhetorical question, he immediately continued. "Since you have finally arrived, let's not waste any more time with idle chit-chat."

Julius eyed the officer, who obviously wasn't willing to vacate the seat that didn't belong to him. A slow, burning fury snaked up his throat and he took a deep breath to swallow it down, since it wouldn't do any good to antagonize the officer by pointing out he was sitting in Julius' seat. Gazing to the young man on his right, he gave a pointed look at the coat on the other available chair. That indecent prick smirked back. At a loss how to behave, Julius returned his gaze to the man in charge.

"So, let's get to the point of our visit, shall we?" he said, ignoring Julius' visible discomfort.

Julius did not intend to humiliate himself by asking whether he was allowed to sit down in his own office, so he stubbornly stood there, his arms crossed.

"There have been irregularities—"

"At my bank? Never!" Julius erupted in righteous indignation, which earned him a scathing glare.

"You speak only when asked, is that clear?"

Seething with anger, Julius kept silent.

"I haven't heard your answer." The officer mocked him and then asked in a voice someone would use with a disobedient child, "Do you understand that you are only to speak when asked a question?"

"Yes."

"Yes, what?"

Julius willed the rage down, fighting hard not to give that obscure commoner a piece of his mind. "Yes, Herr Oberscharführer."

The officer smiled. "I see you have learned your ranks. Perhaps all is not lost in your case." Then he launched into a lengthy monologue about the inferiority of the Jewish race and how one could not expect them to learn even the most basic aspects of life in a civilized society. Finally, he ended his speech with the words, "Fact is, you're a Jew and as such you cannot administer the money of Aryans. It just wouldn't be right."

"With all due respect, Herr Oberscharführer," Julius protested. "This bank has been in my family for over a hundred years and I have served our nation for decades. None of my clients has ever had a reason to complain."

"I hold that to your account. Apparently you did the best within your limited means. But times are changing and we must change with them. Here's the order to sell your bank into Aryan hands by the end of the month, or it will fall to the state." The officer pushed a piece of paper in Julius' direction. "It is in your and the Reich's best interest to put the Falkenstein bank into the hands of a suitable successor. And… if I may give you a piece of advice: do yourself and our nation a favor and leave the country."

With these words, the officer stood up, his younger

companion hastily imitating the action, carelessly flicked cigar ash onto the carpet and rushed from the room, leaving Julius with his mouth hanging agape. This was the peak of effrontery. Telling him, Julius Falkenstein, owner of the quintessentially German Falkenstein bank, Great War veteran and bearer of the Iron Cross, to leave his home country.

Obstinacy overpowered all logical thought. He would not leave! Never, ever, would he follow the ill-meant advice of some Nazi party parvenu who thought he had an inkling about business matters, when all he knew was how to strut around and intimidate hard-working people.

Heaving with anger, Julius suddenly felt his heart palpitate, sending a different kind of panic through his body. At fifty-six years old he was much too young to die. He willed himself to calm down, stepped toward the cabinet, sensing another fit of irregular heartbeats at the sight of the door hanging open, where the SS officer had rummaged, leaving the esteemed cigar collection in horrible disarray.

Without a better idea on how to regain his composure, Julius began to put everything back in order, until a hot flash stabbed at his insides and he jerked his hand back as if it had been burned. Behind the place where the cigar box usually stood, the secret safe lay exposed. It had been tinkered with, but fortunately they hadn't been able to open it. Still, it was awful news.

Julius stared at the space for a long minute, swallowing down wave after wave of surging panic. In the safe weren't only important business documents, but also some of Edith's most valuable jewels, including the precious diamond necklace, a family heirloom, given to his great grandmother by her friend, the princess of Sweden, for her wedding.

Sheer panic crushed over him, pressing on his chest, making it impossible to breathe. He should have taken the necklace to Switzerland years ago. Fighting for air, black dots began dancing in front of his eyes, even as his knees gave way. Then, he heard the soft voice of a woman, whose words he couldn't understand. Forcing his eyes open, the vision was blurred, and his ears rang with a strange buzzing sound. Finally a strong smell cleared the fog in his brain and he recognized his secretary, bent over him.

"Herr Falkenstein. Are you alright?" Worry was etched onto her face.

"I'm fine," he muttered. "I just need to sit down for a minute."

"You gave me quite the fright," Frau Krause said, her face pale as if she'd be the next one to faint. "After the Gestapo left I prepared your coffee, when I heard a rumble. Have you hurt yourself?"

He sensed a dull ache in the back of his head, and touched the spot. It wasn't bleeding. "I don't think so. A coffee would be perfect." He tried to get up, but his legs were still too shaky to follow his orders. To pile onto his humiliation he had to ask his secretary to help him up. "Would you please give me a hand?"

"Naturally." The loyal woman she was, she didn't say another word until she'd helped him settle into his desk chair. "I'll go get your coffee now. Shall I call your wife?"

"No, please don't." He'd rather not inform Edith, she worried too much about his well-being as it was. If she knew the Gestapo had ordered him to sell the bank, she'd intensify her attempts to consider emigration.

He closed his eyes for a second. Outwardly he pretended to anyone around not to be afraid of the Nazis, because they wouldn't touch a person of his stature, in reality though he'd come to accept this wasn't true. Thinking hard, he decided he wouldn't simply up and leave everything behind. He'd been born here long before Hitler had crossed the border and he'd die here, long after the last Nazi was gone. Julius Falkenstein would not succumb to the harassment, however outrageous it might be.

But first he'd fight for his bank. He called his deputy, Herr Dreyer, into the office and recounted the happenings, albeit leaving out his fainting.

"What we have feared all this time has finally happened." Herr

Dreyer had cautioned Julius to transfer the Falkenstein bank into safe, Aryan, hands shortly after the Nuremberg Laws had been put in place. Back then, Julius hadn't wanted to listen, because he was convinced it would never get this bad. Proven otherwise, he now wished he'd taken the precautions Herr Dreyer had suggested when there had still been time.

Even today it pained him to let go of his bank, the family heritage, but he realized there was no way around it.

"You must buy the bank from me," Julius begged his loyal employee.

"We've been through this Herr Falkenstein, I don't have the money," Herr Dreyer protested, visible discomfort on his face.

Julius though, had been thinking about this notion ever since their discussion on this very topic had been cut short but SS men trampling into his office, setting it ablaze and hauling him to Sachsenhausen. "I'll give you a private loan to buy it from me."

Herr Dreyer shook his head. "I couldn't possibly."

"Yes, you can. Hear me out." At this point Julius didn't care much about money anymore. His biggest concern was that the bank could fall into the hands of the government, who'd surely run it into the ground.

He fetched two glasses and poured brandy for both of them. Usually, he didn't drink alcohol in the morning, but today was not a normal day. After the shock of the Gestapo's visit, he hoped it would calm his nerves. Handing one glass to Herr Dreyer, he explained. "We'll draw up two contracts, one for the government and a second secret one just for us. Officially, you'll buy the bank for a price well below its actual worth. You become the owner, keeping me on as director and nothing will change. After the Nazi regime has crumbled, as it will inevitably do, the second contract comes into place and you'll sell the bank back to me for the same price you bought it."

Herr Dreyer pensively swiveled the brandy in his glass. "I've been loyal to you all this time, but I can't do this. To be honest, I'm afraid. What if the Gestapo finds out? What if someone finds the secret contract? They'll hang me for it, and my family as well."

Julius bit his lips. If he sold the bank on the free market, the buyer would take advantage of his precarious position as a Jew and pay a tenth of the current value—actually the going price was between eight and fifteen percent. Perhaps he needed to take a leap of faith and trust his longtime employee to return the property to him once all of this was over, even without a secret second contract? In any case, what did he have to lose? The visitors this morning had made it clear that the bank wasn't his anymore by the beginning of next month.

Either he'd find a buyer himself or the government would seize it.

"Then I guess I'll have to trust in your word as a man of honor. We sign only the official contract. You keep me as director and pay me a monthly sum for the loan for the sales price." It was a bad deal, one Julius would never have engaged in, even a year ago. But times were not normal and this was the best outcome he could devise.

"I'm so sorry," Herr Dreyer said honestly. "Whatever happens, I'll lead the bank in your spirit and take care of its employees. I promise, once all of this is over, I'll gladly return it to you, hopefully in an even better condition."

"Then it's a deal. I'll get the lawyers to work on it." Julius' heart ached as they shook hands.

Later, as he sat alone in his office, staring out the window onto the familiar street below, he almost wept. He had no reason to doubt Herr Dreyer's loyalty and his deputy certainly presented the best choice under the current conditions, yet… it was a terrifying thing to do. Julius' father would turn in his grave if he knew

The Falkenstein bank had been in the family for more than a century. Julius had spent many days in this very office, sitting next to his father, learning the business from a very young age. As he grew older, he'd been given more responsibilities, had managed the branch in Munich, nurtured the employees, modernized the processes.

He'd promised his father to spearhead the family business for the next generation of Falkensteins. And now he was about to betray his ancestors and sign the bank away to an outsider. His heart was breaking at the thought and his only hope was that Herr Dreyer would keep his word.

10

After the driver, they had also lost their housekeeper, not because of another law or because they couldn't afford her anymore, but because her husband had forbidden her to continue working for "the Jews", however well they had treated her for years.

Edith looked at Delia, her personal maid. Even in her staff uniform she exuded grace with her long and fine limbs. Edith could just imagine the young woman going en pointe at any moment to dance nimble-footed across the marble entrance hall. The former prima ballerina at the Berlin Opera might be the worst maid Edith had ever had, but she possessed a very pleasant personality—and she was Jewish, which made her desperate for employment.

"I'll go into town, shopping for groceries." Edith didn't look forward to schlepping the heavy bags with groceries back to the mansion from the nearest bus station. Living on the prestigious Schwanenwerder Island had become quite difficult without access to a vehicle nor staff to send on errands. After redecorating the house into an actual home instead of an oppressive Victorian museum, she had enjoyed living here. Nevertheless, under the current circumstances, it had become rather inconvenient and she planned to suggest that Delia and she move in with Julius in their city apartment.

"When shall I expect you back?" Delia asked.

"Not before nightfall."

"Then you don't want me to cook?"

"No. I'll dine out."

Relief washed over Delia's face, since her cooking was even worse than her cleaning skills. "Anything you want me to do, while you're away?"

"Sweeping and dusting. Oh, and changing the linens in Herr Falkenstein's bedroom." Edith put on her hat and walked out the front door, through the garden filled with evergreen trees. The first harbingers of spring peeked out their colorful heads, snowdrops and crocus filled the otherwise immaculate lawn, reminding her to tell the gardener to get everything ready for spring.

Then she frowned. If they moved to the city apartment, it might not be worth getting the gardens done. They'd have to close the house, put dust covers on the furniture and the paintings; and have someone come over to look after it once or twice a month.

She knew Julius would oppose the idea of her moving to the city, since he considered it a temporary sleeping arrangement for himself. As always, he was unwilling to accept that every single law concerning the Jews was meant to make life difficult for them and wear them down until they raised their hands in defeat and left the country—after paying a hefty tax for "fleeing the Reich."

Deep in thought, she walked out the front gate onto the island's only street that made a full circle around it. Seconds later a vehicle drove up, braking hard when the driver saw her. Edith recognized the car of the Breuninger family and stepped aside, giving a friendly wave. The driver, a middle-aged man in livery, nodded back and put the vehicle into motion. It suddenly stopped again just as she leveled with the back door. The window was cranked down and Frau Breuninger, a petite blonde with pretzel-style braids over her ears, peeked out.

"Good morning, Frau Breuninger." Edith quite liked the woman who moved in the same social circle as the Falkensteins and had been a frequent guest at their mansion. But instead of a greeting, the woman's face contorted into an ugly grimace.

"People like you shouldn't be allowed on the island. You make it unsafe for everyone else!"

"Excuse me?" Edith was too flabbergasted for a more elaborate answer.

"You heard me well. No Jews where upright Aryans live! You better leave before we have you thrown out."

It took all Edith's strength not to erupt into a very unbecoming fit the way Frau Breuninger had done and the only thing she could think of to defend herself, was, "I'm not a Jew."

"Even worse! You Jew-loving whore! A nasty gold digger if I ever saw one. You made your bed with the filthy criminals, now live with the consequences." Just as Frau Breuninger had spewed these hateful words, she tapped against the back of the driver's seat and seconds later, the Mercedes drove away, leaving an utterly shaken Edith behind.

So much for me being safer on the island, she thought to herself, giving a bitter laugh. It was ironic that fate had just given her a solid argument to convince Julius that moving permanently into the city apartment was the only practical solution.

Two days later she waited for her husband to return to the mansion for the weekend. When Julius arrived—on foot, because the guard at the bridge to the island had been unreasonably strict and not allowed the taxi to cross—he looked frightfully tired.

"Shall I brew you a coffee?" she asked.

Julius raised an eyebrow. "What happened to the housekeeper?"

"She left."

"Oh yes, I forgot." He looked indecisively around before he said, "I'll wait in the library."

Edith nodded and scurried away to brew coffee for him. As she walked into the library with two steaming cups of coffee in her hands, Julius made such a forlorn face that her heart squeezed.

"Thank you. It's been a hard week."

She pondered whether she ought to wait for a better opportunity, then decided that things might only get worse, so she forged ahead. "I had a rather nasty run-in with Frau Breuninger."

"The woman from three houses down the street?"

"Yes. Her husband has recently been promoted to some important position in the Gestapo." Edith took a sip from her coffee, thinking of the best approach, since she knew how much Julius hated idle gossip. "She insulted me."

"Oh dear, what did she say?"

"Actually, she insulted you, saying that Jews shouldn't be allowed to live on the island and that we'd better pack up and leave or she'll get us thrown out."

"She can't do that!" Julius exclaimed. "My family owned this house long before she even knew the island existed."

"It doesn't matter. Her husband has connections." Edith finished her coffee and placed the cup on the table. "With the current political climate, the Gestapo can do whatever they want, nobody will as much as raise an eyebrow." She gave him a rueful smile. "I'd been pondering whether to move in with you in the apartment even before this happened."

"Under no circumstances! We will not abandon my ancestral home. This mansion has belonged to my family for a century and I'm not running away, just because some woman thinks she's better than we are." Julius' face had turned crimson red, the vein on his temple pulsating violently, even as he panted for breath.

"Please, don't get so upset. It would be only for a while. It's more practical since you stay in the city most nights anyway and I'm out here alone without a car or staff." Edith cast him a pleading look. "There's not even a grocer's or a haberdashery nearby and I have to walk across the bridge with the heavy shopping bags almost every day."

"Why can't Delia do it?"

"She could. But then who'd do the cleaning, the dusting, the washing and the cooking?"

His answer was an unintelligible grunt.

"Don't you think it would be more practical if Delia and I moved in with you? We could take better care of you and you wouldn't have to stay on your own all week."

"I'm not giving that woman the satisfaction of scaring you out of our home. And that is my last word on this topic."

Edith inclined her head. Right now she didn't have the strength to fight him. Nevertheless, she wasn't going to accept his decision as final.

11

"What's this?" Helga asked as Heinrich pushed a leaflet onto the kitchen table.

"They want our valuables."

"What? Who?" She stopped chopping vegetables, dried her hands on her apron and reached for the sheet of paper. "Why?"

"It's an order. From the Nazi Party."

"Where did you get it?"

"A man was here delivering the mail."

"I thought the mail had already been delivered today." She frowned.

"I guess stealing everything we own warrants sending a messenger."

"You must be exaggerating, Heinrich."

But he wasn't. As Helga quickly read over the announcement, she became light-headed. Not really comprehending what she'd read, she re-read the text slowly, speaking it out loud. "Jews must deliver all gold, silver or platinum objects in their possession, as well as precious stones and pearls to the public purchasing offices within two weeks." She dropped the paper and put her hands onto the table, her knees threatening to give out from under her.

"Sit down, my love." Heinrich put his arms around her, guiding her onto the chair.

"How can they do this?" Helga looked up at him in disbelief, her voice quivering.

"It seems they can do anything."

She gave a coarse laugh. "Isn't it lucky that we don't possess any valuables?"

"We're fortunate to be too poor to be robbed. Who'd have thought?" Heinrich took another chair and moved it against hers, taking her into his arms.

"Our wedding bands!" Helga jumped up in despair, but he held her hand and pulled her onto his lap. "Those are exempt. Though not the necklace I gave you when David was born."

A heavy sadness engulfed her. The golden necklace with a heart-shaped pendant was the only piece of jewelry she owned, and she wore it with so much pleasure. "It'll break my heart to give it away. It holds so many memories."

"You could hide it. Since we didn't register it with the authorities they'll never find out." His head dropped against hers and he murmured, "I'm so sorry, my sweetheart."

"Whatever are you sorry for? Or is this newest atrocity your idea?" She tried to make a lighthearted joke.

But Heinrich shook his head with a grave expression on his face. "All of this is my fault. If you hadn't married me…"

She jumped off his lap, putting her hands akimbo and giving him a stern stare. "Tell me you're not seriously regretting marrying me, Mr. Goldmann!"

"My darling, I love you more than myself." The desperation lurking in his face almost broke her heart. "It's just… you're suffering because of me. As long as you're married to me you're considered of Jewish family. You could keep your beloved necklace and wouldn't be harassed by the government if it weren't for me."

"Without you I wouldn't even have that necklace!" She glared at him. "I wouldn't have spent twenty wonderful years by your side and raised two precious children. So, I never want to hear you utter such nonsense again. Do you understand?" She talked herself into a rage. "I married you because I love you and I promised to stick with you through good times and bad times. And I will!" Taking a calming breath, she caressed his cheek. "Don't you think I'd rather keep you than a necklace, however dear it is?"

Moisture glossed his eyes.

"You mean so much more to me than any material thing ever could... Can't you see that?"

Heinrich gave a slow, pensive nod. "I do realize that, but seeing you suffer and knowing it's because of me, is more than I can bear. I promised to love and cherish you, but I also promised to protect you and take care of you. I'm failing miserably at doing that."

Finally, Helga smiled because she'd discovered a way to ease his guilt. "I'd suffer a million times more without you. It would be pure hell and surely, you can't want that."

He shook his head, undecided. "I love you. Much more than you'll ever know and my most fervent wish is to make you happy."

"Then you have to put up with me, because only being with you makes me truly happy." She returned to sit on his lap, kissing him on the cheek.

"You'd be much better off without me," he whispered against her lips, even as he kissed her passionately.

"I would not. And I never want to hear that nonsense again." Whatever else she wanted to say was washed away by a wave of love and yearning.

With a quick glance at the clock Heinrich said with a wicked grin, "We have at least an hour before Amelie returns from school."

After making love, Helga continued to prepare dinner, while Heinrich gathered the silver cutlery, a silver picture frame—after removing the photograph of their entire family on a day trip to a nearby lake—a delicate silver bracelet with intricate engravings and Helga's necklace on the table, just when the door flew open and Amelie stormed inside.

"What's this?" She stopped in her tracks, pointing at the table.

"This is our family silver," Heinrich said, and Helga, listening in from the kitchen had to suppress a smile at his dry humor.

A clean kitchen towel in hand, Helga turned around to where her most precious possessions lay, and said to her daughter, "The government has issued an order that Jews must turn in their valuables, jewelry, gold and silver."

"But you can't!" Amelie protested, picking up the necklace. "You love it so much."

"I love my family more." Helga gave a sad smile as she began to wrap the things into the kitchen towel. "Things can be replaced, people cannot."

"You don't have to do this. I can go to the designated collection place," Heinrich offered.

"And risk getting arrested or beaten up? No way." Helga put a hand over his. "If anyone enters the police station, it will be me. They won't do me harm."

She didn't speak it out loud. Everyone in the room knew the reason: because she was the sole "true" human in the family, whereas the others were considered subhuman scum.

The next morning, Helga picked up the package and slipped it into her shopping bag. David lingered in the hallway, his broad shoulders filling the doorframe.

"Shouldn't you be off to work?" Helga eyed him suspiciously.

"Baumann gave me the morning off, to make sure nothing happens to you," David answered with a grim expression.

"Me? I'm not in danger."

"I won't let you go to the police on your own. And don't try to talk me out of it."

Secretly, she was relieved, because with the Nazis one could never be sure. So far the officials had always treated her decently, but being married to a Jew, they might get nasty. "Thank you. Are you sure it's alright with your work? You know, we can't afford to lose your income."

"Don't worry, Mutti. Baumann is one of the good guys."

The bag with the valuables felt a lot heavier than it should as she made her way to the police station, her footsteps echoing in her ears. The items inside were more than just objects to her; they were a part of her family's history. Every single piece held fond memories.

Helga straightened her shoulders. Now was not the time to get emotional, since she had no intention of giving the Nazis the satisfaction of seeing her grieve. She forced a smile on her lips and walked toward the officer in charge. With as much hauteur as she could muster, she addressed him. "I'm afraid there has been a misunderstanding. I'm an Aryan. I shouldn't have to give up my valuables."

The officer had a rounded rosy face, similar to an overfed pig. He looked at her with a sympathetic expression. "Well, that is strange. Let me have a look at my list. What's your name?"

"Helga Goldmann."

He flinched and asked after a glance at her wedding band. "You are married, yes?"

"Yes, sir."

"What's your husband's name?"

"Heinrich Goldmann."

His fat fingers moved down the list until he reached Heinrich's name. "Ah here it is. Your husband has been registered as a Jew. Is that right?"

"It is." Helga inwardly sighed. She'd had this same discussion many times with different officials and knew what was coming, still, she clung to the remote possibility that she could convince him to let her keep at least the necklace.

"I'm sorry, Frau Goldmann. Your husband is the head of

family, therefore the entire household is considered Jewish. It doesn't matter whether you are an Aryan."

"But"—she put on her sweetest flirty smile, hating herself for stooping so low—"I'm not asking much, just that you find it in the kindness of your heart to let me keep one piece of jewelry, which is—"

David interrupted her. "A silver bracelet that she was given by her godmother for first communion."

Helga glared daggers at him, since she cared a lot more about the necklace than that bracelet, but he only gave a barely perceptible shake of his head. He took the package from her hands and unrolled it to present the contents to the officer, pointing at the silver bracelet.

Helga's breath caught in her breast as she raced her eyes up and down the gathered items. Her beloved necklace wasn't there. Out of the corner of her eye, she noticed David's merry twinkle. He must have taken it out. Just when and where?

A hot flash rushed through her veins and she wasn't quite sure whether it was fear of being caught, relief that her necklace was safe, or anger at her son for placing them in such a precarious situation. What if the officer decided to search their pockets? Their persons? These things had happened. A policeman could kill a Jew with his bare hands and nobody would as much as raise an eyebrow.

The fat man let his eyes travel over her most precious belongings, boredom showing in his expression. He must have seen much more valuable things than these. Returning his eyes to her, he gave her a commiserating gaze, before he said, "I'm so very sorry, Frau Goldmann, but I can't bend the rules for you. If anyone finds out, I'll get into real trouble." Then, he counted and jotted down every item presented on the kitchen towel and handed her a receipt. "It will be valued by an official appraiser. Next week you can return and collect the payment."

"Thank you." Helga forced herself to stay calm, albeit

suspecting the official price would barely reach ten percent of the actual value.

"When collecting your payment, your kitchen cloth will be returned to you," he said as if this were a huge concession he made.

"Does the Reich not have use for my good linen?" she asked, keeping her voice serious.

He looked up confused, unable to find a trace of mockery in her carefully schooled features. "If you want to donate the linen, you'll have to turn it in at the *Arbeiterwohlfahrt*."

"Well, thank you. I might just do that," Helga answered, feeling the urge to flee his presence. She took David's hand and escaped into the street, where she broke out into laughter.

"Whatever did you do that for?" David asked.

"I couldn't help myself. Though a more pressing question is: what happened to my necklace?"

He cast a mischievous grin. "Safely stored away."

"I certainly hope you don't have it with you!"

"Not anymore," he said, slipping it into her hand.

"God help us if the Nazis find out." The cold metal quickly warming in her palm gave her a sense of comfort, despite the fear.

"We can't just stand by and watch them rob us blind. We have to fight them every step of the way."

Helga sighed. "One day, that'll get you into serious trouble, David. I don't want to suffer through the same agony I did when Heinrich was arrested."

"Nothing will happen to me," he reassured her.

"Let's hope so."

"Why didn't you ask Aunt Feli to keep our silver for us?" David asked just before they reached the tram station, where they had to part ways.

"Felicitas? Why... I never thought about that."

"She might have been able to help."

"Oh well, it's too late now."

"Maybe not..."

She squinted her eyes at her son. "You won't do anything stupid, will you?"

"Mutti, when have I ever done anything stupid?" he answered in mock indignation.

"Promise me!"

"I promise."

The next morning, Helga was about to leave, when a knock came on the door. Dreading the unannounced visitor, she bit her lip, glancing anxiously at the bathroom door, behind which Heinrich was getting ready for work. He'd been hired as an on-call accountant by several Jewish businesses, which meant he worked between five to ten days a month. Underpaid work, but work nonetheless and right now every penny helped.

"It's me. Feli. Open the door."

Helga cocked her head, unbelieving. Her sister was not known to be an early riser and to arrive in Berlin at this time in the morning, she must have gotten up well before dawn.

When Feli stepped inside, she wore a grim expression on her face. "How could you not have told me!"

"About what?"

Feli put her hands on her hips. "David telephoned me yesterday, telling me about the silver."

"Oh, that. The government ordered all Jews to surrender their valuables to the nearest police station." As soon as she'd arrived home the day before, she'd carefully hidden the necklace, since she didn't want to get into trouble with the authorities.

"Did you tell them that you're Aryan?" Feli asked.

"They don't care." Helga was too downtrodden to repeat a lengthy explanation, her sister would know anyway.

"Nonsense. You and I, we'll go to the police station right away and demand they return your possessions."

Helga shook her head. "How exactly will that work? It's a new law."

"You just let me do all the talking." Feli tapped her finger on the party badge fastened to her lapel. "Now let's go, I don't have all day."

Too astounded to protest, Helga reached for her coat and handbag, calling in the direction of the bathroom, "Heinrich, I'm leaving. See you tonight."

Then, her sister pulled her out of the apartment and to the police station, where the same fat, pig-like policeman was sitting at the reception. He seemed to remember her from the day before, because he creased his forehead. "Do you have more things to surrender, Frau…?"

"Frau Ritter, widow of the NSDAP member and mayor of Oranienburg, Ernst Ritter," Feli said, all but shoving her golden party badge into his face.

His demeanor instantly changed. "What can I do for you, Frau Ritter?"

She bestowed a gracious smile on him. "There has been an awful misunderstanding. My sister here,"—she pointed at Helga—"came yesterday and brought in some silverware."

"I'm so sorry, Frau Ritter, as I told your sister, there are rules to be followed and since she is married to a Jew—"

"Nonsense." Feli brushed him off. "Married to a Jew or not is not the question here. The fact is, the silver cutlery is a family heirloom and thus belongs as much to me as to her. You're not going to tell me that Hitler intends for trusted party members like me"—once again she pushed out her breast with the golden badge—"to surrender my belongings."

A sheen of sweat appeared on the policeman's forehead. "Excuse me, Frau Ritter, are you implying the items your sister brought in yesterday are indeed yours?"

"Exactly," Feli said, without hesitation.

Helga recoiled at her sister's blatant lie, furtively catching glimpses of every official in the room, fearing they'd jump up and arrest her any second.

"Well, then… Why didn't your sister say so?" The policeman's voice had lost its booming authority.

"I... I forgot," Helga stammered.

"See how intimidated the poor woman is?" Feli said.

"She shouldn't have married a Jew," the policeman insisted.

Helga felt a surge of anger and defiance scorching her insides. She was tired of being discriminated against and treated like a second-class citizen just because of whom she loved. "I married him long before the Nazis came to power. What do you suggest I should do?" The moment she saw his smug grin, she knew she'd asked the wrong question.

"With all due respect, a beautiful woman like you, educated and with a well-connected sister, has a world of possibilities open to her. You don't have to tie yourself to staying with a man who's causing you so much grief."

"He's not the one causing me grief—" Helga stopped herself at Feli's warning jolt to her side.

"Divorce him and you'll be welcomed back into the German people's community."

"And she will, I'm seeing to it," Feli answered in Helga's stead. "But now back to our little problem. I need my silverware."

"I'm afraid there's nothing I can do. It has already been registered and packed to be sent to a pawn shop."

"My silver. In a pawn shop?" Feli made a pause for impact, until absolute silence pervaded the room, then she continued loud enough for everyone present to hear. "Would you be so kind to call the police chief of Berlin. He's a friend of mine and will be able to solve this unfortunate situation."

The officer's piggy face turned a darker shade of pink. "Perhaps that won't be necessary. Are you able you identify your property?"

"I certainly am."

"I'll ask someone to bring the boxes in, let's say tomorrow?"

Feli raised her chin. "That won't be necessary, I'll have a look at them right away."

"But... but they are in the basement."

"Then I'll go into the basement."

"Civilians aren't allowed down there."

Helga's eyes raced between her sister and the policeman, fascinated at this battle of wills. From experience she knew the policeman had no chance of winning, therefore she was rather enjoying the spectacle unfolding in front of her.

"If you haven't noticed, I've been decorated with the golden party badge, given to me by our Führer personally. When I say I'm going down into the basement to retrieve my property then I'm going to do it. Otherwise I'll need to have a word with your superior about your obstruction of justice."

The policeman's shoulders sagged. "No harm meant, Frau Ritter. I'll accompany you down to the basement to identify your possessions, but your sister has to stay upstairs."

Feli scrunched up her nose, but after a moment of pause, she nodded and said, "That is so very kind of you. I shall recommend your effort to serve the Reich."

Then she disappeared with the policeman through a door, leaving a very nervous Helga behind. About ten minutes later, Feli returned, all of Helga's possessions safely stored in a cardboard box.

As they walked toward Helga's apartment, Feli said, "I suppose I'd better take your stuff with me for safekeeping."

"Thank you so much for doing this."

"No need to thank me. We're family, remember?"

12

David was whistling a tune while lugging a heavy piece of machinery through the workshop.

"Meeting your girl again?" Baumann asked.

"Yes. Is it so obvious?" David couldn't help but break out into a huge grin at the thought of Thea. After going on several dates, chaperoned by his sister, Thea and he had been officially walking out together for almost two months now.

In theory, her mother insisted they didn't go out alone, except on the most harmless occasions like a book reading in the library with plenty of other people present. David found these events equally as boring as Thea did, but she was a very resourceful girl and they always managed to slink away for half an hour to make out.

He'd never hoped in his wildest dreams that she would be so eagerly responding to his advances. In fact, most of the time she was the one pushing for the next step. His face must have given away his train of thoughts, because Baumann said, "Hey, Kessel, stop dreaming, there's work to do."

"Don't worry, boss."

Just before David was due to finish for the day, Baumann took him aside. "Take this warning from an older and more experienced man: if a girl is much too eager, she usually wants to trap you with a child."

David shook his head. "Thea is not like that. She comes from a good home."

"Sometimes those girls are the most devious ones, because they seek a way to escape their overprotective parents and a husband seems to be the best opportunity. Happened to me. Just be careful, alright? I don't want you to get hurt." With these words the middle-aged, working-class man turned around.

David had long suspected that Baumann considered himself more than just a boss to David, perhaps a mentor or even a father figure. He finished cleaning the work area and rushed home to take a bath and rub the grime from his skin, before picking up Thea to take her out to the theater. Officially, Jews weren't allowed to visit libraries, motion pictures, theaters, museums or even public beaches and swimming pools anymore, but since David was a mixed breed, he considered himself exempt from these rules. Even if he were a full Jew, he had no intention whatsoever of obeying the Nazis' ridiculous rules. If someone called him out, he'd feign ignorance and tell them his mother was Aryan.

Thea, too, had never accepted that the Nazi rules for Jews applied to her as well. She was exceptionally beautiful, the epitome of a German girl, with long blonde hair, porcelain skin and blue eyes. Nobody ever suspected her of being anything other than Aryan, and if they ever did, the radiant smile that had mesmerized every boy at the Lemberg school, would be enough to wrap the man questioning her ancestry around her little finger.

Thea loved to be the center of attention. Her incessant flirting with any and all men she met, was a thorn in David's side, even though she always brushed it off, claiming it wasn't her fault.

About an hour before the performance started, he met her in a nearby café.

"Good evening, Thea." He greeted her with a kiss to her cheek, not daring to properly kiss her on her lips in such a public place.

"David, how was your day?" She smiled, taking his breath away. He still couldn't quite believe that this magnificent woman had chosen him of all guys.

"Exhausting. I lugged engines around all day." He grabbed her hand. From experience he knew that she didn't appreciate lengthy explanations about his work. Whenever he talked about the inner workings of an engine, she rolled her eyes and changed the topic.

"I do appreciate you taking me out, especially since I know how little you fancy a romantic comedy." She sidled up to him, her chest brushing against his, sending hot flashes deep into his groin.

"*Bel Ami* is not a romantic comedy," he protested. He'd done his homework and read the reviews about the film they were planning to watch tonight. "It's a splashy satire of the social-political scene in France before the turn of the century, based on the novel by Guy de Maupassant."

For a moment, her face took on the cutest astonished look, then she broke out into laughter. "Well said, David. Maybe you'll become a film connoisseur after all. Although now I'm worried you won't like my surprise."

"A surprise for me? I don't even have a birthday? What is it?"

Her eyes sparkled with excitement as she retrieved a piece of paper from her purse. "This is for you."

David's eyes grew wide as he recognized the ticket in her hand. "Are you kidding me? How did you get hold of that?"

"Let's just say a friend gave it to me."

The idea that another man had given her the ticket clouded his delight, but just for a second. Then he said, "That's amazing. Thank you so much. I've been wanting to go to the International Automobile and Motorcycle Exhibition, but it's been impossible to get tickets."

"Well, it's yours." Her eyes shimmered with love and he

couldn't resist pressing a long and passionate kiss on her mouth, not caring about the public place.

"I should do this more often," she said with a giggle after he released her.

"Thank you so much, again, sweetheart. This must be the most wonderful gift I have received in my entire life." David carefully folded the ticket and stored it in his breast pocket. "But now, let's go."

Hand in hand they wandered down the majestic boulevard Unter den Linden, enjoying the last rays of sunshine on this beautiful spring day. With time to spare, they arrived in front of the motion picture theater, where David bought tickets and soft drinks. They settled on two of the red high-chairs scattered around the foyer and watched other film-goers streaming inside.

"It feels bold, doesn't it?" Thea suddenly said.

"Bold? Because you're keeping our dates from your mother?"

"No." She shook her head. "You know, because..." she lowered her voice to a conspiratorial whisper, "because we're not allowed to be here. I mean, what my mother, or even my father might do to me if they find out is nothing compared to... It's exhilarating." Goosebumps spread on her arms.

David found the situation humiliating instead of exciting. "I hate them. Just because my father, you know... It doesn't give them the right to make my life hell."

Her face fell. "So you think, making my life hell is alright?"

"No. That's not what I meant. They should leave all of us in peace. What have we done to deserve this?"

"Nothing." Her voice was small. "Those who do this to us are wrong, but I hate more..." she looked over her shoulder, dropping her voice to a bare whisper, "...those who have brought this on us."

David's eyes tore wide open. "What do you mean?"

She leaned closer to him, her whisper so low he could barely decipher her answer, despite her nearness. "The Eastern Jews. If those refugees hadn't invaded Germany we wouldn't be in this dire situation and the Nazis wouldn't have had to implement all these rules."

"Are you serious?" He leaned back, staring at her aghast. "You really believe that?"

"Of course." She raised her voice to a normal volume again. "These subjects came to Germany, took our jobs away, brought crime, poverty and illness with them. I hate them."

"But don't you see that this opinion is the source of all our problems? When we feel superior to one group, then another can feel superior to us. And that is the root of all evil." David had listened in on many discussions between his formerly communist workmates. He didn't agree with, or even understand, many of their theories, but he had adopted several aspects of their beliefs: that all people were created equal and nobody should be discriminated against due to their origin, race or intelligence, including the Eastern Jews who'd found refuge in Germany after fleeing from pogroms in their home countries.

"What's so bad about being better than others?" Thea asked him. "Don't you strive to be the best mechanic in your workshop?"

He didn't have an answer to this, and thankfully the bell announcing the beginning of the motion picture relieved him of having to respond.

All throughout the motion picture he could barely concentrate on the plot, trying to reconcile every human's wish to excel with the notion that all humans should be treated as equals. After a while he gave up, deciding this kind of philosophical problem wasn't his strength and he'd rather puzzle over the inner workings of an engine.

When the film ended, Thea gushed about the dashing journalist Georges Duroy who'd saved France from corruption and married the beautiful girl. David half-heartedly engaged in a conversation with her, wishing they could instead expand on what they'd been talking about before the film. But Thea was not a girl for deep thought; she resembled more a butterfly fluttering from blossom to blossom, sipping sweet nectar and never dwelling long in one place.

He delivered her to her apartment building and when she engaged him in a passionate kiss in front of the door, he forgot all his misgivings and enjoyed the pliable woman in his arms.

13

Julius and Edith had been invited to dinner at Silvana's house.

"Good evening, Silvana. You look marvelous," Edith greeted her sister-in-law.

Julius, though, thought that his sister looked much older than her fifty years. The usually so ebullient, brimming-with-energy woman seemed exhausted.

"Where's Markus?" he asked, since he didn't want to dwell on her appearance.

"He had to go to the Ministry of Education for some certificate, he should have been back an hour ago, already." The steep frown on her forehead betrayed Silvana's worry for her husband.

"I'm sure he was held up at the ministry; there are always long queues at every government office." Edith, kind as always, tried to soothe Silvana's worries.

Silvana gave a deep sigh. "I'm sure you are right. The government is giving us a hard time. Every day there's another rule or regulation that makes running the school so difficult. This time, Markus has to apply for a certificate of sanitation, to prove there aren't rats and cockroaches on our premises. Can you imagine?"

"That's pure despotism! I know of no such law," Julius flared, since he made it a habit to stay on top of all legislation.

Silvana rolled her eyes. "Welcome to Nazi Germany, where a bureaucrat can do whatever he wants, as long as it's harassing a Jew."

"Don't be ridiculous. You can appeal against such an order." Julius still refused to entertain the idea that his beloved Germany wasn't a nation of law anymore.

"Should we go inside? It's getting rather chilly," Edith intervened, always eager to mediate between family members.

"Yes, please, come in. Can I offer you something to drink, while we're waiting for Markus?"

"A coffee would be nice, thank you," Edith said, and Julius added, "I'll take a brandy."

They followed his sister into the dining room, which was a shadow of its previous splendor, since they'd had to deliver all their silverware to the authorities. Another absurdity, but at least it was a law not a random malice by some vicious bureaucrat.

"How's the bank doing?" Silvana asked.

So far, Julius had on purpose avoided telling his sisters about his shameful action. He was searching for an evasive answer, when Edith spoke up. "You don't know that Julius had to sell it?"

Silvana tore her eyes wide open, and she turned her gaze first on Edith and then to Julius. "Is that true? You sold the Falkenstein bank?"

A heavy burden settled on Julius' chest, making it difficult to breathe. "Believe me, it wasn't my wish. The Gestapo came to my office giving me the choice to either Aryanize it myself or have them seize it."

"I'm sorry," Silvana said and he was thankful for her not rubbing salt into the wound.

"Fortunately the bank is in good hands with my former deputy, Herr Dreyer."

Silvana raised an eyebrow. "I never thought he'd be wealthy enough to buy such a big business. The bank must be worth a fortune."

Julius pressed his lips into a thin line, until Edith scolded him.

"Don't you think you should tell your sister the truth? After all, her sons are supposed to inherit it one day."

He cast a scathing glare at his wife, because he still reeled from the decision he'd been forced to take. Business-wise it was definitely the worst thing he had done in his life. Unfortunately, Edith was right and his family deserved to know what an abject failure their patriarch was.

"The going rate for Jewish businesses is about ten percent of their actual value, but Herr Dreyer didn't even possess that much." Julius ran a hand through his meticulously combed hair—a despicable habit he'd developed only recently. "He's an honest man, one who will look out for the bank and its employees. And we agreed on a handshake that he'll return the bank to me once the Nazis are gone—"

"You gave the bank away on a handshake?" Silvana gasped.

"Yes and no. We signed an official contract for the sale, but agreed as gentlemen about the restitution." Goosebumps traveled down Julius' back. He'd been tossing and turning at night over that very issue, since he hated putting the bank at the mercy of anyone, even a loyal man like Herr Dreyer, whom he'd known for more than two decades.

"So, what did you do with the money?" Silvana was never one to beat around the bush.

"There's no money."

"There isn't?" Edith looked at him surprised. She had never been interested in finances, and truth be told, he'd never seen the need to teach her about their financial situation. She bought whatever her heart desired and he happily indulged her, making sure there was always enough money in their joint account.

Silvana squinted her eyes. "You just told me you sold the bank. Did you transfer everything to Switzerland? How?"

Julius sighed. "It's more complicated than that. Herr Dreyer didn't have the money, so the bank gave him a private loan."

"He bought your bank with your bank's money?" Silvana shook her head. "Am I understanding this correctly?"

"Unfortunately, yes. He's keeping me on as director. The monthly salary he's paying me has been calculated to include a repayment of the loan. Our lawyer, Doctor Petersen, came up with this idea."

"I really hope this won't come back to bite you," Silvana said. "Why don't you sit down while I go and get you a brandy?"

As she walked over to the cabinet, he spotted a book with the title *"Racial Science of the Jewish People"*, written by the scholar of language and literature, Hans Friedrich Karl Günther, nicknamed Race Günther or Race Pope, because he was the originator of the Nazis' racial ideology.

"You're not seriously reading this drivel?" He pointed accusingly at the book, when his sister returned with a glass of brandy.

"Believe me, I wish I didn't have to. The government insisted we teach our students *proper* history and have made racial ideology and especially Günther's books a mandatory subject. I'm still trying to find a single positive sentence about Jews in that book. I have no idea how to stand in front of my class and tell them to read this."

"Then don't. The Nazis surely won't attend your classes to find out what exactly you're teaching."

"You have no idea." Silvana rolled her eyes. "Even if they don't go to that length, they might have spies in the classroom. Also, they ask children about this stuff, for example during emigration interviews, and if my students don't know the answers, it'll get themselves, their families and our school into trouble."

Julius groaned. It seemed his optimism about Hitler being a short-lived phenomenon had not been justified. Still, he couldn't help clinging to the belief that law and order continued to exist.

"Why don't you close down the school, if the government is giving you so much trouble?" He hadn't approved of Silvana's plan to open a Jewish school in the first place.

"And where shall all my students go?" Her eyes glinted with protectiveness for her charges.

"To some other school."

"Oh, Julius, you're more deluded than I imagined. When will you finally accept the reality?"

Again, Edith jumped in to keep the two siblings from charging into a quarrel. "Have you heard from Adriana?" Their other sister Adriana had emigrated to London years ago.

"Indeed. We telephone almost every week since she's become the official owner of the school."

"When did that happen?" Edith asked.

"A few months ago. It was safer for everyone to have the school under English ownership. The Nazis apparently want to avoid diplomatic trouble with England."

"A very cunning move," Julius said with admiration. He'd never pegged his youngest sister for such a shrewd businesswoman. Perhaps he had underestimated her and she had after all inherited the family's knack for good business.

"Isn't that dangerous? I mean, what if our country goes to war with England?" Edith asked.

For the second time this day, Edith's words surprised Julius. When had his obedient wife who stayed in the background become an outspoken woman who seemed to keep up with current politics. "There will be no war."

"I'm with Julius on this one," Silvana said. "Hitler may want a war, but the German public doesn't. And neither does the English public, or the French. Our nations are still suffering the huge losses we had during the Great War. Forcing us into a new war would be political suicide."

"Which might actually be a good thing then," Edith said, earning her nonplussed stares from both Julius and Silvana.

"War is never a good thing. I was there. It will not happen again. Not so soon after the last one, because the men in power now, even Hitler himself, remember all too well the time in the trenches." Julius took another sip from his brandy and put the empty glass on the dining table. "Furthermore, in the Munich conference last fall Hitler promised peace in exchange for the

Sudetenland. Why would he go back on his word, now that he has got what he wanted?"

"Don't you think that being given the Sudetenland on a silver plate emboldened him to ask for more?" Edith insisted.

Julius couldn't help but feel a spark of admiration. It suited Edith to have her own opinion. "What else could he possibly want?"

"I don't know, the rest of Europe maybe," Edith replied.

Julius snorted. "In his dreams, perhaps, but does he want to go to war for it? He already has the thing he wants most of all: power."

"Enough of politics. Let me brew you a coffee." Silvana disappeared into the kitchen, leaving Edith and Julius alone.

"I like the way you're keeping up to date with politics," Julius said, causing Edith to blush at the compliment.

"I'm afraid, Julius."

Edith had such a forlorn expression on her face, he couldn't help but rub her hand. "Don't be, my dear, there won't be another war. It would be the end of life the way we know it, and even Hitler knows that."

Silvana returned from the kitchen with two cups of coffee in her hands, just as the door opened and a bruised and bloodied person staggered inside. The cups shattered on the floor as Silvana shrieked, "Markus!" and rushed toward her husband. "What has happened to you? Are you alright? How on earth?"

Julius saw Edith blanche, and realized the need to take control of the situation. "Edith, could you please get a dustpan and brush to mop the floor?"

"Yes, of course." She scurried off to remove coffee smears and shards, while he strode toward his brother-in-law, grabbing him around his torso and half-carrying him into the living room, where he eased him onto the sofa. Silvana was a blubbering mess, kneeling on the floor, wiping the blood from Markus' face with her sleeve.

"It's not as bad as it looks," Markus said in a weak voice. "I was just leaving the ministry when three SA men attacked me." He groaned when Silvana dabbed at the gash on his forehead.

"Go, get some fresh water and a clean towel," Julius ordered his sister, and when she didn't move, he called out to Edith. "Bring us two glasses of brandy, fresh water and a clean towel will you?"

When she returned he handed one glass each to Markus and Silvana, before he asked Edith to clean Markus' wounds.

"Now, tell me everything that happened," he asked Markus, even as Edith went to work on him.

"There's not much to tell. They saw me coming out of the building, asked for my papers and when they noted the J on my *Kennkarte,* they started punching me."

"Poor Markus," Silvana muttered. "Shall I call the doctor?"

"No, no, it's just a few bruises. I'll be fine."

"It would be better to have a doctor look at you," Edith insisted. "Just to be sure, and to reassure your wife."

Markus winced when she put too much pressure on his wounds and tried a crooked smile. "If you insist. Call the doctor."

The Aryan family doctor unfortunately wasn't allowed to treat them anymore, but they had found a retired Jewish doctor in the neighborhood who made house visits. After telephoning him, he arrived within half an hour.

Once he had examined Markus briefly he said, "You got off lightly. There's no lasting damage done. You just need rest and time to heal."

Julius paid the doctor for his services and returned to the living room, shaken to his core. Whatever had happened to law and order? This was not the Germany he'd grown up in. The silver lining was that things must soon return to normal, since this folly couldn't last much longer.

Edith raised her voice. "Don't you think you should also consider emigrating?"

"Never!" Silvana called out. "What would our students do? We can't just leave them alone! The Lemberg school is one of the few

Jewish schools left in Berlin. Without us, who will prepare the students for a life in a foreign country?"

Julius thought it ironic that Silvana strove for preparing her students for emigration, while she herself would hear no word of it.

Markus took his wife's hand. "I agree. We can't give up. Even at the risk of our own lives, we have to keep helping these children."

"That's very noble." Julius rubbed his chin. "I never believed I would say this, but perhaps a temporary relocation might be a wise decision."

Edith looked at him with surprise. She'd been trying to persuade him to leave Germany for years.

14

Edith sat on the terrace of their mansion on Schwanenwerder Island, looking at the lush gardens with the tall trees. She had not always enjoyed living there. All too well she remembered the times when the mansion had belonged to her mother-in-law. Back then it had been a dark, cold, damp and depressing place, stuffed with pompous Victorian furniture that would suit a palace or a museum.

Grim-looking ancestors of the Falkenstein family stared down on the living people from their more than head high paintings on the wall. She'd felt a strange chill every time she had to pass beneath one of them, as if they were still alive and frowning upon the slightest error this middle-class girl made during her training to be the new Frau Falkenstein before the wedding to Julius.

The weight falling from her shoulders at being able to move to Munich after their nuptials probably had been heard all across Berlin. When they'd returned to Berlin several years later, Julius had given her free rein to modernize the mansion. She'd done such a splendid job, every visitor had complimented her on the redecoration.

Despite the inconvenient hardship of having to walk into

town every other day to buy groceries—a task that used to be done by staff—she still loved living here surrounded by nature.

Her musings were cut short, when her maid Delia arrived. "Excuse me, *gnädige Frau,* there's a visitor for you."

"Who is it?"

"They didn't say. They looked like Gestapo, though."

Goosebumps appeared on Edith's entire skin, and she gasped for breath. A visit from the Gestapo was never a good thing. After several seconds of not being able to breathe, her head began to spin. Images of herself shackled and bound, bloodied and bruised, flickered through her mind. Despite the fear, she somehow managed to keep her aplomb and calmly asked, "Did they say what they want?"

"I'm afraid not."

"Well then, I guess I'll have to speak to them, if I don't want to escape through the lake."

Delia's eyes opened wide. "*Gnädige Frau,* you can't do that. The water is much too cold. You'd never—"

Edith cut her short. "It was a joke. Where are they?"

"They are waiting in the reception hall."

"I'll attend to them." After a glance at Delia's frightened face, she added, "Perhaps you could go and clean the garden shed?"

Delia nodded gratefully. "Thank you so much. I'd rather not talk to them."

Edith could understand the young woman's dilemma, a former prima ballerina who'd been forced to give up her career because the Nazis didn't allow Jews to dance. The Gestapo wouldn't dare to touch Edith, who was a Christian. At least that was what she clutched at to keep her fear at bay.

In the reception hall, two men in civilian suits were waiting.

"*Meine Herren,* how can I help you?" she asked with as much sangfroid as she could muster.

"Are you Edith Falkenstein?"

"Yes, that would be me."

"Where is your husband?"

"He is at work. Shall I advise him that you need to see him?" Her fear increased multifold.

"That won't be necessary," the older one said. "We've come here with an eviction notice."

She suddenly lost her faculty for speech. Long seconds passed and extended into an awkward silence. Edith felt the tension in the room crush down on her as if it were an actual weight, when the portrait of one of Julius' grim-looking ancestors crossed her mind. For some strange reason it gave her the strength to speak. "Excuse me, *meine Herren,* this must be a mistake. This mansion has been in my husband's family for more than a century."

"This is no mistake." The younger man eyed her with curiosity. "Your neighbors want you gone from the island."

"On what grounds?" Edith was nonplussed, since they had always kept good relations with their neighbors, moved in the same circles, attended each other's parties. Some, like Reginald, had become close friends. On second thought, their friends had emigrated, whereas the other neighbors had turned colder over the years. And recently, Frau Breuninger had said such vicious things to her on the street.

Slowly it dawned on Edith that this eviction must be on her account. Herr Breuninger had made a career in the Gestapo, and would have the authority to issue an eviction notice, independent of the grounds.

"Your husband is a Jew, that is reason enough," the older man answered.

"My husband is living most of the time in our city apartment anyway, since the government took his car away." She knew her remark was pointless, nevertheless she couldn't help to rub it under their noses. "And I'm not Jewish. You can't evict *me*."

"You are married to a Jew." The young officer scrutinized her with a smug grin. "And thus, we can do whatever we want, Frau Falkenstein."

The older man added in a more conciliatory tone. "I'm sure you understand that we cannot have a Jewish family on this prestigious island, where our beloved propaganda minster Goebbels lives."

Edith inwardly groaned. Goebbels had bought the mansion of Julius' friend, the bank owner Oscar Schlitter, for a fraction of its true value. Just recently he'd also acquired the adjacent premises of the emigrated banker Samuel Goldschmitt, and was now having it pompously expanded. Since the Falkensteins would surely never be invited to the lavish parties he was known for, perhaps it was better to leave the island altogether, while they still could.

"What will happen to our house if we leave?" she asked, fearing it would be gobbled up by Goebbels as well and made into another kitschy fairy-tale palace.

"That, Frau Falkenstein, is entirely up to you. The eviction notice gives you until the end of the month to sell the house and leave with all your belongings, otherwise everything except your clothes will fall to the Reich and the property will be foreclosed on."

She gave him a sour smile, musing over the irony that Julius' home would befall the same fate so many of his clients had suffered through at the bequest of his bank, when they hadn't been able to pay their loans. Though in his case there was no loan, no debt to pay, just an act of caprice on the part of the government.

"What happens if I refuse to leave?" she asked, her eyes flashing with fury.

A simple shrug was all the younger Gestapo officer had to offer. "If you choose to align yourself with the Jews, you'll be arrested and taken to a camp with the rest of this scum. We'll take your house, plus everything inside."

The older man intervened, giving her a benevolent smile. "There is a way out for you, Frau Falkenstein."

"Please enlighten me." She slightly bowed her head to listen to his suggestion, although she already knew what was coming.

"Divorce your husband."

She decided to indulge him. "But how does this help? I won't be able to do so before the end of the month, now will I?"

He looked slightly nonplussed, until his eyes lit up. "We could put your divorce on a fast track. I'm sure once the papers are signed, even if the divorce is not finalized yet, we can abstain from enforcing the eviction notice."

Edith shuddered at the casual manner in which he spoke about her twenty-year marriage, as if it was a mere inconvenience, perhaps like the erroneous purchase of a dress, which one then hid in the corner of the wardrobe or gave away to charity. "The mansion and everything in it belong to my husband, won't I have to leave as soon as I file for divorce? Will I find myself on the street, begging the Salvation Army to take me into one of their public shelters?" With satisfaction she observed the officer flinch. Not even a heartless Nazi wished a well-to-do lady like her having to bunk down in a public shelter for beggars and fallen women.

"I'm sure we can arrange something," he offered after a while. "Since your husband isn't allowed to enter the island, he could simply transfer the property to your name after the divorce. Wouldn't that be a solution that suits everyone?"

She could think of at least one person whom this solution wouldn't suit. Nonetheless she dutifully nodded, since antagonizing the Gestapo wouldn't serve her. "Thank you, I'll talk to my lawyer and have it sorted out."

"We're always glad to help, Frau Falkenstein."

"Thank you so very much." She could barely keep a straight face. "Would there be anything else?"

"No. As soon as you deliver the divorce papers, the house will be signed over to your name and you can happily live here forever."

"What a relief." She couldn't wait for them to leave her house. Once they did, she walked into the adjacent library, dropped into the armchair and buried her head in her hands. She had never really considered divorce, although now she contemplated doing it for the sole reason of keeping Julius' parental home in the family. If she was the owner, it would be safe until the Nazi reign was over, which had to end one day, hopefully sooner rather than later. Afterward they could remarry and she would return the property to him—much like the deal Julius had struck with Herr Dreyer.

He would continue to live in their city apartment and she might visit him there on the weekends. It wouldn't be so different from their current situation. Perhaps that was the way out they'd been seeking. It was only temporary.

Then she shrugged. The idea was too ridiculous to even consider it.

15

GLIWICE, AUGUST 30, 1939

Joseph was sitting in a bar drinking beer. Reinhard Heydrich, leader of the Reich Security Head Office RSHA, had given him the top-secret mission to occupy the radio station at Gliwice and send an incendiary speech in Polish at exactly eight p.m. on a yet to be specified date. It was a genius plan.

Hitler would put the blame on the Poles, using the "attack on a German institution on German land" as an excuse to order his planned invasion of Poland in "self-defense".

It was a task after his liking, since secret missions usually involved plenty of action, fighting and even some fun—as opposed to the boring desk work that he'd been doing lately. Especially his short posting to the Sachsenhausen concentration camp, which had been tedious to say the least. Harassing already downtrodden Jews wasn't something Joseph found an adequate occupation for him. He was destined for higher work.

For example, back in 1934 during the Night of the Long Knives, also called Röhm Coup, when his unit had been tasked to prevent a mutiny planned by the SA and had killed the traitors in a cloak-and-dagger operation. He still felt the adrenaline rushing through his veins when he thought of that night. The only other occasion even close to measuring up in importance was the Night of Broken Glass in November 1938, when the Jews received their rightful punishment for killing a German diplomat.

He prided himself to be one of the few SS leaders who had actually gotten his hands dirty. Joseph's musings were interrupted by the sound of the door opening. He broke out into a huge grin, when a man in Wehrmacht uniform entered.

"Good to see you, Knut," he greeted his younger brother.

"Sorry for being late, the briefing went on and on."

"No problem, I was in good company." Joseph nodded at his glass of beer and asked, "Want one?"

"Sure."

He ordered two more beers, before he asked, "So, what was the briefing about?"

Knut rolled his eyes. "You know that I'm not allowed to talk about it."

"Technically, I'm your superior."

"You wish you were! But rank aside, you're not in our unit, so if you want information, get it through the official channels." Knut took a big gulp from the mug the peachy waitress had just put in front of him.

"Well it was worth a try." Joseph laughed good-naturedly. He knew everything about Hitler's plans. After all, he was in charge of inciting the incident, codenamed "*Großmutter gestorben*", grandmother died. He'd wanted to find out whether the Wehrmacht knew, or suspected, anything. For the mission to go smoothly, absolute secrecy was key. He couldn't risk men traipsing round and gossiping about the war about to start.

"But tell me, what are you doing here? I was quite surprised when I received your telephone call," Knut said.

"Nothing special. My unit has been buried in work for months, so our superiors decided to give us a few days off for a fun trip including lots of beer, skittles and beautiful women," Joseph told him the official ruse for the operation.

"Right here at the Polish border of all places?" Knut squinted his eyes. "I'll eat my hat if that's true."

Joseph shrugged. "*Bon appétit*."

"How's the family?" Knut asked. "It's been ages since I've been home to visit."

"Marvelous. Father is enjoying his retirement and mother is overjoyed to have him home every day."

"I can imagine her fussing over him." Knut leaned back in his seat.

"Our sister Carsta is pregnant again."

Knut's eyebrows shot up. "Isn't she a bit old to have another child? She just turned thirty-nine."

"I guess after the first seven you have the knack for it." Joseph laughed. "She confessed that she wishes nothing more than to give our Führer an eighth child, which will make her eligible for the golden Mother's Cross."

"I remember how proud she was when she received the silver cross. Anyway, I thought she and Rudolf were done with having children." Knut was still unmarried at the age of thirty-eight and had never brought a girlfriend home, despite their mother's best efforts to match him up with prospective brides.

"We all live to serve." Joseph's heart swelled with pride that even his little sister was doing her bit for the Fatherland.

"Have you heard from Edith?"

"Not since last November, but I thought you two were talking?"

"We used to, when I was stationed in Berlin. Since I've been posted here we've only exchanged a few letters. Because of the censors, she doesn't write anything of importance."

"I heard they had to sell their mansion on Schwanenwerder Island."

Knut emptied his beer. "Such a shame. It's a nice house and she did a splendid job with the gardens, too."

"Easy for her with the help of how many gardeners?"

"Do you know why they sold it?"

"It seems the neighbors got them evicted because they didn't want Jews living on the island." Joseph lit a cigarette for himself and offered another one to his brother.

Inhaling the smoke deeply, Knut asked, "Are they finally considering leaving the country?"

"No chance. You know how stubborn that husband of hers is. They're living in their apartment close to the city center. If only she'd heeded my advice and divorced that man. It would have saved her so much trouble."

"I guess you can't control with whom you fall in love." Knut made such a forlorn face, that Joseph assumed his little brother was crossed in love.

"Anything I should know about?"

"No." Knut's expression closed, as if he wanted to hide something. From experience Joseph knew it wouldn't do any good to insist.

After about an hour, Joseph bid his goodbyes, because he needed to travel to the neighboring town to meet with SS Oberführer and Gestapo Chief Müller. Before walking to the car, he hesitated for a moment, unsure whether he should return to the hotel and put on his uniform for the meeting, or travel in civilian clothes.

Since Heydrich had instilled in him that they weren't allowed to contact any German authorities in Gliwice, and were not to carry identification showing their affiliation with the SS, he opted for the latter.

"Good, you're here," Oberführer Müller said without further ado. "I take it nobody knows you're here on government business?"

"That is correct, Herr Oberführer. My team and I have checked into the hotel as civilians, supposedly on a skittles trip."

"How bourgeois!" Müller's lip twitched upwards. "Anyhow, please have a seat, I want to go over the details with you. It's absolutely essential that this mission is a success."

"I understand our Führer himself has planned the action, and I can assure you, I've gathered the best and most reliable team for the task."

"All from the security office?"

"No. Some of them are veteran SS men who have been with me for years. One is a native Polish speaker to give the radio speech, two are locals from the area, and one is a first-class radio technician, who has the technical knowledge to interrupt a program in progress at very short notice in a completely foreign station and switch on the microphone to have the Polish-speaker make the speech."

"It seems you have thought of everything."

Joseph relaxed slightly at the compliment. "I have vetted every single man; we have gone through the operation several times, reviewing every possible eventuality."

"Good. Do you have someone inside the radio station?"

"This is indeed the weak spot. Therefore, I personally reconnoitered the site including the entrance area. Fortunately the security measures are lax, so this isn't worrying me much."

"You never actually went inside?" Oberführer Müller rubbed his chin pensively.

"No, sir. Obergruppenführer Heydrich insisted we should under no circumstances attract unwanted attention. My men are experienced enough to deal with whatever we'll find inside the station."

Müller furrowed his brows. "It's not ideal, but being detected would have been a catastrophe. What about the speech you're going to transmit? Where did you get it?"

Joseph straightened his shoulders proudly. "I wrote the speech myself and our Polish speaker translated it. If you wish to see it…"

Müller waved it off. "No need. I trust you. But we'll need further evidence for the local German authorities."

"What kind of evidence are you thinking about?" Joseph believed a radio speech held in Polish, heard by thousands of listeners, many of whom, living at the border, spoke the language, would be proof enough of Poland's aggression against Germany.

"Something more tangible. A canned good."

"Excuse me?"

"That's code for concentration camp prisoners who turn up dead, in our case as a dead Polish insurgent."

Joseph swallowed, reminded of Heinrich Goldmann, whom he'd—in a nostalgic moment—freed from Sachsenhausen. Müller must have noticed his discomfort, because he added, "We're strictly using professional criminals who have received death sentences anyway."

"Good." Joseph didn't want to appear overly empathetic.

"We'll dress him in a Polish uniform and—"

"With all due respect, Oberführer Müller, but I think that's a bad idea. We really can't have a dead foreign soldier in Gliwice. The plan provides for Polish insurgents, a soldier would throw up questions and cause investigations."

Müller wrinkled his forehead. "Alright, you'll get your canned good in civilian clothes."

"How is it going to be delivered?" Joseph had no intention of burdening his team with the logistics of transporting and killing a prisoner on top of everything else they had to do.

"Don't worry, we'll take care of it. Your action starts at eight p.m. sharp, my men will bring it to the station around ten past eight."

"That would work. I'll have two men outside to allow your agents on the premises, but we can't deal with anything else."

"Let that be my problem."

"Is there anything else you need to know?" Joseph itched to return to Gliwice and brief his team on the slight change of plans.

"I think we're clear. As soon as Heydrich gives us both the go, we'll jump into action. Report to me immediately after the successful action."

"Yes, Oberführer Müller."

Müller stood up and Joseph followed suit, clicking his heels. "Sieg Heil!" Several minutes later he settled behind the wheel of his vehicle, giddy with anticipation at the great things that were about to happen.

16

After a day of hard work scrubbing floors in the sweltering August heat, Helga rushed to the bakery to buy fresh bread for dinner. She had almost reached the shop when she spotted Edith, carrying a basket.

"Good evening, Edith," she called out, quite surprised that her rich friend would do her own shopping.

"Oh, Helga, how nice to see you." Edith seemed genuinely delighted. They stood in the queue for a few minutes, exchanging chit-chat. After she had finished her purchases, Edith waited outside, looking over her shoulder. "It's nice to meet a friendly soul. Would you care for a cold lemonade? It's on me."

"That would be wonderful, but I don't have much time."

"Would you rather we met some other day?" Edith looked crestfallen.

"I guess half an hour will be fine, and I really need some cold lemonade. The heat these days has been unbearable."

"Well, then, let's go. There's a nice little café with a shaded garden right around the corner." Edith led the way into a café that looked unspectacular from the outside. She must have been a regular customer, because the waiter greeted her by name and led them into a secluded corner in the garden, shielded from the eyes and ears of other patrons by sprawling ivy.

"Such a beautiful place," Helga mentioned after ordering.

"Julius and I used to come here frequently, but these days… well, he can't come anymore."

Helga nodded, since she'd seen the signpost on the door reading,

No Jews Desired

Despite the secluded table, she automatically looked over her shoulder. "I'm wondering why you patronize this business if they don't want your husband here."

Edith shrugged, guilt written all over her face. "Believe me, I struggle with this. On the one hand I want to shout at them for their awful behavior, but on the other hand, I'm so tired that I need a respite once in a while, especially since I moved to the city center. I miss our gardens so much."

"You moved away from the island?" Helga had never been to the Falkenstein mansion, but she had seen pictures and couldn't imagine someone living on the Schwanenwerder Island voluntarily giving up the glorious surroundings.

"I didn't want to, but…" Edith stopped talking, because the sound of steps announced the waiter bringing their drinks. As soon as he disappeared, she continued. "Our neighbors instigated that the Gestapo kick us out."

"They did?" Helga had never considered that rich, assimilated Jews like the Falkensteins suffered from the same harassment her family did.

"Yes. The mansion and the park have belonged to Julius' family for more than a century, until some up-and-coming Gestapo officer's wife decided she didn't want Jews in her neighborhood." Edith scrunched up her nose. "You know what's ironic? Julius moved out months ago, because they took his car and there's no adequate public transport from the island to his office."

"I'm sorry. The situation gets more depressing by the day." Helga took a sip from the, admittedly delicious, ice-cold lemonade. "Where do you live now?"

"A few blocks from the Falkenstein bank's headquarters. We own an apartment there."

Helga took a moment to process what Edith had just said. "At least the bank seems to do well."

Again, Edith shrugged. "It does. Although my husband's not the owner anymore. The Gestapo forced him to aryanize it, so he sold it to his deputy. Herr Dreyer is a loyal man, who agreed to keep Julius on as manager." As if to apologize she added, "Herr Dreyer actually had to get a special permission to hire a Jew, and it was only allowed because of the many years Julius had been leading the bank."

"These days nobody employs a Jew." Helga's husband had been fired by the Falkenstein bank less than a year ago.

"You must believe me, Julius didn't want to do it, but he had no choice." Suddenly Edith looked very old. "He keeps saying that he needed to protect all his employees, so with a heavy heart he took the decision to sacrifice a few for the benefit of the many."

"Heinrich received a very generous severance package, which we hadn't expected." Helga tried to cheer up her friend, since it wasn't Edith's, or even her husband's fault that the Nazis had come to power and issued all these oppressive rules. She didn't mention that the money had long since been used up and they barely scraped by with her salary as a cleaning lady, David's half-salary at the workshop and the odd job Heinrich was contracted for.

"Honestly, the more I think about it, the more I'm of the opinion he should have stood up for his Jewish employees. Look at him, he's now an ordinary manager of his own bank, who can be fired at whim. Do you think Herr Dreyer will take a stand for him when the Nazis decide he has to go?" Edith was talking herself into a rage. "Did the many need protection? I mean, yes, they were his employees and depended on the salary, but so did the Jews. And has anyone threatened to let the Aryans go? If they lose their jobs, wouldn't they easily find a new one? Don't you think it would have been better to protect the few who really needed it, instead of thinking about everyone?"

Helga put her hand on Edith's arm. "Nobody could have foreseen all the horror Hitler has unleashed on us."

"But shouldn't we do something? Raise our voices?" Edith looked so forlorn, Helga felt the strangest urge to wrap her into her arms and rock her like a child. For obvious reasons she resisted the notion.

"I'm afraid it's too late for that. People should have spoken out six years ago. These days Hitler is more popular than ever. His supporters are everywhere, growing more fanatic on a daily basis. The only thing we can do is to look after our family and friends." Helga felt sorry for the other woman.

Edith furrowed her brows. "My brother Joseph always accused me of living in an ivory tower and not seeing the suffering of the normal people. I'm afraid he was right. I lived in luxury in our mansion and never wanted for anything. But it seems the Nazis have caught up with me. First they took my maid, then the other employees. They took my husband's citizenship, his car, his business, his mansion." She gave a bitter laugh. "Look at me, complaining about having to go shopping all by myself and making do with a former prima ballerina as my only employee to keep our nine-room apartment in top condition. You must be thinking I'm a spoiled brat, whining for nothing."

Helga hesitated for a moment, while a flash of annoyance stabbed her. Edith's situation was so much more comfortable than her own, and yet she seemed to suffer as much, if not more. Then the revelation hit her square in the chest: Edith's situation might be a lot more comfortable, but her fall had been a lot steeper, too. Therefore she said, "Not at all." After a long silence, Helga asked. "Is Joseph still happy in the SS?"

"We're not exactly on speaking terms. He's completely

deluded, he even went as far as to divorce his wife because they found a Jewish great-great-great-grandmother in her family tree."

"Really?"

"Yes, really. Anyway, I haven't seen him since last November." Edith gave a deep sigh. "The only family member I'm in contact with is my younger brother Knut. He's in the Wehrmacht, but has recently been posted to the Polish border because of the simmering conflict there."

Helga had feared a war might happen, especially after Hitler broke the Munich agreement and marched into what was left of Czechoslovakia this past spring. "Do you think there will be a war?"

"Honestly, I don't know. Everyone keeps telling me no, but why would Hitler move troops to the border if he weren't planning something? You can't tell me it's just a precaution, because that man never does anything without a reason."

"Let's hope it never comes to that." Helga looked at her wristwatch. "I need to get going. Thanks so much for the lemonade."

On her way home, Helga mused over everything Edith had told her. Her heart constricted painfully. If war broke out, David was in danger of being drafted and sent into combat.

At home, she voiced her concerns over dinner. David simply laughed it away. "Mutti, the Wehrmacht doesn't want me. I'm a *Mischling,* remember? Unworthy of fighting and dying for the Fatherland."

At a loss for words, she observed her wonderful son, who so stoically suffered from the constant discrimination without ever losing heart, when Heinrich said, "He's right. At least that's one thing we won't have to worry about."

"Who would have thought that I'd thank the Nazis for their treatment of my family one day. Although I still hope war doesn't break out."

Unfortunately all signs pointed to the opposite.

17

Joseph was having coffee with his team in the hotel lobby, when the receptionist approached their table.

"Hauptsturmführer Hesse, there's a call for you. Would you please come with me?"

"Of course." Instantly, the adrenaline rushed through his veins, heightening his senses. His training allowed him to remain calm on the exterior and follow her with a measured stride to the telephone sitting atop the reception counter.

"Please call me back." It was unmistakably Heydrich's voice on the line.

"Give me five minutes." During his reconnaissance, Joseph had identified a public phone not far away from the hotel, where nobody could overhear his conversation. It was a standard security measure not to talk in crowded places. He hung up and walked out the door without a word to his men. They were well-trained enough not to ask stupid questions about his absence.

This call could only mean two things: either Heydrich would give the agreed code phrase, or he would cancel the mission altogether. Joseph fervently wished for the former.

Exactly three and a half minutes later he arrived at the public phone, stepped inside, closed the door and dug for the coins he'd been carrying in his pocket for that exact reason ever since he'd left Berlin several days ago.

Taking a deep breath, he dialed the adjutancy and asked to be connected to Heydrich. Once he was on the line, Heydrich didn't waste time with niceties and uttered exactly two words: "Grandmother died."

A rush of euphoria flooded Joseph's system. The mission was a go, and he, Hauptsturmführer Joseph Hesse, patriot and the Führer's loyal supporter, was the chosen man to make it a success. The future of the entire nation depended on him and his men. It was everything he'd worked so hard for during the past decade.

"I'm so very sorry. Have you already informed her son?" The son obviously was Gestapo Chief Müller.

"He's as disconsolate as I am."

Joseph hung up. The countdown had begun. He looked at his wristwatch; it was a quarter past four. In less than four hours he and his team were going to give the radio speech that would allow Hitler to invade Poland and make it appear as self-defense.

He returned to the hotel lobby as if nothing had happened and settled into his chair to eat the rest of his cake. Judging by their faces, his men had picked up on his inner tension, despite his calm facade and knew the operation was about to start.

They had been waiting for this day, rehearsing the operation over and over, making a detailed action plan and preparing for every imaginable eventuality. This was perhaps the most important task of their lives.

"Anyone up to a good game of skittles tonight?" Joseph asked, giving them the code phrase they had agreed upon.

His heart filled with pride as he looked into the eager faces full of anticipation, loyalty and patriotism. There was no doubt that he'd chosen the best possible men for the job. Tonight they would make history. "Well then, I'll see you at seven sharp in reception."

Then he ordered another coffee, while most of the men dispersed to their rooms to get ready. Each one of them had a unique talent, a special position, but only together as a team would they be able to succeed.

Shortly before eight p.m. they arrived in front of the radio station, a rather drab, greenish-gray cubical building with a red-tiled roof and top-to-bottom rows of windows. It was surrounded by a small park and behind the station building throned the impressive radio tower.

Joseph had been in awe when he'd first seen it: put into service only four years prior, during Christmas 1935, the new radio tower was one hundred and eighteen meters tall, including the antenna, making it the highest wooden construction in all of Europe. But that wasn't the most impressive thing about it: The structure had been nicknamed "Silesian Eiffel Tower", because of the similarity to its big brother in Paris.

It was truly a sight to behold and deserved to become the venue for one of the most important events of present times. Maybe a few months from now, after Poland had been subdued, Joseph might return and ask to mount the tower platform. From up there the view into the newly acquired *Lebensraum* must be splendid.

He brushed off the distracting thoughts, because the next thirty minutes had to proceed with clockwork precision. Later, there'd be enough time to bask in glory. One last glance at his men reassured him they were ready. They had switched into shoddy Polish peasant garb, which the insurgents usually wore to blend in.

"Let's go in," he ordered his men, and from that second onward the operation unreeled according to a set schedule.

The watchmen didn't put up any resistance and within minutes, Joseph's group had forced their way into the radio station. He left two men outside to wait for the arrival of Gestapo Chief Müller's canned good and proceeded with the rest into the building.

Adrenaline sharpened his senses, and he became acutely aware of his surroundings. Trained warriors thrived under duress in combat situations, as opposed to civilians, who usually ran around like headless chickens. Joseph ashamedly remembered the Beer Hall Coup, where he'd vomited next to his dead comrade's smashed head.

No time to reminisce, he analyzed the situation in a split second, identified the door behind which the broadcast room was and gestured his men to advance to it. They threw the door open, weapons at the ready, staring into the panicked faces of the civilian employees.

He felt a twinge of sympathy for the honest German men who were pawns in a bigger game. Hopefully they would choose to fully cooperate, because he would hate having to kill them.

"This is a hold-up!" the Polish speaker yelled first in Polish and then, for the benefit of the employees who might not speak the language, in German.

For emphasis, two of his men fired warning shots into the ceiling. Joseph found it was a nice touch to make the attack seem more realistic and ensure the employees were frightened enough not to play hero and do something stupid.

As he'd surmised, the barked order combined with the shots did the job and the station employees obediently put their hands up behind their heads. Joseph personally herded them into the basement, where he gave short instructions. "Nothing will happen to you, if you cooperate. Understood?"

The civilians nodded.

He left one of his team members to watch them and returned to the broadcast room, where the technician and the Polish speaker were already searching frantically for something.

"What's wrong?" So far the action had worked out perfectly, but minor hiccups were always to be expected.

"We can't find the microphone."

"Has anyone raised the alarm?" Joseph asked, while racking his brain to find a solution for this unprecedented issue.

"No, sir."

"Continue looking for it." Joseph beckoned the technician to approach him. "Is there anything else you can use?"

The man seemed slightly cowed, biting his lip, but after several long seconds he finally answered. "Every station has a thunderstorm microphone for emergencies. We could use that one."

Joseph immediately appointed his longest-serving comrade. "Fuchs, you go to the basement and ask where they keep the thunderstorm microphone." With Fuchs he didn't have to worry about rash actions or uncalled for violence. If needed, he'd efficiently intimidate the civilians, without causing them harm. It was an unspoken understanding that the German civilians shouldn't be hurt, except in an emergency.

Meanwhile, the technician worked on interrupting the ongoing broadcast and Joseph finally had time to survey the heart of the radio station. The walls were filled with wardrobe-big black metal boxes with all kinds of lights, buttons and dials—presumably the technology behind the broadcasting. In the center of the room stood a counter, on top a black telephone, which thankfully hadn't been used to raise the alarm, several cables, and more buttons.

Just as Joseph finished his perusal of the room, Fuchs returned, holding the green emergency microphone in his hands like a trophy. He put it on the counter, and the technician fiddled a bit too long with the connection of the cables.

Joseph repeatedly peeked at the clock hanging on the wall, his nerves strung to breaking point. Thirty minutes was the maximum time they had to get in and out of the station safely. Every minute longer increased the risk of being caught, possibly endangering the operation, and ultimately Hitler's invasion of Poland.

Biting his lip, he visualized the potential exit routes in his mind. The responsibility for his team weighed heavily on his shoulders. It would be a catastrophe if one of them was killed by the local authorities. He also was responsible for the well-being of the radio station employees, hard-working and loyal Germans, who were to be sacrificed only if absolutely needed.

The big hand approached the twelve-minute mark and Joseph cast another glance at the technician, whose forehead was covered with a sheen of sweat. If the man wasn't able to get the microphone up and running within the next eight minutes, Joseph would have to call off the operation. Under no circumstances was he to risk being caught by the local authorities, who weren't privy to Hitler's marvelous plan to blame the Poles for the outbreak of war.

Every cell in his body on full alert, he kept his eyes peeled on the technician, who had turned into the most important man in the Third Reich. In the back of his head, he wondered whether the technician knew about the burden that lay exclusively on his slim shoulders.

Then, a tiny smile showed up on the technician's face as he inserted the cable into yet another hole and a green light popped up, indicating the microphone was ready to use.

"I'm now going to shut off the broadcast and the air is all yours," the technician advised the Polish speaker, who'd already positioned himself next to the microphone, the sheet of paper with the speech in his hand.

On Joseph's nod, the radio program was interrupted at exactly thirteen minutes after eight. He silently counted to five, to give the listeners time to realize something was off, before he gave the sign that unraveled the next scene in their rehearsed performance.

Two men fired shots into the ceiling, faked a short quarrel and then the speaker harrumphed, took the microphone into both hands and announced in a breathless, seemingly agitated voice that the radio station of Gliwice was now in Polish hands, *"Uwaga, tu Gliwice. Radiostacja znajduje się w polskich rękach!"*

The pre-written speech lasted exactly four minutes. Joseph tracked the time, content when it ended three seconds earlier than predicted. It was high time to get out, since it wouldn't take long for the local police to arrive.

On his sign, the technician switched off the microphone and Joseph yelled, "Everyone out! Fuchs, you get Meier from the basement. We'll meet by the main entrance." Then he strode off, exhilaration mixing with relief. The hardest part of the mission had been accomplished, although he didn't allow himself to become complacent, because so many things could still go wrong.

They had seven to nine minutes to make a safe exit. Everything went without a hitch. They assembled near the main entrance, and Joseph counted his men, before he was the last man to leave the building.

Outside, they reunited with the two men who'd been left to watch the premises. A body was lying next to the gate. Curious, Joseph strode over to take a look. At first glance he couldn't distinguish whether the "canned good" was dead or alive, but since Müller was responsible for this part of the operation he did not pursue the disgusting matter by having a closer examination. His part had been done to perfection.

It was such a shame he wasn't allowed to tell anyone, not even his brother Knut, who'd be flabbergasted with admiration.

As soon as the group arrived at the hotel, Joseph discarded his Polish peasant garb and walked to the public phone to give the success message to Heydrich.

"Wish to report. Everything went according to plan," he spoke into the receiver, immensely proud of himself and his team.

Now great things could happen.

18

About six weeks later, Julius was reading the newspaper, which was a chorus of praise about Hitler's strategic genius. The Wehrmacht had invaded, conquered, and subdued Poland in little more than a month—helped by the Soviet Army, which had joined the effort and attacked the country from the East. Just days ago, Goebbels had announced on the radio the division and annexation of the arch enemy, concluding with the promise that the risk posed by Poland's very existence had been rendered harmless.

After remaining in a state of shocked numbness ever since the outbreak of war, Julius found new hope in Poland's quick defeat. Admittedly, not so much for the Poles, but for the rest of Europe. Both France and England had been too slow—serendipitously as it now seemed—in their response. The war was over, before they even managed to send soldiers into combat.

Hitler was a Great War veteran, like Julius himself, and knew from firsthand experience how much misery must be prevented. The Reich chancellor might not care about the Jews, but he claimed to love every German, or more precisely Aryan, in his country and looked out for them as a father would do. Deep in his soul, Julius hoped that this love for his people would be enough to prevent further bloodshed.

If there was the slightest shimmer of hope for peace, Hitler would surely resist dragging out the war. Julius put the newspaper away, clinging to the hope that this was the end of the fighting. Just then, the doorbell rang and Silvana showed up.

"Can I talk to you?" she asked.

The serious expression on her face instantly alarmed him. Although she was all grown up, she still was his younger sister and as the patriarch of the family he felt responsible for her. "Do you have a problem?"

"Who doesn't have problems these days?" She gave a bitter laugh, and looked around the living room. "Can we go to your office? This is not for curious ears."

"Edith is not home."

"And your maid?" Silvana pursed her lips. "I really don't want her to be privy."

Now he was intrigued. Without another word he got up and let his sister into his office, calling out, "Delia, I don't want to be disturbed, not even by Frau Falkenstein."

Delia rushed in from the kitchen, her hair in a tight bun, exposing her long and elegant neck. Her graceful posture stood in a stark contrast to the dough on her hands and apron. "Certainly, Herr Falkenstein. Would you like coffee and buns?"

"Maybe later." Then he closed the door firmly and beckoned for Silvana to take a seat in front of his desk. "What can I do for you?"

"I received a letter from Adriana. It must have been on the last boat across the Channel." Since England had declared war on Germany, telephone calls weren't possible anymore, and even the mail between the enemy countries had been stopped.

"What did she say?"

"She gives you her best regards, urging you to consider emigration."

"You've come all the way here to tell me that?" He raised an eyebrow, expecting a more sinister reason behind Silvana's visit.

"No." She sighed. "The war has complicated everything."

"That, you can say aloud. Not in my wildest dreams have I believed Hitler would go this far. It's been a suicidal move."

"Actually it looks like a very clever move on his part. It's amazing how swift and efficient the invasion of Poland was. People are elated." Silvana echoed his own musings.

Julius rubbed his chin. "The Poles didn't stand a chance, especially not after the Soviet Union invaded them from the East. Hitler and Stalin carved up the country between the two of them, subjugating the people in less than a month."

"It gives us all reason to worry what he might do next." Silvana seesawed back and forth on her chair.

"You mean he's not done yet? What else could he want?" The shock over the war sat deep in Julius' bones, and for the past weeks he'd mulled over the implications again and again, yet he couldn't fathom that Hitler would go further.

Silvana rolled her eyes. "Europe, the world, the moon and the sun?"

"Now you're exaggerating." Julius couldn't help a smile spread across his face.

"Just a tiny bit. Anyhow, what I wanted to talk to you about is the situation of our school."

"What's wrong with it?"

She gave a helpless shrug. "Everything. Adriana cautioned me that since she's the official owner, the school might get seized by the government, now that we're at war with England."

"We're not really at war with them." Julius clung to the notion that peace between the two countries was still possible, now that Poland had been annexed.

"You're deluding yourself. Britain and France both declared war." Silvana was the only person who dared to speak so boldly to him.

"I know." A headache was beginning to simmer deep in his

neck—ever since the beginning of the war he'd felt a growing anxiety, which he carefully blocked out in order to focus on day-to-day tasks, since life had to go on. "It's a technicality, though. They had to declare war to keep their treaty with Poland. Yet they haven't done anything. It'll blow over and everything will return to normal." Julius fervently wished this would happen. Nobody, especially not Hitler who'd experienced the horrors of combat firsthand, could be interested in prolonging this war.

He had gotten what he wanted, wiped Poland from the face of the earth and placed a huge chunk of it into the new General Government, attached to Germany. What else could he possibly wish for? He would not attack France for instance, because the French military was a lot stronger than the Polish one, and located to the west of Germany it would be easy for Britain to come to their ally's help.

Hitler had witnessed the shameful defeat against France and Britain. He'd be clever enough to avoid a repeat.

Silvana snorted. "Keep lying to yourself. This is only getting worse. But back to my school. I need someone to help me with the red tape required to return ownership to me."

"You're asking me a second time to help you ruin your life with such a folly? Why don't you take your own advice and emigrate to England if the outlook here is so bleak?" He said it more forcefully than he'd intended, despite knowing Silvana didn't cope well with being admonished. Before he could calm the waters, she jumped up.

"If you're not going to help me, I'll look for someone else." The next moment she dashed out of his office, slamming the door shut behind her.

Julius stayed seated, knowing from experience there was nothing he could do right now. He'd have to wait a few days until his sister's temper had calmed down. If she hadn't changed her opinion by then, he'd offer to help her.

19

BERLIN, JANUARY 1940

David had felt the outbreak of war like a punch to his guts. Having grown up in the shadow of the Great War with many of their male relatives killed, maimed or missing, his generation was horrified by the prospect of another.

He remembered well the collective shock after the announcement. For several minutes nobody in the workshop had uttered a word, until finally Baumann had spoken up and said, "This is not the end of the world. There's still time for peace negotiations. Nobody, especially not Hitler, is interested in bloodshed."

As time passed, reality had proven Baumann's words wrong. One by one the young fellows at work had been drafted—each of them unable to conceal the sickening shock they felt. David was the only twenty-year-old who'd been spared. Yet, he didn't allow himself to be lulled into a false sense of security. If the need arose, the Nazis would conscript half-breeds as well.

David, though, had no intention to witness it. He'd been putting out feelers and made connections with several Zionist organizations, not an easy task for someone who'd grown up as German without learning a word of Hebrew.

Thanks to the lessons at the Lemberg school, combined with his engineering skills, which he considered the more convincing reason, he had an immigration visa to Palestine lined up. The requirement to be issued the visa was a one-year preparation course, called *hachshara,* which turned out to be a bottleneck, since only so many places were available, even for a gifted mechanic.

One day, as he returned home from work, his father said, "David, there's a letter for you from Luckenwalde."

Since he didn't know anyone in that town, he curiously opened the envelope. His pulse ratcheted up the instant he noticed the official stamp of a training farm owned by the Zionists. With shaking hands he unfolded the letter, his eyes skimming over the contents. When he arrived at the end, he couldn't help punching a fist into the air, shouting, "Yes!"

"What is it?"

David hadn't realized that his father was still standing next to him. Looking up into Heinrich's probing eyes, the courage drizzled out of his bones. His parents wouldn't be happy, for so many reasons. He needed a moment to gather his sangfroid, before he straightened his shoulders. "Father, I have been accepted for a training course at a farm in Luckenwalde."

His father squinted his eyes. "A farm? What about your current job? I thought mechanics was your vocation?"

"It is." A wave of guilt washed over David, since he hated to leave Baumann in the lurch, especially now that many of the younger workers had joined up to the Wehrmacht. He shrugged the feeling off. Baumann couldn't protect him forever, since he had to follow orders from the workshop owner, who surely didn't deserve David's empathy. After all he paid him only half as much as everyone else, because he was only half-Aryan.

The door opened and his mother returned from work. His heart grew heavy, seeing her so tired. Another, stronger, wave of guilt passed through him. Without David's salary, she'd have to work even harder to make ends meet and put food on the family table, since his father wasn't allowed a regular job.

The guilt was quickly dispelled by a surge of rage. If he ever met Hitler face to face, he'd squeeze the breath out of him, even if it was the last thing he did in this life.

"Look what I got." Helga pointed at her bag full of groceries. Following the outbreak of the war, everyone had received ration cards and it wasn't always easy to buy what was needed.

"David wants to do a training course on a farm in Luckenwalde," Father said with a grave voice.

Mother looked between the two of them, a confused expression on her face. "Another apprenticeship? What for?"

David took a deep breath, inwardly preparing for a good telling-off. "It's called *hachshara,* and is a year-long course, preparing the participants for life in Palestine." There, he'd said it.

An awkward silence settled in the room, until his father spoke up. "So, you're serious with wanting to emigrate?"

"Yes. The way things are going here, I don't want to take my chances. I am earmarked for a visa, but finishing this course is a requirement for it to be issued." David put his feet hip wide apart, awaiting protest from his parents.

"It's a great opportunity for you. The way things are going with the war and everything, it'll be a relief to know you're in a safe place."

"We will miss you terribly," Mutti said, her voice laced with sadness. "But we understand your decision and will support you."

David hadn't expected this reaction, because the last time he'd spoken about the possibility of emigrating to Palestine, they'd vehemently opposed it. Encouraged by their acceptance he added, "You could… I mean, I could try to get a visa for you too."

Father shook his head. "Your mother is an Aryan, they wouldn't even consider giving her one of the precious visas. And I will go nowhere without her."

"Your father is right. He and I belong together. But you are young and have your entire life in front of you. You go and use that chance. Maybe after the war we can visit?"

David swallowed down the lump in his throat, determined not

to show he was moved to tears. "I'm not gone yet. For the next year I'll be just an hour's train ride away."

After dinner, he raced to Thea's house to tell her about the splendid news. They might even get married, so she would be allowed to come with him to Palestine when it was time. He already pictured the two of them on the porch of a cute little hut, looking out at the kibbutz farm, where he was in charge of the maintenance of all agricultural equipment, especially tractors and other vehicles.

"David, I didn't expect you today," Thea said as he rang her doorbell.

"I have wonderful news!" he all but shouted.

"Come in, my parents have gone to visit an old aunt and won't be home until tomorrow evening." There was an enticing promise in her eyes.

Today truly was his lucky day. He eagerly accepted the invitation and as soon as the door closed behind them, he found himself entangled in a passionate kiss. Forgetting about the reason he'd come here in the first place, he swooped her up in his arms and carried her to her bed.

Much later, they both lay naked beneath the covers, Thea snuggled against his side. "So, what is your exciting news?"

It took him a few seconds to remember. "I've been accepted on a training program at the Zionist farm in Luckenwalde."

She wriggled herself out of his embrace. "But why? That's so far. What about me? About us?"

Her reaction devastated him. "It's only one hour by train. We can visit each other every other weekend."

"Twice a month only?" Her pout clearly signaled her discontent with the situation. "Why do you even have to go there? Why not stay in Berlin?"

"Oh, Thea, sweetie, don't you remember? This training is a requirement for receiving the immigration visa to Palestine."

Her mouth fell open. "Don't tell me you were serious about working on a kibbutz?"

"Don't you see that this is the solution to escape the harassment we have to endure here at the Nazis' hands?" David was nonplussed, since he couldn't count how many times he'd told her about his plans. Then it occurred to him that she must be sad to lose him. "You can come with me, if we—"

"Me? Never!" she hissed, moving further away from him and taking the covers with her, exposing his naked body. "You don't actually expect me to become a farm woman, do you?"

Now that she mentioned it, he couldn't imagine the lithe, beautiful girl pulling up weeds, or in fact doing any kind of farm work. "You could do something else," he said lamely.

"On a kibbutz? You do realize how basic life is there, don't you? These people are royally backwards. They don't even have electricity and running water."

"That's not true…" David bit his tongue. It was true that the country was quite underdeveloped, which was one more reason they needed modern, skilled people.

"Besides, only Jews live in Palestine."

He gave a croaking laugh. "You're a Jew yourself. Here in Germany we don't have a future."

"I do," she snarled. "This situation is only temporary. Soon enough the Nazis will realize that the likes of me have nothing in common with Jews and everything with Aryans. Look at me! Do I look like a Jew to you?"

"No, you don't." Somehow David felt insulted, because in contrast to her, he looked a lot like the Jewish stereotype with his dark hair, brown eyes and big nose.

"See? I wouldn't want to live in a place infested by Orthodox Zionists."

"That's a prejudice. Some members of the Zionist organization are Orthodox, but there are also many modern, young people who embrace new ideas. People who want to make Palestine a country worth living in. A country that flourishes and allows its citizens a standard of living that can compete with every other industrialized country in the world, even

America, but with better weather." He grinned at her expectantly.

Thea continued shaking her head, even as she wrapped herself tighter in the blanket. "I really wish you wouldn't do this. It will curtail your chances here and make you an outcast."

"We are already outcasts, remember? We basically aren't allowed to do anything anymore in this country." Anger at her stubborn insistence to ignore what was going on crept up his spine.

"I'm not stupid!" She glared at him. "In contrast to you, I believe that the Germans will soon come to their senses and welcome back the likes of me who adapted and didn't make a fuss."

"Well, I'm not going to be pushed around any longer. I've had it! If there's no way for me to overthrow the government, I'll have to suffer the consequences. Emigration is the best way forward. And if it's to a country that welcomes me with both arms, instead of reluctantly issuing a visa for yet another foreign minority, then I'm all in."

Thea's mouth opened wide. "You were planning a coup?"

There had been plenty of talk among his communist friends, although nothing had come out of it. Every time they seemed to take a step forward, the Gestapo showed up, arrested someone and they started from scratch again. In any case, he wouldn't confide in Thea, since this was a secret he'd not even shared with his sister.

"Of course not!" he protested.

"That's good, because I wouldn't want to be together with someone who actively opposes the government."

"Even if the government is unjust?"

She gave a little pout. "Life is not always just. We need to make the best of it."

David furrowed his brows and she added, "I hate the restrictions as much as anyone else, but you'll see, the Nazis will soon come to their senses. People like you and me are not their enemies."

In order not to enrage her further, he dropped the topic. "So, are you going to visit me in Luckenwalde?"

Again, she flinched as if she'd been bitten by an insect. "Certainly not." Then her expression turned softer. "I'd love you to come visit me whenever possible."

"I'll certainly do that." A small doubt crept into his heart. Since he couldn't expect a gorgeous woman like Thea to live on a farm, would he want to move to Palestine without her? The nagging voice in his head was silenced, when Thea threw off the blanket. Mesmerized he stared at her naked body and softly caressed her breasts. For now he would concentrate on the present.

A year was a long time and so much could happen.

20

Edith prepared coffee for herself, eying the dwindling supplies. Since the outbreak of the war, imports had plummeted and the remaining coffee beans had been seized for the Wehrmacht.

Since moving into the city apartment without a garden and only nine rooms, she had done away with many things: social events, parties, invitations to opera premieres, new evening gowns or dresses. Her only pieces of jewelry were a few golden necklaces and modest matching earrings, because the precious items had either been sent to Switzerland or been hidden away after Jews had been forced to give up all their valuables.

She hadn't bought a single pair of shoes, a dress or even a hat since the introduction of the *Reichskleiderkarte,* the clothes ration card last November, which had to suffice for three people, because neither Delia nor Julius received clothes cards.

Pouring coffee into a cup, she pursed her lips. A freshly brewed coffee combined with a sweet bun was the only luxury she couldn't imagine doing without. She inhaled the rich, earthy and slightly bitter scent with notes of chocolate, caramel, nuts and spices. Instantly her energies were revived, and somehow the world looked less daunting.

Edith settled at the kitchen table, eyed the sugar bowl, its contents dwindled as well, and gave a deep sigh. Starting right now, she'd enjoy her coffee without sugar. Tentatively, she took the first sip, bracing herself for the sharp acidic taste. She slushed the hot liquid on her palate, astounded when the bitterness gave way to a more mellow and rounded flavor.

Her second sip held the same experience, albeit somewhat more pleasurable, since her taste buds were adapting to the new situation and discerning unfamiliar fruity and even floral tastes. Yes, she decided, she could definitely do without sugar, but certainly not without coffee.

After she'd drained the one cup she allowed herself every afternoon, she got up to do the dishes, wondering why Delia hadn't returned from grocery shopping. Her maid was long overdue, giving Edith a queasy feeling. These days anything out of the norm was a bad sign.

The dishes were washed and dried, and still no sign of Delia. Edith fought the urge to go and look for her maid, when the door opened and a visibly distraught woman walked inside.

"There you are, I was getting worried." A huge burden fell from Edith's shoulders.

"*Gnädige Frau*, I'm so sorry, I couldn't get any of the things you asked for." Delia was near to tears. "At the registration office, they gave me these new cards." She handed three cards to Edith, two of them stamped with a big red J and about half the detachable coupons.

Edith didn't need to decipher the words on the card to understand the meaning. True to Nazi ideology the authorities had come up with yet another means of discrimination and cut the food rations for Jews. Perhaps they should be thankful that Hitler hadn't removed their eligibility for groceries altogether, the way he'd done with clothing. "Why couldn't you buy at least the things on my card?"

Delia might be a talented dancer, but she didn't possess one ounce of shrewdness. "I'm so sorry, *gnädige Frau*. The saleswoman told me that Jews have to buy in special shops, and that she wouldn't serve me anymore even if she were allowed to."

"Such crap!" Edith burst out, immediately regretting it. "I'm so sorry."

"It's alright, from now on I'll do the grocery shopping myself." Edith gazed at Delia. "Perhaps you should go outside as little as possible."

Delia nodded with a frightened expression on her face.

"Now, go and do the laundry. Don't forget to iron Herr Falkenstein's dress shirts. Meanwhile, I'll go to the grocer." Edith inspected the Jewish ration cards, groaning when she saw how little goods they were allowed to buy and muttered under her breath, "How does the government think a person can survive on that?"

Then she put on her coat, grabbed her purse and a shopping basket and left the apartment to step into the paternoster elevator. She still hadn't gotten used to living with several parties in the same house and started when the elevator door opened on a lower floor and a neighbor greeted her. "Going shopping, Frau Falkenstein?"

"Yes. Herr Krause."

"Shouldn't your maid be running the errands?" he asked, peering into her basket.

Since Edith didn't know his political loyalties, she politely answered, "I quite enjoy shopping, even with the rationing."

Fortunately the lift arrived at the ground floor, so he didn't have the time to ask more nosy questions. Edith hurried off to the grocer's about a block away. There, she gathered the things she needed, including a rare package of sugar and walked to the cashier.

"Your ration cards, please," the friendly saleswoman asked, ripping off the required part from Edith's booklet. "There's not enough on here for the potatoes. Do you have another card?"

"Of course." Edith handed over Julius' booklet.

The cashier's face fell the instant she noticed the J stamped across it. "Jews have to shop in dedicated stores."

"I'm not a Jew," Edith said.

"Well, but... this card... we don't accept them here. If you want to buy goods for Jews, you'll have to use a dedicated store."

"You're not seriously telling me that I need to go to another store, just because I'm buying something for a Jew?" Edith gave the woman her most scathing stare, which usually worked to cow people. Not this time, though.

"That is exactly what I'm saying." The cashier puffed herself up. "If you want to use ration cards for Jews, you need to go to a shop for Jews. We don't accept them here, we're a reputable store!"

Edith had heard enough. As much as she wanted to talk back, she knew it wouldn't change a thing and would only cause her grief in the future. "Well, thank you. So, where can I buy groceries for Jews?"

"I wouldn't know that," the cashier said haughtily, before she added, "If I were you, I wouldn't do this."

"Do what?"

"Buy things for this pest, it's unpatriotic to be a *Judenfreund*."

Edith gave her a tired smile. Being called a friend of Jews had turned not only into a curse word, but even a threat to one's one safety. "My husband is a Jew."

The woman flapped her hand to her mouth, but the "Heavens!" was still loud enough to turn heads in the store. Suddenly Edith felt as if a pack of wolves were closing in, ready to lunge at her and tear her into pieces. She took a deep breath, ready to fight them off.

"Under these circumstances, I'm afraid we cannot serve you." The cashier pushed Edith's severed ration coupons back toward her.

"You're refusing to sell groceries to me, even though I have perfectly valid coupons?" Edith's voice sounded high-pitched.

"We make it a habit to do business only with honest Germans, not with Jew-loving whores."

Being called a whore was a new low in her life. Shame burning its way up her skin, Edith grabbed the coupons, leaving the groceries on the cashier's desk and stormed out of the shop. She ran for two blocks, before she stopped holding her stitching side, and muttering to herself, "Looks like I have to find a new business to patronize."

From that day on, Edith did all the shopping. She found the stores designated for Jews, who gladly took her Aryan ration cards as well and always gave her good service. Unfortunately with the new coupon cards, there was never enough food, and certainly not of the quality Julius was used to.

Therefore she resorted to the black market, buying most of their needs in a less official way. The prices, though, seemed to increase faster than during the Great Depression and the ensuing hyperinflation.

Edith remembered well the times in Munich when she'd stuffed her purse with bills just to go out for coffee and cake. The only difference was that back then Julius had provided her with a seemingly inexhaustible supply of fresh money, whereas these days she was running fast through her monthly allowance.

About two months later, Julius told her over dinner, "You have spent all the money in our bank account."

Money had never been an issue in their marriage. There had always been more than enough of it. Julius had showered her with expensive gifts and made sure she never lacked a thing.

A new dress? Go and buy two.

A pair of shoes to match? Get yourself the Italian ones made of genuine leather.

A necklace to wear with the dress? Don't forget to buy the matching earrings and bracelet as well.

Edith looked up from the steak she was about to cut. Since the Falkenstein bank had been mandated to dissolve all accounts pertaining to Jews, she had opened an account in her name, where a monthly sum was paid into. "I was going to talk to you about this, I need a higher allowance."

"Whatever for?" Julius mouth twisted angrily.

"For food."

"Food? Good woman, have you gone completely insane? How can you spend my entire salary on food?" His voice boomed over the dinner table, causing Delia to peek into the dining room. On Julius' wave of dismissal, she disappeared again.

Edith, though, wasn't cowed and answered him in the condescending tone she'd learned from his mother. "There's no need to exaggerate. I admit, I've been spending more than usual, a lot more indeed, because I had to resort to the black market."

"The black market! That's illegal!" he yelled at her.

"Would you rather I let you starve?"

"Now you're the one exaggerating." Julius' voice tempered, but his eyes were glaring daggers at her. "Like everyone else in Germany, we have ration cards, which suffice the daily needs of an average adult."

"I have such a ration card," she corrected him, raising her chin. "You and Delia receive the one's stamped with a J for Jew."

"So, there's a J on it, and some luxury items cannot be bought anymore. But the authorities have determined the calorie needs for types of citizens, including heavy workers, toddlers, or pregnant women. The different types of cards make sure the national supply is spread evenly according to needs. This has been done to avoid a famine, similar to the one we had during the Great War."

She looked at him, incredulous. "Have you ever actually seen one of the Jewish ration books?"

"I have read the announcement when they were issued, detailing what I just explained to you." His expression had lost the haughtiness and turned into bewilderment.

"What you call luxury items are indeed day-to-day foodstuffs like meat, milk, sugar and eggs. Also, the allocated quantities certainly aren't enough to properly feed an adult." She couldn't help to issue a potshot. "Especially a discerning gourmet like you.

To keep your meals up to your usual standard, I had to buy extra food."

Julius blanched. "But running through my entire salary? How do you suppose we pay for all other expenses? Delia's salary, utilities, taxi fares, clothing?"

"Well, that's why I was going to ask you for a higher allowance. I need more money to pay for everything." She couldn't understand why he'd turned so stingy.

"More money? There is no more money. Today Herr Dreyer had to fire me, because I'm not allowed to work in my own bank anymore!" His voice had risen again. "I have no salary, so there's no more money to deposit into your account."

It took a few seconds for the reality to trickle in, then it was Edith's turn to blanche. "Why haven't you told me before?"

"Because it just happened today." Julius seemed to deflate a few inches.

Edith needed a few seconds to recover from the blow. "But he's still going to repay the loan you gave him, right?"

His face turned into a stony mask. "Since the repayment of the loan was included in the salary, the answer is no."

At a loss for words, Edith looked at the browned crust of her steak, cutting into it to expose the pink, juicy interior. She pierced her fork into it and put the piece into her mouth, chewing slowly to savor the tenderness of the prime piece of meat. It might well be her last one for quite a while. When she had swallowed it, she took up her glass of red wine, taking a soothing sip.

She'd never thought about money, it had just always been there. She had no idea, where it came from or where Julius had stored it. Then, she cocked her head at Julius. "We do have cash reserves somewhere, don't we?"

He gave a pained sigh. "We do have plenty of cash piling up in Swiss and English bank accounts—unfortunately none of it is available to us from within Germany. We also have valuables stashed away safely, but I'd rather not sell them for frivolous things like food."

Edith didn't think to eat was frivolous, but she resisted making a snide remark. "Well, then I guess we'll have to live on what the ration cards allow us to buy."

"Just like everyone else." Julius cut a piece of his steak, putting it into the mouth, his eyes glowing with delight. "We'll manage. It surely won't be as bad as you make out."

"No more meat for you, but loads of potatoes," she answered, full well knowing how much he loved a well-cooked steak.

"I can manage with potato dumplings and a duck." He smiled smugly, giving Edith the impression that he thought he'd won this argument.

"I'll go to the lake in the park first thing in the morning and fetch a duck for you. It might not be as soft as you're used to, but a duck is a duck, isn't it?" He stared at her open-mouthed and she added, "We should rather enjoy our last delicious meal for a while."

21

Her landlord was lingering in the hallway when Helga returned from a grueling day working.

"Frau Goldmann, can I speak to you for a minute?"

"Of course, what is it about?" She didn't like the expression on his face and wished Heinrich were home. But her husband had found a temporary—illegal—job with a shop owner on the other side of Berlin and usually arrived home well after midnight.

"I'd rather discuss this in your apartment," the landlord said.

Despite the queasy feeling in her stomach, she nodded, because what else could she have done? As she opened the door, Amelie was in the kitchen, cooking dinner, and Helga's heart jumped with relief. "Amelie, I'm home. Our landlord is with me," she yelled into the kitchen.

Amelie turned around and stepped into the shabby living room to greet Helga and the visitor. "Good day, Herr Trost. Mutti, I'm going to finish making dinner, holler if you need anything." Then she returned to the kitchen, leaving the door wide open.

Herr Trost made himself comfortable on the sofa, which doubled up as a bed for Helga and Heinrich, before he spoke.

"Frau Goldmann, you know how much I appreciate your family as tenants."

That was news to her. "And we appreciate you letting us live here."

His face turned into a grimace. "You've always been punctual with your payments, and if it were my decision..." Helga blanched, expecting the worst. "I really liked having you in the house. Not everyone is as clean and meticulous as you are. In fact, I must say with your arrival, the entire house community took a turn for the better..." He waffled on and on.

"Herr Trost, would you please get to the point," she interrupted him exasperatedly after a while.

"I'm so sorry, Frau Goldmann. This is a new law." He pulled out a sheet of paper with a government announcement. "By the end of the month, all Jews have to move into designated Jewish-only houses in Jewish quarters."

"I'm not a Jew," she protested automatically, in spite of knowing that it didn't matter. She had married a Jew and thus was treated as one most of the time.

Helga took the paper from his hands, the letters swimming in front of her eyes. Not really comprehending, she asked, "You're kicking us out?"

"As I said, if it were my decision, I'd love to keep you as tenants, but the government is forcing my hand."

"How long do we have?"

"Look, I really feel for you. Officially I must evict you by the end of the month, but if you happen to stay here a few weeks longer, I'll make sure not to notice, as long as none of the other tenants complain."

It was probably the best outcome she could hope for. "Thank you, Herr Trost."

After the landlord had left, Amelie stepped in from the kitchen. "I listened to your conversation. I'll ask Frau Lemberg what to do, she has good connections in the Jewish community."

Amelie, who would soon turn eighteen, was attending the last year of the Lemberg school, learning to be a seamstress, even though she would have preferred to follow in her father's footsteps and become an accountant. Unfortunately the need for German accountants in the possible receiving immigration countries was next to zero, whereas a good seamstress was welcome most anywhere.

The next day, Amelie came home from school with the news that only apartments or houses owned by Jews were qualified to accept Jewish tenants.

At Helga's question, how to possibly find one, Amelie answered, "Frau Lemberg said the Jewish Council is collecting addresses and making a list. Everyone who can't find a place is encouraged to go to the council, who will then do their best to assign a living space to every family."

"They'll be overrun with applicants." Helga pursed her lips. She didn't doubt the good intentions of the Jewish Council, nonetheless she'd rather not depend on them. After thinking for a few minutes she said, "You'll register us with the council and I'll go visit Felicitas first thing tomorrow morning."

"What about your work! What if they fire you?" Amelie asked fearfully.

"They won't fire me, since they'll never find another person whom they can pay as little as they pay me." At long last, her precarious status might be good for something. The next day Helga called in sick and traveled to Oranienburg to ask her sister for help.

"Helga, what a surprise! What brings you here?" Felicitas greeted her.

After exchanging the latest news about the family, Helga came to the actual reason for her visit. "There's been a new law, stipulating that Jews can rent apartments only in houses owned by other Jews."

Feli's face fell. "I heard about that. Honestly I don't believe it applies to you."

"Why would you think so?" Helga couldn't fathom how her

sister managed to stay so naïve. As a long-standing party member she should have realized years ago what Hitler's intentions were.

"Ach, you know. It's just Heinrich who's Jewish."

Helga rolled her eyes. "Don't tell me you didn't realize that women don't account for anything with the Nazis, therefore his status is what counts, not mine."

"Don't be unfair. I'm a woman and I have an important role in the party."

Only out of respect for your late husband, they let you do the busy-work while keeping you far away from the roles of true power. Helga didn't voice her thoughts, after all she'd come as a supplicant. Forcing a smile on her face she concurred. "Agreed. Anyway, I came here to ask for your help."

"I don't know any Jewish houseowners in Berlin."

"Amelie is registering us with the Jewish Council, so we're hoping to be assigned a living space before long, but they are swamped with applications and it might take a while. Since we have to evacuate our current apartment within the next couple of weeks, I was wondering if we could stay with you for a while."

Feli's face clearly showed her discomfort with the request. "You know how much I love you, but four people in my house?" The house was actually a mansion with at least fifteen rooms.

"David is living on a training farm in Luckenwalde, so we're only three."

"Still, three of you. You know how much the people gossip around here. It wouldn't show me in a good light, trying to circumvent a national law."

"Please, Feli. It wouldn't be for long." Helga would rather hide in her sister's mansion than take up her landlord's offer to *illegally* stay in their current apartment. It didn't matter how careful they were, the neighbors were prone to find out quick enough and spiteful as they were, they'd enjoy nothing more than ratting the Goldmanns out to the authorities.

Visibly fighting with herself, Felicitas finally agreed. "If push comes to shove, you can certainly visit with me, although it can by no means be a permanent arrangement."

"Thank you so much!" Helga fell around her sister's neck. "We might not need to seek shelter with you, but if we do I promise it'll be for a short time only. I'm sure the council will quickly assign a living space to everyone." In fact, she wasn't at all as optimistic as she made it sound. During the past years Helga had learned to take things one day at a time. If and when things happened, she'd deal with them and not fret beforehand.

Felicitas invited her for lunch and packed a huge basket with groceries for Helga to take home, which was a godsend, since the new ration booklets for Amelie and Heinrich didn't allow anyone in the family to get up from the dinner table with a full belly.

"Keep a stiff upper lip," Felicitas said, after accompanying Helga to the train station.

"I will. This cannot last forever."

"It's just until we've won the war, then Hitler will ease the restrictions against the Jews." Feli shrugged. "You must understand the difficult situation he's in, having to keep an entire nation on its toes."

Helga kissed her sister on the cheek without an answer, while she inwardly reeled from the affront.

22

Julius was angry with himself. He'd been so proud of his ability to consider all eventualities, yet all the preparation hadn't been enough. He'd never anticipated the lengths to which Hitler and his cronies would go. Hell, he'd not even believed that little man with his comical moustache would last longer than a few months in power.

Seven long years had passed and for the first time in his life Julius felt helpless. There was nothing he could do to help their situation. After being fired from the Falkenstein bank, he'd buried himself inside his home office, leaving it only for meals, usually lashing out at Edith.

He knew the situation wasn't her fault, but since he didn't have anyone else to take out his frustration on, he often lost his temper with her. Herr Dreyer had promised to provide him with cash whenever he could without raising suspicions with the authorities and a trusted friend had sold a few pieces of Edith's jewelry, putting the money into her bank account.

In spite of this, the reserves were dwindling fast. Soon, Julius might be forced to sell another piece. He walked across the room to the hidden safe, opened it and took out the diamond necklace, which had once belonged to his mother.

It was a spectacular piece, worth more than a bank director earned in a year. His fingers caressed the cold metal, which warmed under his touch. As he moved the necklace in his hand, the diamonds caught a ray of sunshine, reflecting it back in all colors of the rainbow.

No, he would not sell this magnificent necklace. Ever. He returned it to the safe, wondering whether that was a good hiding place. If the Gestapo decided to search the house, they'd find the safe easily enough and would force their way inside. On the other hand, smuggling the necklace across the border to Switzerland had become much too dangerous. If he or Edith were found with it, they'd inevitably go to jail for stealing valuables from the Reich. He snorted at the irony. Julius Falkenstein stealing his own diamond necklace because he refused to sell it for a fraction of its worth to the lying and cheating Nazi bastards.

A rap on the door interrupted his musings. "Come in."

Delia stepped into the room, holding an important-looking envelope in her hands. "Herr Falkenstein, there's a letter for you."

"Thank you." He reached for his letter opener and sliced the envelope open. Within seconds he balled his free hand into a fist. "Bloody bastards! This is my apartment!" Then he crumpled the letter and threw it into the wastepaper bin.

Over dinner Edith asked him, "Delia told me there was a letter from the Gestapo. What did they want?"

"Nothing."

She pursed her lips. "The Gestapo never sends letters wanting nothing."

"This is my home!" He speared a potato, without duck, and shoved it into his mouth much more violently than he'd intended.

"Are they going to evict us?" Edith gasped.

"On the contrary, they ordered me to notify the Jewish Council of any spare rooms that can be assigned to tenants."

"Strangers living with us in this apartment?" Edith glanced around the dining room. Compared to the mansion they had owned on Schwanenwerder Island this apartment was tiny, consisting of six rooms, a kitchen and two bathrooms, one for the family and one for staff.

"It's ridiculous. How are we supposed to host another family in here? Are they going to share the bathroom with the maid? And what about the kitchen? Shall we take turns cooking and eating? No." He shook his head. "I'll inform the council that unfortunately we don't have spare rooms to rent out."

The next day, he and Edith dressed to go out and walked—because he refused to set foot on public transport, but didn't want to afford a taxi—to the Jewish Council. After the half-hour march he arrived exhausted, puffing heavily. Terror etched into his face as he noticed the stairs they had to climb.

"What floor is it?"

"Fourth, it says."

Edith gave him a sympathetic glance. "Shall I go up alone?"

"No." For fifty-seven years he'd never had the time nor the inclination to pursue sports, his only hobby had been cigar smoking. Pausing several times to gather his breath, they reached their destination ten minutes later. Julius passed the people waiting in the hallway and knocked on the door of the council.

"Hey, there's a queue. Go to the back and wait your turn like everyone else," a woman scolded him.

"You must not know who I am," he told her, not unfriendly.

"For all I know, you're a wretched Jew looking for housing, just like the rest of us."

Had he really sunk so low? Not enough that this woman didn't recognize him, who'd once belonged to the elite of Germany, no, she assumed he had joined the rank of beggars for a roof over their heads.

Edith put a hand on his arm, apparently trying to keep him from throwing a fit. Inwardly groaning, he looked at the woman with a jovial expression. "*Gute Frau*, you are much mistaken in your assumption. I'm not looking for a place to live. On the contrary I've been summoned to offer space for people like you."

She didn't have to know that he was going to refuse to live with complete strangers in his apartment.

"Oh," she said.

Moments later, someone left the council office. Julius seized the opportunity, put a hand on the small of Edith's back and stepped inside. The man sitting behind the desk wore a long beard and the traditional kippa. When he looked up, he gave Julius the shock of his life. The man was one of the leaders of the Jewish community in Berlin and until recently had been a very powerful, vigorous and charismatic man—now he was reduced to an exhausted shell of his former self.

For a split-second his eyes shone with recognition, before they returned to their former dullness. "Herr Falkenstein, I surely didn't expect to see you here. Are you in need of a place to live?"

"No, Herr Knobloch, in fact the Gestapo sent me here with the request to rent out rooms to other families within my private apartment."

"Is the apartment owned by you?"

"Yes."

"How many rooms does it have?"

Julius didn't like where this was going, so he cut the interrogation short. "I've come to explain that I won't be able to sublet rooms. You'll understand that our apartment simply doesn't offer amenities for more than one family. There's only one kitchen, one dining room and two bathrooms, the smaller not even a full one."

Herr Knobloch nodded pensively. For several long seconds he didn't speak. "Herr Falkenstein, have you seen the queues outside? Each person represents an entire family of three or more people. By the end of the month, none of them will have a roof over their heads if we can't assign a living place. You, indeed, are in a very fortunate situation."

Julius didn't think he was fortunate. After all he had been forced to sell his ancestral home and make do in the much smaller city apartment. He suppressed a groan as he realized in hindsight that instead of transferring most of the proceeds to Switzerland, he should have kept the cash at hand. In all his astuteness, he hadn't foreseen losing his bank, and soon after his job, effectively joining the rank of the unemployed.

It seemed, he wasn't as prepared to weather the Nazi reign as he'd always assumed. The insight was like a slap in the face.

"You will agree with me that these people would be elated having to share a kitchen and bathroom, if it means not living on the street?" Herr Knobloch said.

"Perhaps they would." Julius pressed his lips into a thin line, racking his brain how to get out of the corner Herr Knobloch had maneuvered him into. Julius didn't want to appear as the proverbial heartless Jew who was interested solely in his own benefit. He was a generous man, giving vast sums to several charities and going above and beyond for the well-being of his employees. Unfortunately, right now he wasn't in a position to help, because for the first time in his life he had to economize. "My wife and I are both Christians. We don't follow any of the religious traditions, and thus the food we keep in the kitchen is not kosher. Therefore, I believe your applicants would be much better off living with like-minded people."

Amusement sprinkled Herr Knobloch's eyes, giving a glimpse of his former enthusiasm. "Have you ever considered that there are families in a similar position? Jews, who converted to Christianity, hoping it would save them from persecution?"

"I did not convert out of fear," Julius protested. "In fact, I converted the day I came of age, which was almost four decades ago, long before Hitler ever set foot in our country."

"Unfortunately I don't have the time for a philosophical discussion. My duty is to help my compatriots. How many rooms are you offering to sublet?"

"None." Julius gave the insolent man a cold stare. "I would help if I could, but for several reasons I simply cannot offer to host complete strangers in my home."

Herr Knobloch answered with an equally cold stare. "That is a very unfortunate stance, because as soon as I report my lists to the Gestapo by the end of this week, they will wonder why you didn't heed their order." He pointed at the paper still in Julius' hand. "We both know the Nazis expect full cooperation, thus they might visit you to see for themselves how many families can live in your place."

Julius inwardly fumed. "Are you threatening me?"

"Not at all, Herr Falkenstein. I'm merely stating the facts. Go and find two or three families to live with you among your acquaintances and report back to me by the end of the week. Otherwise I'll assign tenants to you. Good day!"

Seething from the contemptuous treatment, Julius was barely able to utter, "You will hear from me!" before he turned on his heels and rushed outside, Edith following suit. He was so agitated, he raced down the stairs in one go, arriving at the ground floor bathed in sweat, his heart throbbing against his chest.

23

Edith reeled from his scene at the council, coming across as an utterly selfish man, which in reality he wasn't. Throughout his life he'd always provided for other people. Despite him doing this, admittedly, in a sometimes patronizing way, Edith knew he had a good heart and genuinely cared for other people.

She chalked it up to his rigid upbringing that most of the time he didn't show how much he cared. Today though, she was ashamed of him.

Julius seemed unfazed and walked silently beside her, panting hard due to the unaccustomed exercise. As he unlocked the door to their apartment, he finally raised his voice. "I'm afraid I've made quite a fool of myself."

Edith barely suppressed a grin. "That is very true."

Julius settled onto the sofa in the living room, shaking his head. "Would you be so kind and brew a coffee for us?"

"Of course." One glimpse at his pensive face and she knew he was mulling over the events at the council and needed some time alone. She walked into the kitchen, pressing her lips into a thin line as she spooned the last coffee into the machine. Her contact at the black market hadn't been able to deliver anything last week, at least not at the price she was prepared to pay.

"Here you go." She offered a cup to Julius, who sat on the couch in the same position she'd left him a few minutes earlier.

"Thank you." He took the cup from her and beckoned her to sit next to him. "I hate the idea of sharing our personal space with strangers." He put the cup on the coffee table and rubbed his chin. "If we still lived in our mansion, it wouldn't be a problem to designate one wing for tenants… but here?" He cast her a pleading look.

"It's not ideal, I agree." Edith shrugged. There wasn't much they could do. The Gestapo ordered, the citizens obeyed. "It doesn't have to be forever."

Julius snorted. "Aren't you the one who keeps telling me to stop deluding myself? The way I see it, this order will stay in place for as long as that madman is Chancellor."

"So, what are you going to do?" A twinge of sympathy hit Edith, since this must be so much harder on him than it was on her.

"If we're forced to host someone, we might as well live with a family we know and trust."

"Are you thinking of Silvana?" Edith loved her sister-in-law, but she couldn't imagine the two siblings living under one roof, too different were their views.

"Oh no, certainly not." Julius shook his head, the furrowed brows echoing her own sentiments. "You know my sister, it wouldn't work well with us. Besides, I don't believe she needs a place. I'd rather have a non-practicing family live with us…" He bit his lip, giving Edith the impression there was more to it.

"It does make things easier if we don't have to heed religious rules."

"Yes and…" Julius clearly needed more time to put his thoughts into words, so she took a sip from her coffee, signaling there was no need to hurry through the conversation. He did the same. Upon emptying his cup, he said, "There's been that nagging feeling that I could have done more."

"More about what?"

"Back then I genuinely believed it was the correct thing to do, but now…" He shook his head in misery. "I should have protected those who needed it most, instead of looking after the majority of my employees."

Edith had no idea what he was talking about.

"Well, long story short. Perhaps you could ask your friend Helga Goldmann if they wanted to move in with us?"

Edith all but toppled over at the unexpected suggestion. Then, she realized how much guilt Julius must be feeling over having to fire all his Jewish employees, including Heinrich Goldmann, his head accountant, whom he held in great esteem for his impeccable work ethics.

When she didn't answer, Julius said, "Will you ask her?"

"Definitely." She smiled. "I believe the Goldmanns are a great choice. I'll ask Helga."

The next day she met with Helga for dinner in a popular restaurant she wouldn't have set foot in less than a year ago. Unfortunately, her usual posh places had all put up signs saying "Jews not welcome." If they didn't appreciate her husband, she wouldn't give them her business either.

To be honest, even if she were tempted to enter one of the famous restaurants she used to frequent, she couldn't afford them anymore.

"How nice to see you, Helga," she greeted her friend as they met in front of the restaurant. If Helga was surprised about the choice of location by the former society lady Edith Falkenstein, she didn't show it.

"It's so good to talk to a kind soul once in a while." Helga's face spoke volumes about the day-to-day harassment she must receive and once again Edith was reminded of how privileged her situation still was—in spite of all her problems.

They ordered the only meal on the menu available with ration coupons. Since she wasn't sure how to broach the delicate topic, she engaged in small talk, until she grew exasperated with herself and laid down her cutlery. "Look, I was wondering whether you are affected by the new housing law as well."

Helga's face fell. "Indeed we are. The council is overwhelmed with so many applicants, and so few available apartments. Why do you ask?" Then, recognition crossed her face. "You're not being evicted, too, are you?"

"Oh no. On the contrary." Edith leaned back to inspect her friend. She didn't actually know that much about her. After losing touch with each other following their respective marriages, they had reconnected several years ago and kept up a loose contact since. As they moved in different social circles—used to move, Edith corrected herself—they had met occasionally without becoming close friends again.

She knew Helga's husband Heinrich was Jewish, but had never met him, despite him working at the Falkenstein bank upon Edith's intervention. She also knew Helga had two children, a boy and a girl, who must be grown-up by now.

Deep down she wondered whether it was such a good idea, or whether living with complete strangers, with whom one didn't have to talk, was preferable? She scolded herself, because by now it was too late to have second thoughts.

"I don't understand," Helga said.

"My husband received a letter from the Gestapo ordering him to sublet a room in our apartment to another family."

"I see."

"Understandably, we were not pleased. The apartment is tiny compared to our mansion, and has only one kitchen and one dining room. The bathroom would have to be shared, too. We tried to tell the Jewish Council that our place isn't well-suited to host more than one family, but Herr Knobloch insisted that it must be." Edith gave her a timid smile. "I thought, maybe, I mean, if you need to leave your place..."

Helga looked at her, completely nonplussed. "You're offering me to move in with you?"

"It would only be until you've found something more suitable, because as I said, the place is not really fit for two separate families."

A huge grin appeared on Helga's face. "Am I dreaming? This must be the best thing someone has said to me during the past month. You can't imagine how despondent I have become, since the Nazis issued that new rule. Heinrich has been queuing up at the Jewish Council to be assigned a space, I've been running from pillar to post, asking anyone and everyone for a place to live, and even Frau Lemberg is at her wits' end. So many of her students need new places and even with the connections she has, it's nothing more than a drop in the ocean."

"Is it?" Bashfulness spread through Edith, since she never for a second considered the situation to be this bad. Instead of whining about her own fate she should have telephoned Silvana, and asked how she could help. Edith vowed to be a better person from now on.

"You have no idea." Helga shrugged, her shoulders slumping.

"Perhaps I've been too naïve. In any case, my offer stands. You can move in with us, if you wish. Although you'd have to pay rent." Edith offered an embarrassed smile.

"Of course. We can pay. Heinrich has the odd job here and there, and I work as a cleaning lady for an insurance company."

"Don't think me a greedy person, please. I normally wouldn't charge, but..." She wished she didn't have to speak about such a delicate topic. "Julius has been fired, therefore he doesn't have a regular income anymore and our wealth is tied up in illiquid assets."

"You don't have to explain yourself." Helga stopped her with a wave of her hand. "I understand the circumstances very well."

"You can move in anytime. Delia, our maid, will show you your room and everything you need to know."

"Thank you from the bottom of my heart," Helga said.

. . .

A few days later, Edith met with her brother Knut, who was on furlough.

"You look tired," he greeted her, forgoing the niceties.

"And you look splendid," she answered, offering him her arm to link. "Where do you want to go?" Three years her junior, he'd always been the "little brother", the one she mothered, whereas she had looked up to her older brother Joseph in admiration—until recently, that was.

"What about a café? I know one that has real coffee, only for men in uniform and their lovely company."

"Real coffee, now that is a treat I won't say no to." She fell into step with Knut as he led her along the boulevard Unter den Linden, pondering how much her life had changed. Just before they arrived at the café, she stopped him. It was an awkward confession she had to make. "There's one thing... I can't pay."

His expression was more compassionate than shocked. "Has it become that bad already?"

She bit her lip while nodding. Ever since marrying Julius she'd been the one to generously bestow gifts on her family, helping them out during the Great Depression, loaning Carsta money for the down payment on a house, using her connections to get Joseph a job—anything. And now she had to ask her little brother to pay for the coffee. It was humiliating.

Knut seemed to read her thoughts. "It's about time I did something for you."

"Thank you."

As they settled inside, sipping deliciously smelling real coffee and taking bites of the most delicious pie, Knut lowered his voice. "Why are you still here?"

"Me?" Edith looked around. "Are you in a hurry?"

"I don't mean the café. I mean the country. Shouldn't you"—he glanced over his shoulder to make sure nobody was within earshot—"be somewhere safe across the Channel."

"We've been looking into options, but the war has complicated things." She felt stupid having to tell him that Julius refused to acknowledge the gravity of their situation.

He gazed at her pensively for several seconds, before he bent forward and whispered, "It's going to get much worse. Promise you'll talk to Julius? Beg him to leave the country."

"I will."

"Good." He leaned back again. "I'm worried about you. Very much so."

"Let's talk about something else, shall we?" On his nod she asked, "How are our parents?"

"Getting old, but holding up well."

"I miss them. I often wonder whether it was right to cut all ties."

Knut took her hand. "You did what you had to do."

"Do you think they would be open to talking to me again if I visited?"

"Difficult to say." He shook his head. "You know Father, he'll expect you to crawl to the cross and admit that you were wrong."

She had anticipated that much. "I guess you're right… and I certainly won't do that. Though I do miss them. Also Carsta, my nephews and nieces."

"She's just delivered the new baby a week ago, his name is Henrik."

"I suppose you won't give her my congratulations," Edith said resignedly.

"I can if you want."

"Perhaps, yes. The baby boy doesn't have any fault in this, so please give him a kiss for me."

"Carsta misses you too, I believe."

"Has she said so? I wrote several letters to her, but she never responded." The tiniest shimmer of hope entered Edith's soul. Despite sporadic differences in the past, she and her sister had always cared for each other—until Hitler had spoilt everything with his hateful rhetoric.

"Not really, at least not in my presence. Probably because Joseph is always there when I visit. And you know how he is."

Ever since that fateful day in 1923 when he'd participated in Hitler's Beer Hall Coup, Joseph had been sliding into an abyss of delusion, radicalization and unconditional admiration for the Führer. Meanwhile it was much too late to expect logic or reason from him, since he saw everything through the lens of the Nazi ideology—where even the grossest atrocity and the most twisted thought made sense.

"How is he, by the way?"

"On the rise. He's been promoted to Sturmbannführer and has become Heydrich's right hand."

An icy hand squeezed Edith's heart. Heydrich was the mastermind behind all the harassments thrown at Jewish people. Knowing that her own brother was an instrumental part of it knocked the breath out of her lungs.

Knut seemed to have observed her shock, because he said, "I'm sorry."

"It's not your fault."

"I know. I just want to say you can count on me, anytime, with anything. I'll do whatever I can for you."

"Thank you." At least one member of her family hadn't stopped caring for her.

24

LUCKENWALDE, SUMMER 1940

The Zionist training camp didn't meet David's expectations. On the first day he'd been tasked with menial farm work: tending livestock and clearing the fields of weeds.

Every morning he got up with the chickens, did five hours of boring, mind-numbing, backbreaking farm work, before attending theory sessions in the afternoon. These consisted of religious studies, Hebrew, Jewish traditions and culture. To say he was not happy would have been a huge understatement.

The one thing he looked forward to were the meetings in the evening, when the group sung folklore songs, presented poems, even performed small stage plays. He loved making friends; there were so many interesting young people from all social classes and political directions in Luckenwalde.

During one of the evening sessions, he sidled up to another guy his age, Michal, who had a vast knowledge about Palestine, or Israel, as some people called it.

"So, what exactly is the Aliyah?"

Michal was a friendly guy, who'd been raised in a very traditional way. "Aliyah is the Jewish return to the Land of Israel from the diaspora," he explained.

"That means Israel is the same country as Palestine?" David asked.

"Haven't you learned anything at school?" Michal asked good-naturedly.

"I went to a public school, where they were more concerned in teaching us the Horst-Wessel-song." David remembered bashfully how he'd been singing the Nazi battle song at the top of his lungs, because it had given him that exhilarating sense of belonging. At least until his Latin teacher had ruled that an interbred Jew wasn't worthy of belonging or singing, or participating in his class.

Henceforth David had carved out a miserable existence in the penalty bench at the back of the classroom, until his mother had enrolled him in the Lemberg school, where he'd attended his first ever lessons on everything Jewish, including the Hebrew language.

"I see. It's complicated. The short version is that Israel will become our own country, a sovereign state that belongs just to us Jews. There we'll all be able to live in peace among friends. Finally, we won't be a homeless people, but a nation of our own, where everyone scattered in diaspora around the world has the right of citizenship."

"Does that include people like me who are half-Jews and not very religious?" David had to ask.

"It means every Jew and eligible non-Jews, such as children, grandchildren and spouses. We will be a nation based on love, not on hate or racism."

"So, my mother, who's an Aryan would be allowed to come with us?" David was getting giddy. As much as he was prepared to emigrate on his own, he would rather have his family accompany him, especially his father and sister, who were in peril in Germany. Unfortunately Heinrich had made it clear that he wouldn't go anywhere without Helga.

"In theory, yes. Right now, we have to restrict the immigration because we don't have our own state yet. Palestine, which will become Israel, is under the British protectorate and they are letting in as few people as they possibly can. Therefore we need to immigrate illegally, which is called *Aliyah Bet*." Michal grinned. "This, obviously, is dangerous, so only the people best prepared for such a perilous journey and the hard times of pioneering in the state of Israel can participate. That's what the *hachshara* is for: To prepare us for what's coming."

"I see."

David's disappointment must have shown on his face, because Michal put an arm around his shoulders. "Don't be sad. It's just for a while. In a few years you'll be able to bring over the rest of your family."

David nodded. "How does the actual process work? How do we get there? Which town? And what will we do?"

"That's a lot of questions." Michal laughed. "Let's start with the how: we take a ship. Usually, the passengers have to travel by train or perhaps by riverboat to the ports in Italy and Romania and from there the ship sets a course for Palestine, most likely to the ports of Tel Aviv or Haifa. From there, we will be distributed to wherever we are most needed."

"That sounds promising."

"It is."

"One more thing." David knew that Michal wasn't one of the decision-makers, nevertheless he might give him advice on how to tackle his most urgent problem.

"Just one?" Michal grinned from ear to ear.

"Yes. Or perhaps, no. I have finished an apprenticeship in mechanical engineering and I believe my abilities to repair machines would be very useful for our new nation. Yet, in the time I've been here, all I've done is manual farm work. It's not that I don't want to do my bit, it's just that I could be of so much more value if I were allowed to do mechanical work."

"Oh, man. You'll have a rude awakening. In the average kibbutz there is no mechanical equipment, they only use manual labor."

"Really?" David's eyes became round.

"Yes. Trust me on this. Life in Palestine is a lot more basic than even on this farm. You could even say the place is backwards. Which obviously is the fault of the British and the Arabs who do everything to keep us from flourishing."

"I see." David didn't like Michal's assessment of the situation, since he'd been looking forward to being the repairman in charge. Nevertheless he decided that wasn't a reason not to emigrate. The situation in Germany was getting worse on a daily basis and he desperately wanted to leave. If he had to become a farmhand, so be it.

25

Several months later, another summons fluttered into the house. Julius eyed the envelope with suspicion, wondering whether the Gestapo had found out about his efforts to receive a visa for England and now claimed their share of his fortune.

He snorted. There was no fortune left, at least not in Germany and not to his name. The only thing he officially possessed was the apartment where he lived—together with the Goldmanns and another family. Should the government steal whatever it was worth, he wouldn't shed a single tear once he was living comfortably in an old English mansion.

The letter wasn't about him seeking emigration. Instead it summoned him to visit the labor office for Jews. Julius furrowed his brow, assuming that must be a mistake. He wasn't seeking employment, therefore he had no intention to action the request.

"You must go," Edith insisted when he told her.

"Why should I? I've been a business owner all my life, until the Nazi scum forced me to sell my bank and later had me sacked. Whatever do they think? Do they really want to give a job to a man approaching sixty years?"

"Probably not, but you know how the Nazis are. If you don't

go, the Gestapo will knock on our door, which will only cause unnecessary grief."

She kept begging, until he finally relented. "Alright, I'll go there first thing in the morning."

"Shall I accompany you?" Edith asked.

Despite knowing that she asked out of genuine concern for his safety, he couldn't keep his temper and lashed out at her. "*Herrgottnochmal! For God's sake,* I'm not a child! I'm very well able to go to the labor office on my own."

"It's just..." She shrugged. "I worry. Who knows what those people at the labor office will do to you?"

"What? Send me to a concentration camp?" he scoffed at her, even as a chill ran down his spine. He'd long stopped being haughty.

"It wouldn't be the first time," Edith said matter-of-factly. "They don't need a reason either. Being a Jew is crime enough."

He managed to get a grip on his temper, which was getting worse by the day. "I must apologize. Thank you for caring, although it is absolutely unnecessary. Nothing will happen to me."

She gave him a terse smile, obviously not quite believing his answer. To be honest, he was slightly scared himself, doing his best not to show his fear to anyone, especially not to Edith. She had enough worries of her own—all due to him.

Being a burden weighed heavily on his conscience and made him angry. Every day more so. He'd begun to resent her for their reversal of roles: because she was the one to protect him, to shield him, to manage things for him, hell, even their bank account was in her name.

During their entire lives together it had been the other way round, from the moment when he'd fallen in love with the shy girl so many years ago, he'd taken the lead. Had courted her, introduced her into a completely different world, indulged her, protected her, given her everything she could ever have asked for.

Meanwhile the Nazis had turned him into a helpless child, a person not trusted to do anything: not owning or driving a car, not handling money, not running his own business, not patronizing restaurants, not going to the theater or just anywhere else. He depended almost entirely on Edith—and he hated the feeling.

"Are you even listening to me?" she asked.

He raised his eyes to look at her, for the first time he noticed the wrinkles around her eyes, the exhausted look in them, a few gray streaks in her hair and he wondered, whether he was the reason for them. If she had divorced him years ago, when her family had suggested—or rather demanded—it. Would she then be happier? Looking radiant, because she could live a life without all the hassles that came with being married to a Jew.

"Do you want to get divorced?" he asked.

"Why would I?" Her expression was more confused than upset.

"You'd be so much better off without me."

"Have my family talked to you?" She eyed him suspiciously.

"No." He shrugged. "To be honest, I feel guilty because you're going through all this because of me. You're still young enough to find another man, one with whom you might have the passionate love we lost so long ago."

For a second, a wistful expression flit across her face. "No. I married you. For better or worse. Even if I wanted to, I wouldn't leave you right now, because being married to me is what keeps you safe."

"And I hate it!" he flared up, just to slouch back again with guilt. "I'm sorry, Edith."

"Don't apologize," she said, sweet and composed as ever. "This is the Nazis' fault. They are running the country into the ground and all of us with it."

"Millions of Germans would disagree with you. Hitler has conquered Austria, Czechoslovakia, Poland, Norway, Denmark, the Benelux countries, most recently France, with little casualties for the Wehrmacht. The average German is in a flush of victory, Hitler's popularity is unparalleled—almost on par with God himself." He smirked sardonically. "It seems you stand pretty much alone with your opinion, except for the Jews, of course."

It was true. Almost every day there was some sort of victory celebration, a military parade or a rousing speech by propaganda minister Goebbels, and the German public was cheering.

"All of them will have a very unpleasant awakening," Edith said, much to his surprise.

"Since when do you have so much political insight?" he teased her.

"Since I've become an outcast in this oh-so-glorious New World." She deadpanned him. "We should emigrate."

"I'm afraid you're right. I've already made enquiries. But even with my connections, it'll take some time. Six months at least, perhaps a year."

"Why haven't you told me?" she asked.

"I didn't want to raise your hopes if nothing came out of it."

Her lips pressed into a thin line, before she said with only a slight trace of anger in her voice, "You're not still believing you have to protect me?"

He frowned. "I'd like to cling to the illusion that I still can."

Edith seemed moved by his admission, because she put her hand over his. "A year is not that long, we can manage. But please, keep me updated on the process, will you?"

"Promise." He couldn't help but feel relieved. Edith had begged him to emigrate for almost a decade. Yet, he'd never realized how serious she had been, since they had so much to lose. Edith especially would have difficulties adapting to the new environment without friends or family, no work to keep her occupied, and not speaking the language. It was one of the reasons why he'd resisted the notion.

These days they'd reached a point when there wasn't much to lose. He, certainly, wouldn't shed a tear, although the prospect of emigration and having to start over in a foreign country, even in England, which he knew quite well from extended stays during his youth, was daunting.

If the situation hadn't become so utterly unbearable, he'd never have pursued it for real. He was German and his place was in Germany, independently of what the Nazis did or said.

"For now, I urge you to go to the labor office and hear what they have to say. You wouldn't want them to torpedo our emigration efforts just because you were too proud to answer a summons."

He nodded wordlessly, hating to admit that she was right. Being stubborn would only throw a spanner in the process. He'd play the good citizen—although he'd long ceased to be a citizen of the Reich— and do the labor office's bidding.

The next day he walked the long way to the labor office, pausing every ten minutes or so, because his legs were giving him trouble, since he wasn't the young man he used to be.

He was completely exhausted when he finally reached his destination and needed to put a hand against the wall to steady himself while fighting for breath. Bile crept up his throat, making his anger soar and pushing heat into his already burning cheeks. He dug his fingers into the soft flesh of his palm, warning himself to keep his composure. It was hard to do in light of the glaring injustice: at his advanced age the Nazi thugs had forced him to walk instead of sitting comfortably in the back of his Mercedes the way he'd done all his life.

What gave them the right to treat him, along with all Jews, so miserably? What was their justification to take his car away, his house, his business, his job, his very lifeblood? A red haze descended upon him and he swore not to stay in this country a minute longer than necessary—not while the Nazis were in power.

Germany didn't deserve his loyalty anymore. He'd up and leave, watching with schadenfreude at how Hitler ran the country and its people into the ground, as Edith had predicted. Affection for his wife warmed his heart and he promised himself to keep his temper under better control. She was the person least deserving to be treated badly. It wasn't her fault the Nazis had come to power, and it certainly wasn't her fault that they managed to stay there. She did her best to keep him safe.

Once he'd caught his breath, he made to climb the stairs to the entrance door and knocked on the door with the sign *Administration.*

"*Herein,*" a male voice called.

"*Guten Tag.*" Unused to being a supplicant, Julius pondered whether he should introduce himself by name. In his former life, which seemed lightyears away, the people he dealt with usually knew who he was.

"How can I help you?"

"I got a letter to present myself here." Julius showed him the paper.

"Ach, you're a Jew." The official's friendly face became dismissive, while handing the paper back as if it were poisonous. "You need to go up to the fourth floor. Last office on the left. That's where they deal with your kin."

Julius spared himself the *Thank you* that good manners required and left the office grumbling. He spotted an elevator further down the hall and was about to step inside, when he saw the huge sign next to it: *No Jews allowed.*

In an outburst of mulishness, he disregarded the sign and searched the button for the fourth floor, but there were only one, two and three. Obviously, an elevator forbidden for Jews wouldn't go all the way up to the floor where the authorities dealt with the likes of him. He shrugged, acutely aware of his blood heating up. That was the exact reason why he preferred to stay home these days instead of venturing out into a world which hated him.

On the third floor he stepped out of the elevator, groaning with dismay as he noticed the stairs leading up to the next floor: a ramshackle wooden construction resembling more a ladder than actual stairs. Sweat trickled down his temples as he realized he had to brave this monstrosity in order to get to where he needed to be. It was beyond humiliating.

Just in that moment a young man, a boy actually, sat on the wooden handrail and swooshed down, landing on both feet with a loud thud right next to Julius. He broke out into a grin. "Sorry for that, I didn't see you."

"Nothing happened." Normally Julius would have given the boy a lecture about proper behavior, but what good did that do in a country that had lost its moral compass?

The boy scrunched his nose, skidded away, stopped, turned and squinted his eyes at Julius. "Do you need help going up? I mean these kind of attic stairs can be quite scary if you're not used to them."

Despite loathing having to admit his shortcomings, Julius gave a relieved nod. "That would be very kind of you. My legs aren't what they used to be."

With the help of the boy he reached the top of the stairs, where he had to duck his head, since the roof was so low. Apparently the attic of this building had never been intended to be used as an office. *Good enough for Jews though,* he thought bitterly, and stopped in front of the only door.

"Wait," a voice boomed answering Julius' knock.

About five minutes later a visibly distressed woman scurried out, leaving the door open for him. It was the most peculiar setting. Behind the huge desk sat a big man in uniform with a reddish face. Since there were no seats for visitors, Julius had to stand, and in spite of not being very tall, he ducked his head between his shoulders. It was a rather uncomfortable position to stand in, which must have been carefully designed by some vile Nazi bureaucrat.

If he'd needed another reason to leave the country, the treatment he received here did the job.

"Papers!" the man barked and Julius handed him the letter he'd received. "Are you daft? Your *Kennkarte*!"

Julius felt himself flush at the insult. Barely able to suppress his ire, he reached into his pocket, fumbling with trembling fingers for his identity card.

"Name?" the man asked, even as he read the *Kennkarte*.

Julius had half a mind to call him out for being not only daft, but an imbecile. Alas, it would not be wise to antagonize the official. "Julius Falkenstein."

At hearing the name, the man looked up and said, "What a coincidence, my brother has a managing position in the bank of the same name."

I doubt he was promoted on his merits, Julius thought, feeling the stab of loss. This bank had been his home, his family, his very livelihood for so many decades, he'd loved it almost more than he loved his wife.

"Date of birth? Address?" The man rattled down questions he could have easily answered by looking at the damn identity card in his hand.

"Do you have any special talents?" he finally asked.

"Talents?"

"Did you learn a useful profession? Anything of value for the Reich?"

"I have vast knowledge in running a business."

"That's what every Jew claims to know about. A certificate perhaps? Or a recommendation from a former employer?"

"No. As I already said, I was running my own bank for decades." Julius couldn't resist the subtle hint at the Falkenstein bank, which his counterpart didn't seem to notice. "May I ask what you need this for?"

"You truly are daft, right?" The man looked at Julius with disdain, before he elaborated. "This is the labor office, what do you think we do here? We allocate work."

"I'm not looking for work—"

The man interrupted him with a wave of his hand. "Work-shy riff-raff. That's what you are! Bloodsuckers, vermin, a disgrace to our country! It's about time you did your bit."

Julius was quickly losing his countenance and he wasn't going to let this parvenu steamroll over him. "On the contrary. I fought for Germany in the Great War. The bank your brother works for? My ancestors built it, my father made it into the biggest bank in Germany and I managed it for many years, before…" He stopped himself a split-second before using a derogatory term for the Nazis. Taking advantage of the other's bewildered expression he added, "I'm nearly sixty years old and my health isn't the best, therefore I decided to retire last year and sold the bank."

The official didn't seem to understand, because as cool as ice he shuffled several lists on his desk, until he finally said, "Ha. There it is." He took Julius' summons, wrote a few words on it, before he signed and stamped the paper and handed it back. "You'll present yourself at this packaging company tomorrow morning."

"Why? But I…" Julius stammered, flabbergasted.

"Or if you'd rather be arrested for refusing to work?" he drawled.

Julius shook his head. "No, no." He knew there was no arguing with a government official, especially not when you had that ugly J stamped across your *Kennkarte*, making you out as a subhuman non-citizen. How he loathed being in this position!

The next day, Edith accompanied him to his workplace, because he still found the public transport confusing. He'd vowed never again to use it after that first disastrous experience, but there was no way around it. Walking the distance was simply impossible. Even a taxi was out of the question; they'd become scarce and costly after the outbreak of war.

Edith promised to pick him up in the afternoon, at least for the first few days, and once again he felt like a first grader who needed parental supervision at all times.

"Thank you," he mumbled, unable to look her in the eyes. She deserved so much better than him.

"No need. I can do the shopping on my way back, so it's really not a big deal." Ever since the Goldmanns had moved in, Edith had assumed the task of doing the grocery shopping for both families, because Frau Goldmann worked long hours and returned home utterly exhausted. At first, he'd opposed, feeling Edith was being taken advantage of, until he understood that she yearned to be of use.

Despite never working a single day in her life, in their old lives as part of the upper class, she'd been occupied overseeing the household and organizing their busy social schedule. Now, she had only Delia to manage.

He stepped into the factory, reporting to the personnel department, where a haughty twenty-five-year-old man in SS uniform showed him to his workplace folding carton boxes. The work was tedious and boring. Several times he cut his fingers on the sharp edges. When he finished the pile of unfolded boxes, he stood there waiting for new ones, until the foreman barked, "Don't sit around doing nothing. Get new boxes!"

"Where?" Julius looked around, ashamed at his utter helplessness, until a man at the station next to him took pity on him. "Come with me, I'll show you. I'm Arnold Klemper, by the way."

"Julius Falkenstein." Together they walked to the other end of the big factory hall. While Julius was happy to leave his station to stretch his limbs, his eyes became wide with shock as he noticed the huge piles of carton stored.

"How do we get them to our stations?"

Arnold laughed good-naturedly. "We lug them."

Julius thought he must have misheard, but there was no doubt, because Arnold grabbed the cable holding one of the packs together with his huge, calloused hands and walked away.

Dismayed, Julius glanced at his raw and bleeding hands, before he followed suit. An excruciating sting cut through his hand, when the cable touched the raw skin of his palm. Julius pressed his jaws together to prevent himself from crying out loud and walked away, just to be stopped cold in his tracks by the weight of the pack. What had looked so easy when watching Arnold had turned out to be an almost impossible task.

He threw his entire weight forward, just to stumble and all but fall over, when the heavy pack finally moved, since he wasn't prepared for the lack of resistance once his burden was sliding across the floor.

Panting and gasping, he hadn't even made it halfway across the hall, when Arnold returned and wordlessly took the pack off Julius' hands. Back at their stations Julius gave him a heartfelt thank you.

"You'll get the hang of it soon," Arnold said.

"I'm not so sure."

The other man stared at him with a serious face. "You better had, or you'll be punished with work that's a lot worse."

After five seemingly endless hours, when Julius felt he wouldn't survive another minute, the foreman came to announce lunch break. Too exhausted to keep up Julius walked several steps behind his colleagues. When he passed the canteen for Aryan employees, several men in fine suits stepped out and he found himself face to face with one of them.

"Herr Falkenstein," said the surprised man, whom Julius recognized as a former treasury expert at the Falkenstein bank.

"Herr Glanz, what a surprise," Julius greeted him.

Herr Glanz looked at him pensively, waving at the foreman who'd stopped to scold Julius for being late. "Go ahead, he'll catch up with you later." Then he addressed Julius. "Come with me."

As they settled into his office, Herr Glanz offered coffee and biscuits. "Never in my wildest dreams would I have expected to see you here. When I heard you'd sold the bank, I assumed you'd left the country."

"I probably should have." Again, Julius wished he'd listened to Edith and left years ago. Inwardly he promised himself to increase his efforts to speed up the issue of a visa for England.

"You are part of the latest bunch the labor office sent us?"

Julius nodded. "Today is my first day. And if I may say so, my old bones aren't up to the heavy work."

Herr Glanz laughed. "Neither would mine be. We may be able to juggle numbers all day, but lugging those carton boxes? That's for tougher men than we are." Then he grew serious. "I'd love to offer you a post as head of treasury, God knows we need an expert like you. Unfortunately my hands are tied." He worried his lower lip, gazing up and down at Julius. "Please don't feel offended, Herr Falkenstein. I have great respect for you... the only position I can offer is assistant in the accounting apartment, if you would accept?"

Normally, such an offer would have been an affront, yet, nothing seemed to be normal these days. After working half a shift in his current post, the accounting department held the allure of a paradise island in the Caribbean, therefore Julius nodded. "I have recently retired, but the labor office deemed me much too young and sent me back into the workforce. Believe me, I'm beyond grateful for the offer and gladly accept."

"I won't be able to pay you more than you would receive in the factory," Herr Glanz said with a bashful shrug. "We have our orders..."

"Having a job I actually know how to do, which won't break my back, is more than I can expect under the current circumstances."

"Then it's settled." Herr Glanz grabbed the telephone and called for someone from the accounting department to introduce Julius to his new task.

It was work he could have done with his eyes shut. While Julius was grateful for the serendipity, it also stung. The Nazis had reduced him to a beggar, happy to catch the scraps they threw at him.

26

The insurance company closed over the holidays, and Helga was on vacation for an entire week. Edith had confided in her that her husband was finally taking emigration seriously, therefore she wanted to use this year's holiday season to celebrate with friends, since it might be their last time together.

Edith had invited the other tenants as well, but the Gerbers had already made plans with relatives. Since Silvana Lemberg and her husband would visit, they decided to make it a joint celebration. Coincidentally this year the first day of Chanukah fell on Christmas Eve.

They had pooled their ration books, including those of the Lembergs, and Helga had been tasked to shop for the things obtainable with coupons, whereas Edith and Silvana would visit the black market with a few of their valuables.

Helga looked at Heinrich as they stepped onto the suburban train to the outskirts of Berlin. It had been her husband's idea to do the shopping in a rural area where the shop owner didn't know them and might not realize what the stamped J on their ration cards meant.

"That is a hilarious idea," Helga had said, when he'd first suggested it.

"Not at all. The people in those tiny villages aren't on top of the latest rules and regulations, and they often don't care for the Nazis." Heinrich spoke from experience, because he'd become akin to a traveling salesman, offering accounting help to small shop owners on the outskirts. That meant he was on the road most days and got to meet many people.

"So what are we going to do when they ask? That red J stamped across the ration book isn't very inconspicuous."

He put his arms around her, whirled her around and said, "What has happened to my astute wife?"

"Maybe she's too exhausted these days to conjure up street-wise tricks." Helga leaned against him, wishing back the times when life hadn't been so cumbersome.

"Come on. Don't make such a sad face." He kissed her on her lips until Amelie entered the room—now home to all three of them. Reluctantly letting her go, Heinrich looked at his daughter and said with a smirk. "We'll tell them the J stands for *Jugend*, or youth."

Helga had her doubts. "You actually believe we can pull this off?"

"Pull what off?" Amelie asked.

"Passing your ration booklets as one for youth instead of Jews," Helga explained.

"We absolutely can." Heinrich stood in the room, radiating utter conviction. "It's merely a matter of belief and authority. You know how much the Germans love to obey."

Helga shook her head. "I'm not sure…"

"Let me do all the talking, sweetheart." Heinrich took her hand, rubbing his thumb across her palm.

"What if they don't believe us?"

"Then we better run fast." He pointedly peered at her feet stuck in old slippers and added, "I suggest you change into sturdier shoes."

Finally Helga found a reason to laugh. "I didn't plan on going out in my house slippers."

"Everything will be just fine." He wrapped his arms around her, pressing her tightly against him, kissing her long and hard.

"Eek. You behave worse than the lovey-dovey boys at our school," Amelie complained, evoking a fit of giggles from both of her parents.

The halting train brought Helga back to the present.

"This is our station." Heinrich grabbed her hand, jumping from the train. As soon as they left the platform, he carefully draped his scarf around his neck. "How do I look?"

"Stunning as always." She giggled, growing serious again a few seconds later. "Are you sure this is safe for you?"

"Getting cold feet, my love?" he teased her.

"Never." Helga squared her shoulders. It wasn't herself she was afraid for—in contrast to Heinrich she didn't have anything to fear. After a while she relaxed and appreciated the landscape.

She had never been in this part of the city and looked in wonder at the beautiful trees lining the streets, the idyllic red-brick station building and the peaceful atmosphere. Out here they didn't encounter a Swastika flag at every corner and certainly no men in SS uniform striding up and down with an important gait. "It's beautiful here."

"It is. Let's go." Heinrich took her hand, and a sudden exhilaration spread through her limbs. It felt like a thrilling adventure and Helga tried to remember the last time she'd been so mischievously excited. When she and Heinrich had sneaked into a dark alley to exchange their first kiss, back in high school? Or maybe the first time they'd left their children with her sister Felicitas for the weekend and Heinrich had taken her to a cozy little hotel at the seaside?

She involuntarily sighed, causing Heinrich to look at her.

"Don't worry—" He stopped midsentence, eyeing her dreamy expression and impishly adding, "Why do I get the impression you're anything but worried?"

"I was thinking of our getaway to the seaside." A sensual groan escaped her throat.

"That was wonderful, wasn't it?" He squeezed her hand. "I miss those times."

"Me too. Everything has become a struggle; I'm so sick and tired of it."

Heinrich's face fell. "I'm so sorry, my love. When I proposed to you, I promised to make you happy. It looks like I failed miserably. You shouldn't have to suffer because of me."

"I am happy with you, with our children. I'm just sick and tired of the Nazis, and their existence certainly isn't your fault."

He looked crestfallen. "But you wouldn't have to worry about them if it weren't for me."

"Stop that nonsense right now! Do you genuinely believe I'd condone the affliction they cause if I were married to a Christian? Do you believe me that shallow and selfish?"

"No, I don't." His face was a grimace of sorrow. "It's just, I can't in good conscience watch how you are hurting."

"Oh, my darling. Being with you is what keeps me together these days. Without knowing your embrace waits for me at the end of a horrible day, I don't know what I'd do."

Meanwhile they had reached the grocery store. Heinrich stopped and took her face into his hands. "No more defeatist talk. We need to give our best performance." He kissed her swiftly. "Ready?"

"Ready."

"Remember, let me do the talking."

It was exactly the way Heinrich had promised and ten minutes later they were back on their way to the station with two bags full of produce needed for a combined Christmas and Chanukah celebration.

Helga was holding her side, which hurt from giggling so hard. "Did you see the shop owner's face when he saw the ration books? He had never seen one with a J before."

"I told you so." Heinrich helped her onto the suburban train that arrived. Out here the wagon was empty, but no doubt it would get crowded as they approached the city.

"And when you told him, 'How do you not know this is a special card for youngsters?'" She broke out into another fit of giggles as she imitated Heinrich's authoritative voice. "That was marvelous. Simply marvelous." Since they were alone in the wagon, she pressed herself against him. "This is just one of the one million reasons why I love you so much."

Heinrich's eyes shone with emotion. "I love you too. I just wish—"

"Shush." Helga put a finger to his lip. "Don't spoil the moment. Let's pretend we're without a care in the world."

"We could also pretend to be newly enamored."

"Hmm… are you going to take me into a back alley to steal a kiss?" Her skin prickled with anticipation.

"I just might… although"—he pointedly looked at her thick scarf—"it's much too cold outside. If we hurry up, we can sneak into our room before Amelie returns home."

Helga leaned against him, enjoying the comfortable silence between them. After a while she said, "Isn't it ironic that we're going to celebrate together: Jews and Christians, practicing and not, rich and poor, despite all efforts to get us apart?"

"It feels incredibly good to score one off Hitler."

The train rolled into a station, where several passengers stepped inside. Instantly Helga was on her guard again, afraid to utter a wrong word and betray their shenanigans—or that her husband was Jewish, therefore she decided to switch the topic to something inconspicuous. "I'm so happy David will be coming home over Christmas. I miss him."

"He's grown-up. It's normal that a child leaves its parents' house." Heinrich was the voice of reason.

"I know, but I still miss him. Why did he have to go so far away?" Even to her own ears, she sounded miserable.

"Luckenwalde is hardly far away. You can count yourself glad that he hasn't—" Heinrich stopped himself before saying "emigrated to Palestine", and, after a glance at the other passengers, concluded his sentence, "Moved to the other end of the country."

Helga nodded. As much as she wanted David to be safe, she loathed the idea of him crossing the Mediterranean into some unknown faraway place where she might never be able to visit him.

27

David returned to Berlin for the holidays with fantastic news: despite not having completed his *hachshara,* he'd been granted passage on a ship destined for Palestine. The exact date to set sail wasn't yet known, the organizer calculated early spring.

Ever since he'd received the news, David was on cloud nine, simmering with excitement for the departure together with his newfound friends at the farm. His parents would be less enthusiastic at the news, albeit supporting his decision to leave the ever-worsening conditions in Germany. Now he just needed to convince Thea to follow him later in the year.

He dropped his bag next to Amelie's bed, and made to leave again.

"Aren't you going to wait for our parents to return? Mutti will be here any minute," Amelie asked.

"I've got something to do, it won't take long." He deliberately avoided telling his sister more details.

She put her hands on her hips, gazing at him sternly. "Where are you going?"

"None of your business, but if you must know: to Thea's."

She scrunched her nose. "Shouldn't you wait until after the holidays?"

"I have only a few days off, remember?" He urgently needed to see his girlfriend. They hadn't been able to telephone each other, and her letters had been sparse and stilted, which he chalked up to her not being comfortable to write with the censors reading every word of it.

"Why don't you give her a call instead?"

"What is wrong with you?" David eyed his sister suspiciously. "Is there a reason why you don't want me to see Thea?"

Amelie squirmed beneath his scrutinizing gaze. "For God's sake! If she hasn't told you, it seems I must."

"What are you talking about?"

"She is walking out with some other guy."

"That's not true!" David refused to believe his sister's words. "She would never. We're in love."

"Don't get angry at me. I'm just the messenger. I wanted to spare you the heartache, but if you must, go and see for yourself." With these words, Amelie turned around, leaving him staring at her back.

It was not true. It could not be true. He loved Thea and she loved him. A doubt crept into his heart. What if this was the reason her letters had been so distant? Had she found someone else? If she had, why hadn't she told him? He shook his head, feeling forlorn.

In a sudden hurry to get clarity, he grabbed his coat and hat, and rushed over to Thea's place a few blocks away. After "the great move" as he called the displacing of Jews into so-called Jewish houses in Jewish quarters, nearly everyone he knew from the Lemberg school lived nearby.

He rang the doorbell at her apartment building, racing upstairs, where Thea's father stood in the door. "David Goldmann, right? It's been a long time, we already thought you gone."

"Not yet. I'm still in Luckenwalde for training."

"What can I do for you?"

David stood straighter, towering over Herr Blume. "Is Thea home?"

"Unfortunately not, she's walked out with her young man."

Fighting against his emotions, David somehow managed to thank Thea's father and trudged down the stairs. Just as he opened the main door, Thea entered—alone. When she saw him, anxiety passed across her face, before she stubbornly put out her lower lip.

"I hadn't expected you here."

"That's what your father told me. He mentioned you have a new boyfriend." David's blood was boiling with rage and if it weren't for his good upbringing, he'd have pinned her against the wall and choked her until she begged for forgiveness.

Thea blanched, before quickly regaining her composure. "You disappeared to that farm, leaving me high and dry. What did you expect?"

"Now it's my fault?" He shook his head in disbelief.

"I had no other choice, since I wasn't going to pine after a man who couldn't be bothered to stay by my side."

"You're being unfair." David was barely holding on to his temper. "I asked you to come with me."

"To a farm? Do I look like a yokel to you?" She pursed her lips.

Suddenly he found her repulsive. "No, you look like an adulteress to me."

"We're not married," she answered dryly.

"You could at least have told me." The fight had seeped out of David.

She shrugged. "That's not something to share in a letter."

"Did you ever plan to tell me? Or did you rely on the grapevine to give me the news?"

Again, she shrugged. "I figured you'd find out somehow, if you hadn't already found yourself another girl or two. There must be girls on that farm, eager to snatch a man before going on the passage across the sea."

His fingers itched to slap her in the face, once again his education kept him from doing so. He just wanted to get away from Thea. Forever.

"I'm not a cheater." Then he turned around and rushed off, walking for hours in the cold, trying to reconcile his image of the sweet, lovable Thea with the cold, treacherous version of her he'd learned about today.

"David Goldmann, is that you?" Frau Lemberg called out when he finally returned to his parents' place.

"Yes." He had great respect for his former headmistress, so he swallowed down his anger. "Are you coming to visit the Falkensteins?"

"Hasn't anyone told you? We're celebrating the holidays together. We've been preparing this celebration for weeks." Another detail nobody had seen fit to inform him about.

"I just arrived. Can I help you?" he asked, pointing at the heavy bags in her hand.

"Yes, that would be nice." She handed him her bags and held the door open for him and her husband, who was lugging an even bigger bag. Before they reached the landing, she held him back, asking, "You look a bit shaken. Is everything alright?"

"I'm fine," he reassured her.

Frau Lemberg, though, was perceptive and clearly noticed his trembling lip. At school, she had never been fooled by whatever excuse her students came up with, since she had an uncanny ability to distinguish truth from lie. "If there's anything I can help you with, I'll be here all night."

"Thank you." It was a nice offer, even though he had no intention to tell his former headmistress that his girlfriend—also a student of hers—had just ditched him after walking out for God knew how long with some other lad. "There's nothing, really."

Upstairs, everyone was already waiting for them.

Frau Falkenstein greeted the Lembergs, before she addressed David, "Your mother has been worried, you've been gone such a long time."

"I'm old enough to look out for myself," he stubbornly responded, overwhelmed by the sympathy. If only Thea had as much concern for him as these virtual strangers.

"You certainly are. Although these days anything can happen, especially if a bored police patrol checks your papers." She didn't have to add *and finds out you're half Jewish,* for him to understand.

"I'm sorry, I should have returned earlier."

"Let's forget it! Now's the time to celebrate. At least for a couple of hours we all want to pretend life is a bowl of cherries."

David's mouth watered as he visualized the sweet, juicy cherries growing next to the farmhouse. "Cherries in winter. That's what life should look like!"

After a fantastic celebration, David fell onto the mattress on the floor—for lack of a bed—and slept for twelve hours straight. The hard farm work, plus the long evenings with social interaction had taken its toll.

He came down hard with a stomach flu. Three days later he was admitted to the Jewish hospital with complications. When months later he finally recovered enough to be dismissed, his ship to Palestine had sailed, his ticket had been given to another very lucky chap.

28

BERLIN, SEPTEMBER 1, 1941

Germany was two years into the war, and Hitler seemed to be invincible. Edith groaned every time she witnessed a victory parade after the Wehrmacht successfully invaded yet another country: North Africa, Yugoslavia, Greece. In June, Hitler had attacked what had been his strongest ally: the Soviet Union.

From one day to the next the former friends had become enemies, for what reason exactly, nobody knew. Except of course, the Führer's hunger for land and power.

With their savings dwindling fast, because buying on the black market was expensive, Edith had considered taking a job, but Julius had not allowed it. She shook her head; it seemed to be the last shred of his pride: that his wife did not need to work, because he could provide for her, when in fact, he could not.

So she resigned to cooking for the entire shared household, which now included David. The poor boy had been utterly devastated, after receiving the notice that the ship had sailed without him. He'd walked around like an undead for weeks, never once smiling or even uttering a word.

To add insult to injury, he hadn't been allowed to return to the Zionist farm. Instead he had been ordered by the labor office to return to his previous workshop, which these days worked exclusively for the Reichsbahn.

For David, it had been a blessing in disguise and he'd made peace with his bad luck. Edith greatly admired the young man for being able to get up and dust himself off, unsure if she would have the strength to do the same in a similar situation.

His boss Baumann was short of skilled men and soon promoted him—unofficially of course—to head engineer. Thus David became the only man in the brigades of Jewish forced workers to freely roam the premises.

Edith pursed her lips. *Räder müssen rollen für den Sieg,* wheels must roll for victory, was a popular slogan found not only on the locomotives themselves, but also on posters all over the city.

Her maid Delia, too, had been forced to take up external work several months ago, apparently household chores for a mixed family didn't advance the Reich. The poor thing had been sent to a munitions factory where she toiled ten hours a day, six days a week.

Thinking about the former prima ballerina, bottled-up rage pushed to the surface and Edith violently chopped the vegetables into thin slices. Such a magnificent talent wasted. Before all of this, which seemed like nothing but a dream, she and Julius had often attended the performances of the Berlin Opera House Unter den Linden, and had been mesmerized by the dancers, among them Delia.

"How is this going to end?" she murmured to herself, adding a pinch of precious salt to the potatoes. She'd been forced to learn how to cook after finding herself without staff and being responsible to cook for a household, which had grown to twelve persons, including their other tenants, the Gerbers, practicing Jews with three children.

She was still musing about how to make the meal go further, when her thoughts wandered back to her adolescence. During the starvation winter of 1916–1917 Edith's mother had served them nothing but barely palatable turnips, alongside bread stretched with sawdust. Her body convulsed at the memory, and she blinked a few times to dispel the troubling images. It wouldn't come to that a second time, would it?

"That's for the dishes." Helga came home from work, putting scraps of soap onto the kitchen counter. Ever since the Jewish members in their household didn't receive coupons for soap and shaving foam early this summer, Helga *accidentally* put ends of the curd soap she used at work into her pockets.

"Thank you, but you really shouldn't do this. What if you get caught?" Edith said.

"For stealing a morsel of soap? It's small enough to claim it clung to my clothes after scrubbing dirty footprints from the marble floor." Helga flopped into the only chair in the kitchen, scrutinizing her hands. "I wish I could afford hand cream."

"You can have mine. I rarely use it," Edith offered, but Helga shook her head.

"I can't possibly accept that. It's much too expensive."

Edith shrugged, she wasn't going to insist. By the time it was empty she probably wouldn't be allowed to buy a new one.

At the rate the Nazis pushed out laws prohibiting one mundane thing or the other for Jews, they'd soon not be allowed to breathe the air. Whoever worked in the Ministry of Justice's Department for Jewish Affairs had been on a roll this year: the prohibition to buy soap was followed by an order to cut all telephone lines for Jewish families—and hand over the telephone sets to the authorities without compensation.

This had been followed by a ban to use privately owned libraries, which basically banned Jewish people from reading any books at all, because state and university libraries had been off limits since before the beginning of the war.

And who these days had money to spare to buy books? Even buying newspapers and magazines was forbidden for Jews, who had to rely for their information solely on the radio—Edith secretly wondered how long until the Nazis would take that from them—or the only allowed Jewish newspaper *Das Jüdische Nachrichtenblatt*.

"Have you heard the latest?" Helga asked.

"What is it now?" Honestly, Edith would rather not know what atrocity the Nazis had deliberated this time.

Helga pulled out a newspaper from under her blouse and read, "Starting September first, all Jews six years and older are forbidden to show up in public without the Star of David."

"What exactly is a Star of David?" Edith turned around to look at Helga.

"It says here: the Star of David is a palm-sized six-pointed star made of yellow fabric with the black inscription 'Jude'. It is to be worn visibly, sewn firmly onto the left side of the chest of the garment." Helga rubbed her chin. "Apparently we have two weeks to implement this newest chicanery."

"Now isn't that nice?" Edith said sarcastically. "What happens if someone refuses to wear that stupid star?"

Helga pushed her finger down the lines. "Obviously the government has thought of everything: anyone who is in caught without the star shall be liable to a fine of up to one hundred fifty Reichsmarks or to imprisonment for up to six weeks."

"That's a lot of money." Edith shook her head, nobody she knew could afford paying the fine, so prison it would be for most everyone. "Does it say where to get those patches? Knowing the Nazis, I assume they have figured out a way to make it as cumbersome as possible."

Helga shook her head. "No, it doesn't say. Just some comment by the newspaper desk how convenient this will be, because the Jews won't be able to go unnoticed anymore."

"Now that is concerning. Just imagine anyone can distinguish at first glance who's Jewish and who isn't." An icy shudder raced down Edith's spine, as pictures of random passers-by spitting on Jews, or SS men beating them up just for fun entered her mind. What a horrible new world it was.

One after another, the other household members came home. David, who possessed just the right amount of shrewdness to be the first one to find out these kind of things announced, "The fabric printing company Geitel & Co has reportedly been printing one million Stars of David in their factory building in Wallstrasse, so a friend and I sauntered over there to find out more." He grinned and pulled out a bunch of yellow stars from his pockets.

"David, please tell me you didn't steal them!" Helga asked.

He waved off her reproach. "The Nazis have been robbing us blind, it's only fair to get a bit back."

Edith looked anxiously at Julius, who didn't tolerate such behavior. To her utter surprise he didn't seem to care.

"I had to share with my friend, that's why I only got these five." David looked around as if apologizing, because eight of the eleven persons present were required to wear this abhorrent sign.

Herr Gerber grabbed one of the yellow batches, grimacing with disgust. "I'm not going to wear this atrocity! Look at it! Even the letters are a mockery, misappropriating Hebrew letters." He threw it back onto the table.

His wife reached for the piece of cloth. "Please, Lennart, you must wear it or they'll send you to prison."

"I'd rather go to jail than make a fool out of myself," Herr Gerber said valiantly.

"I've been to a camp, I'd rather not repeat the experience," Julius said, taking one of the yellow patches and holding it to his chest. "I really hope our emigration visas will be issued soon."

Edith sensed an awkward pause in the conversation, because the other two families didn't have the hope to emigrate. Therefore she decided to return the discussion to practicalities. "Let me get a clasp pin to fasten it."

"That's not allowed," Amelie said, turning all heads to look at her since she didn't often speak up.

"What?" someone asked.

"According to what we were told at work, you have to sew them on tightly. Our boss gleefully said he'll check our stars in the morning by trying to put a pencil between the stitches. If he succeeds, the culprit will forfeit one week's salary and has to work double shifts." Amelie gave a miserable shrug.

"So each of us needs more than one star?" Heinrich said. "Where do we get them?"

David raised his voice again. "Geitel & Co only produces them, distribution is done via the Jewish community offices, where you can buy a star for ten Pfennig each."

"Ten cents?" Lennart Gerber hissed. "This is fraud! Making us pay for the privilege to wear this abomination? I'm not standing for it."

Everyone in the room knew Herr Gerber was all talk and no walk. He'd never openly oppose the Nazis.

"How many do we need?" Edith asked.

"Two per person I would assume," Julius suggested. "For a winter and a summer coat. Deducting the five David has kindly organized,"—he gave the young man an appreciative glance—"that leaves eleven still to be bought at ten cents each, for a total of one Reichsmark, ten cents. Not charging David for his share, that makes it sixteen cents per person."

"How did you calculate so fast?" one of the Gerber children asked.

"I used to own a bank, numbers are my passion." A flicker of energy appeared in Julius' eyes, making him look a decade younger.

"Who is going to buy them?" someone asked and all eyes focused on Edith, who was the only one in the household not working or attending school.

"Me? No? I'm not sure I'm the right person."

"I'll do it. I pass the Jewish Council on my way to work anyway," Amelie offered.

When Edith and Julius retired to their bedroom, she said, "The Gerber boy was very impressed with your quick calculation."

He looked at her pensively for a while. "I love working with numbers. They don't lie and they don't disappoint you."

She nodded, knowing he was thinking about those people who'd dropped him like a hot potato, despite having benefitted from his generosity for years.

Shaking his head, he added, "I would never have thought that one day I'd become a penny-pincher. It pains me that I couldn't offer to pay for all those darned stars."

"Don't feel guilty. Everyone understands."

"I still hate not being able to be generous."

"You are generous. You're giving these families a home," Edith reminded him, before she slipped into bed, waiting for him to occupy his side. "Do you have an idea how we can contact your sister Adriana to see whether she has been able to send the affidavit?"

Julius rubbed his chin, suddenly looking very old. "There's no way to place a phone call or even send a letter from anywhere in Germany to England since our countries are at war."

"I've been racking my brain about this problem the entire week." The desolation sucked all energy out of Edith, since without Adriana's affidavit they'd never be allowed to emigrate.

After a long silence Julius said, "There might be a way."

"How?" She was all ears.

"Our friend Reginald. He's in the Hamptons, and since we're not at war with America, we can telephone him."

"Have you forgotten that the government took our phone line away?" she said bitterly.

"Oh right. And you can't feed the public phone fast enough with nickels and dimes to keep the line working." He furrowed his brows, until he slowly formulated his thoughts: "Here's an idea. American war reporters can telegraph back home through the American consulate. I happen to know one from better times. If he'd agree to contact Reginald, who in turns calls Adriana, we could get in touch with her."

Edith suppressed a groan at the hoops they had to jump. "We should at least try it."

"I'll visit with him after work tomorrow," Julius promised.

29

A few days later, Heinrich returned from work with a black eye.

"Whatever happened to you?" Helga immediately fussed over him.

"Nothing. I fell."

"You fell? Under the bus or what?" She observed his facial expressions, sure he was hiding something from her.

"It's really nothing." He escaped into the bathroom, seemingly hoping she'd buy his ludicrous story, which wasn't about to happen. When he returned, freshly washed, she stepped into his path, putting her hands akimbo. "Does this have anything to do with that yellow star you're wearing?"

He gave an awkward shrug, which was enough for her to realize her worst fears had come true. "Tomorrow I'll accompany you to work."

"That really isn't necessary," Heinrich protested.

"It absolutely is." She glared at him. "I'm not going to lose you because some bastard feels like beating you up."

"Oh, darling." Heinrich wrapped his arms around her. "You'll only get yourself into trouble. I couldn't bear it if these thugs harmed you because you were trying to protect me."

To be honest, Helga was terribly afraid of this exact scenario, though she would never admit it. Therefore she feigned poise. "They won't harm me. They don't hit Aryan women."

Heinrich wanted to respond, but at noticing the determination in her eyes, he slumped his head. "If you insist."

"I do."

The next morning, she got up extra early to drop him off at his workplace before racing to her own. As soon as they stepped onto the tram, she was confronted with a situation even more awful than she had imagined. Helga had expected hostile looks or nasty comments. A man in a business suit spitting at them, was an utter shock.

"What's worse than a Jew?" The stranger looked around, craving attention from the other passengers. Then he answered his own question. "A Jew-loving German woman." The entire crowd broke into jeers and laughter.

"What's worse than bestiality?" another man asked with an ugly smirk. "Banging a Jew."

Another round of rowdy howling erupted. Helga's cheeks burned hot at the vulgar insult, wanting to disappear from the face of the earth. She clung to whatever dignity she had left, holding her head high, staring straight ahead, pretending she didn't hear their taunts.

Next to her, she sensed Heinrich tensing, every muscle in his body strung tight. Out of fear that he'd pounce at one of the strangers—which would inevitably rouse the rabble and they would come out losing—she grabbed his fingers behind her back.

How horrible the world had become in the matter of just a few days. That dreadful yellow star seemed to give everyone who harbored evil feelings permission not only to voice them, but also to act upon their hatred.

"This vermin shouldn't be allowed to ride in the same tram car as we do," a woman's voice called out.

"Right. Why do we have to breathe their foul air?" someone asked.

"Push them out! Push them out!" the crowd chanted, closing in on them.

Helga choked in panic, already imagining herself and Heinrich lying on the street with another vehicle approaching fast. She was sure she was going to meet her maker any minute, when out of nowhere a man in a Wehrmacht uniform showed up and said, "Leave them alone!"

"What gives you the right!" one woman screeched. She was quickly silenced by the rest, who kowtowed to the uniform more than they wanted to kick those they believed to be inferior.

The crowd dispersed and Helga stood face to face with the Wehrmacht soldier in his late twenties.

"Thank you so much." Her lips were trembling so hard, she could barely pronounce the words.

"I'm so sorry I can't do more," he said, visibly distressed.

"You might have saved our lives, that is a lot," Heinrich said.

The soldier looked between both of them, slightly shaking his head. "You oughtn't to go out together, it riles them up."

Helga was about to answer that without her by his side, her husband had been beaten up the day before. One glimpse into Heinrich's pleading face, and she kept this to herself. "Thank you again so much for your help."

The soldier stood next to them without speaking another word. Strangers gave them the evil eye, though nobody dared to go any further in his presence. Finally, she and Heinrich disembarked, a sudden sense of relief settling over her as she stepped out of the hostile environment.

"You're not going to work anymore!" Helga vented, knowing full well that wasn't an option.

Heinrich was a picture of misery. "You know that's not possible. In any case you shouldn't come with me. I don't want you to get hurt."

"We could buy a bicycle for you?" she suggested.

"With what money?"

"For all that's holy, there must be a way! I'm not going to let you go by tram every day to be treated like scum. If that soldier hadn't arrived, I'm sure the mob would have thrown us through the windows."

"Now you're exaggerating, my darling." For a moment waggishness appeared in his eyes, reminding her why she'd fallen in love with him so many years ago. "We're much too big to fit through the tiny window openings."

Despite her worries she had to laugh, too funny was the image of Heinrich getting stuck midway through the tilted window.

"I love it when you laugh," he whispered into her ear. The good mood quickly dispelled when passersby approached and Heinrich fearfully raised a hand to his chest—to cover the ugly stain branding him as a subhuman, a person without rights, whom everyone could trample over without feeling guilt or fearing repercussions.

Helga was near to tears, recognizing that from now on this would be their daily routine: watching over their shoulders at every step, fearing a punch coming out of nowhere, threatening their very lives. "We're talking about this when I pick you up after work."

"You're not seriously considering doing this again?" Heinrich asked her, aghast.

"You bet I am. Remember that I swore to love you in good times and bad? Hitler has no idea what I'm capable off to protect my family!"

A small smile appeared on his lips. "My brave, upright darling."

Three short bursts of a siren sounded from the building, indicating it was time for the workers to begin their shift.

"I'll be waiting for you right here tonight," she called after him. Then she stepped back onto the same tram line they'd traveled earlier. Alone, it was a completely different experience: nobody taunted, insulted or threatened her. Nobody even took any notice of her. She was simply one more passenger in the crowded car. Helga wanted to crawl into a hole and cry.

Instead she pulled herself together, wrapped her light summer coat tighter and stepped of the tram when it reached her station. Taking it one day at a time, that was all she aspired to.

30

Joseph fought with himself. What he was about to do could cost him his career. Despite everything he didn't want his sister Edith to get hurt. She might be stubborn, unreasonable, weak and deluded, but she was still his sister. He had to warn her.

"It'll be one last attempt. If she doesn't heed my advice, then there's nothing else I can do for her," he said to himself. "Tomorrow I'll pay her a visit."

The next morning, he left his uniform hanging in the wardrobe—an SS officer visiting a Jewish house would attract unwelcome attention—and dressed in a smart business suit, before he asked the driver to drop him off several blocks away from Edith's building.

Several times he was tempted to turn on his heels and leave her be. She wouldn't like what he was going to tell her. *Why do I even care?* he asked himself. His sister had brought this hardship on her herself. If only she had heeded his advice to divorce this man. No, stubborn as she was, she refused to listen to reason.

Secretly he admired her determination not to waver in her convictions and do what she thought was right—if only her idea of the right thing aligned with the truth.

If only she could see the great future Hitler had planned for the German nation, including her. If only she could free herself from the Jewish spell under which she stood, and which caused her to twist the truth, feeling treated unjustly.

He shrugged. This was his last attempt to make his sister see the true path. If she chose to believe in the Jewish conspiracy theories making the Nazis out to be the boogeyman, then she was irrevocably on her own. Even her big brother could only so do much.

Walking up to the formerly majestic building he was shocked to see it so dilapidated. The next second, he wondered why he had expected anything different. The building's tenants were exclusively Jews, among a few forlorn souls like Edith, therefore its decayed condition was natural. It was yet more proof that these vermin were dirty, lazy and cunning.

The entrance door gave way after a short push, popping open as if by an invisible hand. His heart beat faster as he entered the entrance door standing ajar, hoping it wasn't too late to coax his sister back onto the path of virtue. Since he'd never been to their city apartment before, he checked every doorplate to find the correct name.

Reading one Jewish last name after another, dread crept down his spine making him shudder. He was a courageous man, but walking right into the lion's den gave even him the chills.

Finally, he reached their floor and knocked on the door, hoping Edith was alone at home. It took several seconds, before her wary voice called out, "Who's there?"

"Me. Joseph."

Quick steps paced toward the door. Then it opened slowly just a few inches, until she recognized him.

"It really is you," Edith said amazed.

"Yes. May I come in?" He took off his fedora, holding it in his hands like a shield, the strangeness of the situation seeping into his bones.

"Sure." She cast him a wary look, even as she stepped aside. "Are you alone?"

"Yes."

"Why are you here?"

"I..." His well-rehearsed speech had vanished from his brain, leaving a huge blank. "It's... it's good to see you." To gain time and recover his wits, he stepped into the corridor, fiddling with his fedora.

He peeked into the living room, taking in the clean but worn-down carpet, the cheap furniture, the many wardrobes crowded against the walls, and the complete absence of knick-knacks, silver decorations, or expensive paintings. It was so different from their previous homes both in Munich and Berlin, he'd feared he'd knocked at the wrong place. But the beautiful, yet exhausted-looking woman in front of him was definitely Edith.

The past two years hadn't been kind to her. Streaks of gray showed in her hair, wrinkles etched around her eyes, and her soft, white hands looked raw and red as if she had been scrubbing dishes for days on end.

"What happened to your maid?" he asked, nodding at her hands.

"Got drafted to forced work by your ilk." Edith put out her lower lip the way she'd always done as a child when she'd wanted to rile him up.

"I'm not here to fight, on the contrary—" He broke off. What he was about to tell her was top secret and would get him into serious trouble if it ever came out. "Can I have something to drink, please?"

"Would water be sufficient? There's nothing else." The way she said it, made it sound as if Joseph were to blame for her situation.

"That's perfectly fine."

Edith disappeared into the kitchen, giving him the opportunity to scrutinize the living room more closely. It resembled more the common lounge at the SS barracks than a family home. He squinted his eyes at the assembly of different styles and colors of almost everything. When she returned to hand him a glass of water he asked, "What happened to your furniture?"

"We had to sell it."

"And all this stuff? What do you need this for?"

She rolled her eyes. "How come you don't know this? We've been ordered to sublet. There are three families living in this place."

His eyes widened. Of course he knew about Jewish housing conditions and how cramped they lived, yet somehow he hadn't expected that his own sister was affected by these rules. "Well..." When their eyes met, he was transported back in time to their adolescent days. The awkwardness between them fell away. "Oh, Edith, I'm so sorry. I never wanted this for you. You should have heeded my advice and divorced this man."

"Is that your reason for coming? To commend me to divorce my husband?" Her voice was cold as ice.

"No." He shook his head. "I came here to warn you."

"Again? Another threat to get what you want?"

Made desperate by her hostility, he ran a hand through his carefully slicked back hair. "Not at all. I have information that I must tell you. How you act or don't act upon it, I don't care. But first you must swear never to mention my name in connection with that information."

She perked up her ears. "What is it?"

"Promise first."

"I promise never to mention your name. Satisfied?"

He decided it was enough. Edith wasn't anything if not loyal, proven by her pathetic determination to stay married to that Jew. "I realize you've been planning to emigrate."

"How do you know?" she interrupted him.

"Let's just say I know the right people." He smiled smugly.

"I forgot." She pursed her lips

He almost reconsidered at the hostility in her behavior. Inwardly, he groaned. He hadn't taken this risk to leave her without issuing his warning. "Anyhow, you need to hurry up the process. There'll be a law forbidding Jews to emigrate pretty soon, possibly before the year ends."

She snorted. "That's not true. Hitler hates the Jews and wants them gone."

"Yes and no." He fought with himself over how much to tell her, then opted to give the least information possible. "Our Führer still distrusts them, but"—he glared at her, hoping to convey the urgency—"he won't let them leave to regroup and destroy Germany from abroad."

Edith stared at him in disbelief. "What's he going to do to them?"

"I can't say. Just this much: you really don't want to find out. So, please, leave the country, before it's too late." He emptied his glass, took up his fedora and said, "I've said too much already. Remember: I was never here." In a sudden burst of emotion he bent forward and kissed her on the cheek. "Godspeed, Edith."

31

David rounded the corner a few blocks from home, disappeared into a narrow alley and slipped out of his jacket. He turned the inside out, before he slipped into it again, since he had no intention to show up at work with the humiliating yellow star flaunting on his chest.

His parents would be aghast at the notion of defying the Nazis in such a bold way, pestering him to obey and suffer in silence the way they did. He snorted. What good had being law-abiding citizens done them? None at all.

In contrast, Amelie had been open to his suggestion and the good seamstress she was, she had altered his jacket, and hers, so that it could be worn inside out.

Moments later, he stepped out onto the main street the stigma on his chest safely hidden on the inside. Instantly, the sun seemed to shine brighter and the birds to chirp louder. His step became cheery; instead of ducking his head between his shoulders, wary of hostile passersby, he proudly strode among the rest of the Germans as if he belonged.

When he arrived at work without the obligatory star, Bauman, the old communist, merely lifted an eyebrow. "You be careful, Kessel."

"I will, Baumann."

"If the personnel department finds out, I know nothing. Can't be bothered to control what everyone wears outside the shop."

"Thanks." David adored the much older man and would never want to cause him trouble for being complicit in David's fraud. If someone found out his ruse, David would rely on his quick wits to talk himself out of the dicey situation.

For now, he walked onto the shop floor, whistling a tune. It didn't do any good to rack his brain over things that might or might not happen. He much preferred to wait and trust in his intuition.

Overnight, several worn-out engines had arrived from the Reichsbahn and David immediately went to work. Here, he forgot about the hardships, the harassment and his other problems. Here he was happy. Returning after his hospital stay had made him realize how much he had hated the farm work in Luckenwalde.

Of course he was disappointed at having missed the ship to Palestine. While his name sat on the waiting list for another ship, he busied himself doing the work he loved: tinkering with machines. Once he arrived in Palestine he'd make sure to find a way to work with engines or other mechanical repairs, instead of harvesting crops. Whatever the Zionists in Berlin said, an emergent country must need technically apt citizens like him.

In the evening he decided to take a detour home and mix with the perambulators along the boulevard Unter den Linden, maybe chatting up a pretty girl and inviting her for a soda. Or at least sitting in the café, reading the newspaper he wasn't allowed to buy anymore, while watching the other patrons.

When he stepped from the tram and walked toward his favorite café, he bumped into Thea. She looked as radiant as ever, although when she recognized him, a flicker of fear crossed her face, while her hand shot up to her chest.

Automatically his gaze followed the path of her hand and landed on her left breast. It took him a second to understand why she'd been so afraid: no yellow star blemished her jacket.

He was going to reassure her, when she in turn noticed the missing mark on his own chest and dropped her hand. Giving a silly giggle to overplay her moment of shock, she said, "Hello, David. What a nice surprise to see you here."

Despite wanting to hate her for dumping him, her sweet smile mesmerized him, and his resolve melted away. He would be forever under the spell of this woman.

"No worries, I'm not going to tell on you."

"Me neither." She pointedly looked at the space where his star of David should be sewn on. Then she stepped nearer, looking around before she whispered into his ear, "Aren't you afraid about what happens when they check your papers?"

Instantly the old attraction hit with a vengeance, her nearness making him woozy. Somehow he managed not to beg her to return to him. Instead he coolly shrugged. "Aren't you?"

"They rarely check beautiful young women with blonde hair. On the other hand, men looking the way you do…"

Her reminder of the precarious situation he was in caused goosebumps to break out on his arms. Since he wasn't about to admit his tricks to her, he simply said, "There are ways to avoid being checked." Before he could stop himself, the next words tumbled out of his mouth. "Would you care to drink a soda with me?"

Thea cocked her head, her blonde curls dancing around her shoulders. "Yes, why not. To remember the good times we had."

Going inside, David grabbed a copy of *Der Stürmer*, the vile Nazi magazine, from the rack and laid it on their table. In his experience a man with the party mouthpiece was never bothered, harassed or asked for papers.

Thea raised her eyebrow, but didn't comment and he didn't care to explain. After ordering their drinks, he asked, "What are you doing now?"

"I was pressed into working for Siemens. It's awful." She looked as if she wanted to break out in tears. "At least my mother is with me in the same company."

"Your mother, too?" David shouldn't be surprised, since every adult Jew, even senior men like Herr Falkenstein, were forced to work for the Reich.

"Yes, she's taking it surprisingly well. And you?"

"I got sick and was in hospital for close to three months at the beginning of the year." He swallowed down the lump in his throat before he continued. "I missed my ship."

"I'm sorry." She looked genuinely sad. "You were so looking forward to it."

"There's always another boat going." He tried to cheer himself up, adamant not to shed a single tear in public. Thea's spectacular smile made his insides go wobbly all over again. He took it as an encouragement and probed. "Are you still together with that lad?"

She shook her head and bestowed another of her magnificent smiles on David. "Not with him. He wasn't half as nice as you are."

Joy flooded David's heart at the possibility of a second chance for the two of them.

"I now realize it was a hasty decision to break up with you." She paused, fidgeting with her hands. "You must understand, I was, still am, in a terrible situation and I had to do what was best for me."

David touched her thumb, wanting to indicate that he understood. "We're all under a lot of stress, due to *them*. I don't blame you."

"Thank you. When you left for that farm, I panicked. On the one hand I simply couldn't imagine ever moving away from my parents, especially not… you know… so far away, and on the other hand I couldn't stand the idea of having a boyfriend and not seeing him for weeks on end. I really need to have my man close by." She raised her face to meet his eyes, begging for understanding.

David's heart leapt with joy. "Now that I'm back in Berlin, we could walk out again?"

"I'd love to, but…" Her face fell. "It's not possible." She held up her other hand, featuring a small band on the ring finger. "I'm married."

"You…" The rest of the sentence got stuck in his throat, only a miserable croak coming out. He harumphed and tried once more. "You just said, you're not together with him anymore."

"That's right. I married another one. His name is Ralf."

He didn't care one bit what name her husband had. He valiantly fought against the disappointment and the pain threatening to smother him, as he was sucked into a maelstrom squashing the air from his lungs. "Congratulations." The coarse voice didn't sound like his own. He clung to the table, desperately grappling with taking his next breath. Somehow he came up from the dark depth, looking at the unmoved face of the utterly beautiful woman he adored so much, feeling the acute agony over losing her a second time.

David needed to leave this place if he wanted to cling to his sanity. "I better leave or I'll be late." He left the money for the drinks on the table and fled from the café, promising himself never to return to the place of his personal Waterloo.

Walking home instead of taking the tram, he scolded himself on the long march for being a complete and utter idiot, falling twice for the same selfish girl. Instead of reeling over the humiliation, he decided to be grateful that she'd found another dork to marry.

32

At work Julius had been given two days off to run errands and used them well to make the last arrangements for his and Edith's imminent emigration.

What had been a relatively easy feat for his sister Adriana and her husband Florian, had turned into a daunting task. Because Germany and England were at war, the British had closed all consulates in Germany, thus issuing visas for German citizens only in embassies in Spain, Portugal, Vichy France or Switzerland.

Julius shook his head at the many hoops the bureaucrats had made him jump through and he shuddered at the thought of how many times he'd had to ask Adriana to transfer one fee or another to someone to quicken the process.

When Adriana's affidavit had finally been received, validated, certified, and processed in the embassy in Switzerland, the diplomats there had insisted on Julius and Edith being physically present to receive their emigration visa. This, of course had added another layer of complications, because with a "J" stamped on his passport Julius needed a visa for Switzerland.

Thus, he had begun the process all over again, greasing palms to receive a tourist visa for himself, for the sole purpose of stepping into the British embassy in Zurich, where he fervently wished to finally receive his ticket to freedom.

After months and months of letters going back and forth, he finally held the coveted piece of paper in his hands. He instantly raced to the Swiss embassy near the Reichstag and really and truly received the precious stamp in his passport. He couldn't wait to give Edith the fantastic news.

She waited for him in a café and jumped up the moment she saw him coming down the street. For a second, rage pulsed through his veins, because he wasn't allowed to sit next to his wife and order a drink.

"How was it?" she asked, jumping up and linking arms with him.

"Good."

"So, we have reason to celebrate?"

"Yes. I got the visa for Switzerland. It's contingent on receiving the emigration visa for England and only valid for three months."

"That should be more than enough," Edith said.

Julius, though, was more skeptical after the amount of red tape he'd gone through. "We'll see. In any case, I'll apply for the tax certificate tomorrow and then we can book our train tickets."

"Thank God. It's taken long enough."

"I should have considered emigration earlier, everything would have been so much easier." It was hard for him to admit that he'd been wrong and he braced himself for her inevitable *I told you so*.

Edith, though, was much too kind to dwell on his mistake. "We're about to leave, and that's all that counts. How long until they'll give you the tax certificate?"

"A couple of weeks at most." He couldn't help but feel nostalgic. Once they left Germany, there was no way to return, at least not in the foreseeable future. "I would have sworn to high heaven that Hitler wasn't stupid enough to start another war."

"Nobody could have known." Edith slowed down to walk around a puddle.

"You did."

"I didn't know, I feared that this lunatic is capable of anything."

He rubbed his chin. "I should have listened to you."

"In hindsight, everything becomes clear." Edith sounded tired.

It occurred to him that this situation must be so much harder on her than she let anyone know. Again, he felt guilty for causing her so much grief. "Once we're in Switzerland I'll treat you to a five-course dinner in Bern's finest restaurant."

"That would be nice. I barely remember the taste of a steak cooked to perfection." At the next street corner they waited for a vehicle to pass and she looked at him. "Can't you rush the expedition of the tax certificate? I keep thinking about what Joseph told me."

After giving it some thought, he shook his head. "The risks far outweigh the benefits. I don't trust your brother. Has it never occurred to you that he might have ulterior motives?"

"It did. In fact, I confronted him with my doubts. His answer seemed sincere." She stopped and looked at him pleadingly. "Please! What is the problem of speeding up our departure as much as possible?"

"We don't want to appear desperate."

"But we are desperate!" Her voice had a shrill sound to it.

"One week more or less won't make a difference. I have my visa to Switzerland, you have your passport and we'll be leaving this country in no time at all. I'm afraid to draw unwanted attention if I put too much pressure on the expedition of the tax certificate. I'd hate to arrive at the border and find out someone has instigated an inquiry and we have to return to Berlin for another signature."

"Perhaps you're right," Edith admitted. "I'm still nervous. Joseph was very clear that we need to hasten our efforts."

"Did he tell you why?" Julius probed, sensing Edith's despair.

"No. He said it was top secret."

"That makes me think he was trying to frighten you, otherwise he'd have told you a specific reason."

"It doesn't work that way," she said hesitantly.

"You know as well as I do that your brother has fully embraced Nazism."

"Why would he come to our place and warn me if it weren't serious? Do you think he took that risk for nothing?"

"What risk?" Julius paused for a moment, since his right knee was acting up again. He looked forward to not having to work ten hours a day anymore once they arrived in Switzerland.

"An SS man visiting a Jewish house."

He snorted. "Serves him right. Why shouldn't they suffer the consequences of Hitler's follies, too?"

Edith glared at him, but softened her tone. "Please. Just let us get out of here as soon as we can."

He nodded. Maybe it was time to take a more pragmatic approach and forget about making arrangements for the things he left behind. Should someone else care about their apartment. Then a worrying thought crossed his mind. "What shall we do with the necklace?"

"Which necklace?" Edith's hand automatically flew to her bare neck. Ever since Jews had been forced to give up their valuables she'd stopped wearing jewelry, except for her wedding band.

"My mother's diamond necklace."

Her eyes became big. "I thought you'd sent it abroad."

"I couldn't. It reminds me of my parents, so I kept it in the safe in our apartment. But now I'm wondering how to smuggle it out of the country."

"It's much too dangerous," Edith answered, pale as a ghost. "We should leave it here."

"Under no circumstances will I hand this precious piece over to the Nazis." His voice boomed, slightly too loud and both he and Edith automatically looked over their shoulders to see whether someone might have heard him.

"We could give it to someone to keep safe for us," she suggested.

"But whom? Who is trustworthy enough to get his hands on a necklace easily worth a quarter million Reichsmark and not steal it?"

Edith knew how much he cherished that particular piece of jewelry. After giving it some thought she answered, "Your sister Silvana."

"Indeed, I trust her and Markus implicitly, but we'd put them in an untenable situation, since they aren't allowed to own precious stones."

"Right, I forgot." Edith looked crestfallen. "We could leave it in the safe, hoping nobody will discover it?"

"Never. The way this war is going, bombs will be falling in Berlin, despite all of fat Göring's assertions to the contrary."

"You truly believe this?"

They had reached their apartment building. The elevator had long ceased working, so they climbed the stairs. Slightly out of breath he answered, "It's a risk I don't want to take. The necklace can't stay in the safe while we're gone.

"I could wear it," Edith suggested. "Sometimes the obvious is the least suspicious."

"Normally I would agree with you, though not in this case. At the border they will scrutinize our papers and whether it is legal or not, the Nazi scums will try to rob us of the last possessions we own. They'll simply steal the necklace from you. No, we have to hide it somewhere."

"In our luggage?"

That gave him an idea. "I'll ask the leather worker who made our suitcases whether he can arrange for a secret compartment."

"Is he trustworthy?" Edith objected.

"I'll ask Silvana to make the inquiry for me."

"If he talks, the Gestapo will make the connection to you soon enough, she's your sister after all."

"What do you suggest then?" They had reached their apartment, and he yearned to sit down, putting up his legs. He might have to hasten their departure, not because of Joseph's ominous threat, but because his health was deteriorating fast and he needed the reprieve.

"The Goldmanns?"

"They are our tenants," he said.

"The leather maker doesn't know that."

"Hmm. Let me think about it." He unlocked the door and immediately settled on a chair, thinking hard.

33

Helga watched the crowd gathered in the apartment: her entire family, the Falkensteins and their former maid Delia, the Lembergs, the Gerbers, and Herr Dreyer, the new owner of the Falkenstein bank with his wife.

Rumor had it he'd given Herr Falkenstein money to pay the ridiculous cost of the *Reichsfluchtsteuer,* the tax penalty for fleeing a country which didn't want you. The surprise visitor, though, was Edith's brother Knut, a Wehrmacht soldier currently posted in Berlin, doing whatever secret thing with the Abwehr.

Helga vaguely remembered him from school, where he'd been three years beneath her. Never before had he shown up at the apartment, and she'd assumed he had cut all ties to Edith like the rest of her family had done, due to her liaison with a Jew.

Mentally she thanked her sister Felicitas who'd always stood by her and continued to support her whenever she could with money, food or clothing coupons.

"I'm going to miss you," Helga said to Edith, who looked radiant in her travel dress, a dark blue two-piece suit with matching coat, hat and gloves. As soon as the Falkensteins had gathered the required papers and permits to leave Germany,

Edith had been smiling constantly, seeming to grow younger by the day.

Today's gathering was to celebrate and bemoan the departure of yet another befriended family for a better future abroad. While Helga was happy for them, she also envied Edith for the carefree life ahead of her once she left Hitler's oppressive Third Reich.

"Don't be sad." Edith gave her an unusual hug. "Julius has promised to work on sending you an affidavit as soon as we reach London."

"You don't have to do this." Helga was moved to tears, since she never expected such generosity.

"But I want to. You've become such a good friend over the years, and who knows better than I do what you're going through under the Nazi reign?"

"Thanks for letting us stay in the apartment." Frau Gerber sidled up with them. "We were so worried that you'd sell the place."

Edith nodded. The thought had crossed Julius' mind. For several reasons, not least of them out of concern for the tenants who'd become friends, he had decided to transfer ownership to his sister Silvana.

The Lembergs would keep on the current tenants and use extra rooms as an emergency location for Jewish families in need of a temporary place to stay.

"I'm so happy and sad at once, I really don't know what to say." Silvana approached the other women. "First Adriana and Florian, now Julius and you. It seems I'll be the sole sibling left in Germany. It'll be so lonely."

Helga noticed how Silvana was fighting against her tears and quickly said, "You're always welcome to visit us, Frau Lemberg. Edith has been a good friend, and I would love to extend that friendship to you as well."

"Thank you so much." Silvana dabbed her eyes. "I better get us something to drink."

To celebrate the occasion, everyone had chipped in with

ration cards. In addition Herr Falkenstein had raided his secret stash of precious brandies, making the gathering a feast they hadn't seen in years.

Much too soon, Herr Falkenstein announced, "It's time for us to leave."

"I'll take you to the train station, courtesy of the Wehrmacht," offered Edith's brother Knut. Helga didn't miss the irony that an official Wehrmacht vehicle would escort a Jewish family to the train station so that they could flee the country.

Everyone shook hands with the Falkensteins, Delia broke into tears, and the Gerber children intoned *"Muss i denn, muss i denn zum Städtele hinaus"*, a popular folk song that originated in Swabia, which had become very popular among soldiers and for farewells.

Then the Falkensteins were gone. After all the guests had left and they had cleaned up the apartment from the remainders of the party, Helga leaned against Heinrich. "I need to go for a walk."

"I'll come with you." Heinrich seemed unusually serious, which she chalked up to the occasion.

When they walked toward a nearby park, she said, "I'm happy for them, but I'm also sad. Edith has become such a good friend. Having her support has been a true blessing." She thought she sounded too materialistic and added, "For so many things, but mostly for having someone who shares my experiences and can commiserate."

"Yes." Heinrich increased his pace, without uttering another word.

"Their departure leaves an empty spot, don't you think?" She didn't wait for an answer. "Every time someone leaves, it reminds me of our own precarious situation."

"Hmm." Heinrich seemed to be mulling over something. From experience she knew he'd tell her when he was ready. For now she didn't mind, since she needed to express her own feelings to recover a clear head.

"It's just… I feel trapped. Everyone around us ups and leaves. Sometimes I believe we'll be the last ones to stay. You know that saying: 'The last one turns off the light.' That's exactly how I'm feeling. It's so sad, not only for us, for everyone. Jews and non-Jews. Germans and foreigners. Everyone is suffering, even the Nazis themselves, they just don't know it yet."

Heinrich paused and gazed at her, his face grim. "I want a divorce."

"What?" Helga's heart squeezed with brutality, almost knocking her over. "Why?"

"It's for the best."

"For the best?" She had to hold onto a nearby tree to keep from toppling over. For almost a quarter of a century she'd loved this man with every fiber of her body, heart and soul, and now he asked for a divorce. "I don't understand. Don't you love me anymore?"

His eyes filled with sadness. "I love you more than my own life."

"But why... why do you want a divorce then?" Helga was struggling to utter the words, unable to comprehend what he was saying.

"To keep you safe. When you're not married to me any longer, you can have a normal life. You won't be treated with contempt everywhere you go. You can get a decent job, buy enough food and wear nice things. You won't have to live in crammed quarters in a place shamed by everyone, stigmatized by the yellow star across the door, which gives the Gestapo free reign over everyone inside. Without me, you'll be so much better off. I can't in good conscience keep this from you. I wouldn't be able to look in the mirror for the rest of my life if something happened to you—because of me." Heinrich's shoulders slumped, seemingly exhausted from his passionate speech.

Despite the shock coursing through her veins, she felt empathy for him. At least until that sentiment was crowded out by rage. The anger she'd bottled up inside during the years since Hitler had come to power sent sharp tingles from head to toe, her entire body burning as if it were set ablaze.

The injustices, the harassments, the worries, the lack of decent food, the constant fight for yet another day, it all accumulated in this instant and caused her to explode. "This is what you think? After all those years we've lived through, bad times and good, now you toss me aside like a piece of trash?"

"Please, darling—"

"Don't 'darling' me!"

"Helga, please. Calm down. I'm doing this for you and for our children. Once I'm out of the picture they won't be considered Jews anymore, won't have to wear that damn yellow star. Won't get harassed on the street, beaten up, made to work overtime without pay, not given breaks or even a warm soup in winter. Don't you want them to have the chance for a better life?"

A chill ran down her spine at the realization how much truth was in his words. Logic demanded she grant him his wish. Love though, knew no reason. "Right now I'm the only person standing between you and the Nazis. Without me, you'll have no protection whatsoever. Who says your boss won't kill you the next time he beats you up? When he realizes there's no German wife to hold him accountable?"

"I'll be fine," Heinrich whispered.

"No, you won't! Do you really want me to choose between you and our children? Don't you think I can protect all three of you?"

He gave her a rueful smile. "This is as hard for me as it is for you."

"Obviously it's not or you wouldn't make such a heinous suggestion." She turned on her heels and stalked away. After walking off her fury she returned to the exit of the park, where Heinrich was standing all dressed up and with nowhere to go.

"Helga, please," he begged her.

She came to a stand a step away from him, glaring. "You really think it's so easy, do you? If I had wanted to divorce you, I would have done so many years ago. I'd have caved in to the constant pleading of so many well-meaning friends. Did you know that even the director of Amelie and David's public school advised me to do just that, so they wouldn't be ostracized at school?"

"You never told me." His eyes were cast downward.

"I didn't tell you because I never considered it even for a split-second. And you know why?" She was much calmer now, having realized that all her pent-up anger was directed toward the Nazis. Heinrich was the last person she should take it out on. "Because I love you. I've never loved another man in my entire life. You were the first one and"—she paused to look deep into his eyes—"you will be the only one until the day I die. I will do whatever it takes to keep you safe, whether you agree with it or not. So, no, I will not grant you a divorce. And this is my last word!"

"I'm sorry, sweetheart." Tears welled up in his eyes. "You looked so miserable after the Falkensteins left. I couldn't bear it; I had to give you a way out of this. I wanted to make you happy again."

Now it was her turn to fight the tears. "Oh, Heinrich. Do you have any idea how much more miserable I would be without you by my side? Lying in your arms every night is what allows me to keep on fighting, to deal with everything that's thrown at me. Loving you is worth so much more than better food or a new dress."

She sensed that he wanted to object and put a finger to his lips. "Don't say anything. Even if I would miraculously be embraced by the German community again, do you really think I would be happy? With all the horrible things the Nazis do? Do you believe I want to be a part of that? No. I'd rather die than give in to their pressure."

"I love you so much." Heinrich wrapped her into his arms, sending love and warmth into every single cell of her body. "Please forgive me for underestimating you."

"You are forgiven." She smiled. "But only this one time. If you ever mention the d-word again, you won't be getting off scot-free."

After a long and passionate kiss they walked home, hand in hand. Happy despite all the hardships.

Deep in her soul, Helga harbored the hope that her friend Edith would come through with the affidavit and give them the chance for a better life abroad.

Until that day, she'd stay and fight. Every step of the way.

A LETTER FROM MARION

Dear Reader,

Thank you so much for reading *The Berlin Wife's Choice*. If you enjoyed it, and want to keep up to date with all my latest releases, just sign up at the following link. Your email address will never be shared and you can unsubscribe at any time.

www.bookouture.com/marion-kummerow

As always this story is a mix of facts and fiction. I have kept closely to real events and timelines, but my characters and how they react to events are entirely fictional. Sometimes they are inspired by a real, existing person, often they are a combination of several true persons.

The Kristallnacht on November 9, 1938, in English called the Night of Broken Glass, is often considered as the beginning of Jewish persecution, although the bullying, boycotts, and marginalization had begun almost immediately after Hitler's coming to power in January 1933.

It is perhaps the event that dispelled all doubts among the Jewish community about what the Nazis were up to. Obviously nobody imagined how horrible it would become, yet it created an urgency to leave the country if at all possible.

Less than a year later, due to the beginning of the war, this route all but closed down. To show how the conditions gradually worsened, I picked just a few of the laws and rules meant to exclude Jews. All the regulations, however far-fetched or ridiculous they may seem, have indeed been issued in reality, although the reactions of the Falkensteins or Goldmanns to the rules are entirely fictional, just like the characters themselves.

My favorite villain, of course, is Joseph, closely followed by Thea (about whom you'll read more in the next book of the series). Avid historians among my readers will recognize that his attack on the radio station in Gliwice closely follows true events.

I reconstructed the happenings from an interview in the German magazine *Der Spiegel* with former Sturmbannführer Alfred Naujocks in 1963. Naujocks and his team were responsible for the mission—and his recounting of the events became the inspiration for Joseph and his men.

As you know from history, the mission was a success. Blame was put on the Polish side, and the next day the war started.

Thea Blume stands exemplary for a large group of assimilated Jews who never considered themselves to be Jewish at all, and sometimes had a rather complicated relationship with their own Jewish identity. She—and Julius too, by the way—feels completely German.

In reality, many of the assimilated Jews despised the Orthodox Jews, who were mostly poor refugees from the East, for being backwards and bringing misfortune over them by affiliation.

If you've read my series *Margarete's Journey*, you've met Thea in *Daughter of the Dawn* and can probably imagine what happens to her in the next installment of German Wives, titled *The Berlin Wife's Resistance*. Without giving spoilers I can tell you that she and David will meet again.

Forced Aryanization of businesses was another issue during the Nazis reign. It's not entirely clear whether the government planned this as a means to finance the war, or if this just happened. In any case, many Christian business owners took advantage of the opportunity and "bought" Jewish businesses for a fraction of their values.

The Nazis quickly caught up on the practice and perfected it, issuing several rules to make the theft easier. One of them decreed that in case of deportation to a camp outside Germany, which started by the end of 1941, all possessions of that person were automatically forfeited. An astute reader may realize that the government expected deported people never to return.

Squeezing money from the "greedy Jew" was one of the Nazis pet peeves, which started as early as 1938, when the Jewish community had to pay a penalty of one billion Reichsmark for the destruction caused during the Night of Broken Glass. But that wasn't the only infamy.

The seizing of gold, silver and jewelry was another way to make money. The scene where Felicitas goes with Helga to retrieve the family silver, claiming it's hers, apparently truly happened, as recounted in the memoirs of Gad Beck, *An Underground Life: Memoirs of a Gay Jew in Nazi Berlin*.

One of his aunts was my inspiration for Felicitas: a woman who loved her sister and Jewish husband dearly, but who also was one of the first persons to join the Nazi party. Gad Beck also mentioned the *hachshara*, the preparation course for a life in Palestine in his book. There were several Zionist training farms in the vicinity of Berlin, although to my knowledge none in Luckenwalde.

I have a lot more planned for the Falkensteins, the Goldmanns, their friends and relatives. And, at the personal request of my daughter, there will be a cute animal in the book. *The Berlin Wife's Resistance* will be out on January 19th, 2024.

Marion

KEEP IN TOUCH WITH MARION

www.kummerow.info

- facebook.com/AutorinKummerow
- twitter.com/MarionKummerow
- instagram.com/MarionKummerow
- goodreads.com/MarionKummerow

Made in the USA
Middletown, DE
06 January 2024

47371557R00145